"I wanted you from the first second I saw you."

Lauren's heart sped up at the look in his eyes. "I never knew why. I was so not your type. Before me, you went with all the beautiful, wild girls."

"You were different."

She waited for him to elaborate, but Shane remained silent. "Different how?" she prodded, annoyed with herself because she shouldn't care.

He thought for a moment. "Honest. Genuine. Real."

"You make me sound like a Girl Scout," she complained.

"I don't think what we did together was in any Girl Scout handbook," he said lightly. "In fact, being on this beach with you reminds me of the night we—"

"Don't go there," she warned.

"Why not?"

"Because I've already been there today," she confessed.

"Really?" His brown eyes sparkled wickedly. "It was a good night."

"Yes, it was," she admitted, meeting his gaze, the delicious heat of their memories dancing between them. Her fingers bit into the hard rock she was sitting on, as she forced herself not to get up and fling herself into his arms and see if it was as great as she remembered. "Stop looking at me like that," she ordered.

"You're looking at me the same way. It's still there, Lauren—no matter how much we want to deny it."

[Turn the page for praise of bestselling author Barbara Freethy's heartwarming romances]

"Freethy has written a suspenseful and captivating story, weaving in human frailty along with true compassion, making every page a delight."

—Reader to Reader Reviews

"Angel's Bay is a place I'll want to visit time and again. . . . Freethy has done a beautiful job of weaving a compelling story while having the patience to fully develop characters who will become our friends, characters with whom we will share joys, sorrows, and all of life's adventures."

—Romance Novel TV

"A well-written, captivating story, with good pacing that will leave you satisfied as it unfolds. There is a little bit of everything—romance, mystery, and inexplicable events—a fascinating story sure to make your summer reading a pleasure."

—Romance Reviews Today

And for award-winning author Barbara Freethy

"Barbara Freethy delivers strong and compelling prose."

—*Publishers Weekly*

"Fans of Nora Roberts will find a similar tone here, framed in Freethy's own spare, elegant style."

—*Contra Costa Times* (CA)

"Freethy skillfully keeps readers on the hook."

—*Booklist*

"Freethy's star continues to gain luster."

—*Romantic Times*

BARBARA FREETHY

*On Shadow
Beach*

POCKET **STAR** BOOKS
New York London Toronto Sydney

Pocket Star Books
A Division of Simon & Schuster, Inc.
1230 Avenue of the Americas
New York, NY 10020

This book is a work of fiction. Names, characters, places, and incidents either are products of the author's imagination or are used fictitiously. Any resemblance to actual events or locales or persons, living or dead, is entirely coincidental.

First Pocket Star Books paperback edition April 2010

POCKET STAR BOOKS and colophon are registered trademarks of Simon & Schuster, Inc.

For information about special discounts for bulk purchases, please contact Simon & Schuster Special Sales at 1-866-506-1949 or business@simonandschuster.com.

The Simon & Schuster Speakers Bureau can bring authors to your live event. For more information or to book an event contact the Simon & Schuster Speakers Bureau at 1-866-248-3049 or visit our website at www.simonspeakers.com.

Designed by Jill Putorti

Manufactured in the United States of America

10 9 8 7 6 5 4 3 2 1

ISBN 978-1-4391-0157-5
ISBN 978-1-4391-2698-1 (ebook)

In memory of my mother,
who shared her love of reading with me,
and is surely an angel now.

ACKNOWLEDGMENTS

Thanks to my writing friends with whom I enjoy lunches, chocolate, and lots of wonderful, sometimes crazy, brainstorming sessions. You know who you are and how much you mean to me. Thanks also go to my wonderful editor, Micki Nuding, whose enthusiasm and support are always appreciated, as well as to my astute and insightful agent, Karen Solem.

Thanks to my family for their never-ending support and to my tennis friends, who keep me sane and fit by running me around on the tennis court. I couldn't do it without all of you!

One

Just like before, the front door was ajar, every light in the house was on, and a game show played on the television. Lauren Jamison put down her suitcase, feeling uneasy.

Thirteen years had passed since she'd been home, but the living room looked the same: the brown leather recliner by the fireplace where her dad read the paper every evening, the couch her sister, Abby, used to curl up on and write in her journal, the table by the window where her mother and little brother, David, played board games. The furniture remained, but all of the people were gone. All except one.

"Dad?" she called.

The answering silence tightened her nerves. She needed her father to appear, to remind her that this *wasn't* like before. Because thirteen years ago she'd returned home late one night, an innocent seventeen-year-old, and found the front door open, lights blazing, and her mother sobbing hysterically. Nothing had been the same after that.

The whistle of a teakettle drew her toward the kitchen, but the room was empty. She turned off the stove and moved into the hall, checking each bedroom. Her father's room was cluttered with clothes. Only the faded floral curtains betrayed her mother's once important influence on the décor. David's bedroom had been turned into an office that was covered in dust and papers. The room at the end of the hall had belonged to her and to Abby.

The door was closed, and Lauren's steps slowed. Her father might have redone the room, boxed up Abby's things and given them to charity—or the room might look exactly the same as it had the night Abby died. Her heart skipped a beat.

She tapped on the door. "Dad? Are you in there?"

When he didn't reply, she opened the door, scanned the room quickly, and then pulled the door shut, her breath coming hard and fast. Abby's side of the room was frozen in time, as if it were still waiting for her to return. Lauren let out a long, shaky breath, then turned away.

Where the hell was her father? She'd called him that morning and told him she was coming, and he'd seemed fine. But according to the neighbors, who had sent numerous letters to her mother over the past three months, her father's Alzheimer's was getting worse. It was time for someone in the family to come back and take care of him. Her mother had refused. She'd divorced Ned Jamison eleven years earlier, and she had no intention of reuniting with him now. David was back east at college. So Lauren had returned to Angel's Bay to deal with a man who was little more than a stranger to her. But he was still her father, and she needed to find him—she just wasn't sure where to look. She had only spent a half dozen weekends with her dad since she'd left home at seventeen, and all those visits had occurred in San Francisco. Where would he be on a Friday night? She didn't know who his friends were anymore, what he did, where he went.

Or did she?

Her father had always been a creature of habit. During her childhood, he'd spent most of his time in three places: home, the bait and tackle shop he'd run until two years ago, and his fishing boat *Leonora*, named after his great-great-great-grandmother who'd been one of the founders of Angel's Bay.

Lauren headed out the front door toward the marina, which was only a few blocks away. Buttoning up her sweater, she hurried down the street. It was seven o'clock and there was already a chill in the darkening September sky. Soon there'd be pumpkins and Halloween decorations on every porch, but for now the neighborhood was quiet.

While some of the homes had been remodeled, the streets were very familiar. She'd been born in Angel's Bay, and this neighborhood was where she'd taken her first steps, learned to ride a bicycle, roller skated into the Johnsons' rosebushes, gotten her first kiss in the moonlight, fallen in love . . . and fallen out of love.

She blinked away the sudden moisture in her eyes and picked up her pace. She had a great life in San Francisco now, an interesting job and good friends, and she had no regrets about leaving her hometown. She just wished that she hadn't had to come back.

By the time she reached Ocean Avenue, she was breathless. She quickened her pace as she passed the Angel's Heart Quilt Shop, where she and Abby and their mother had partaken in the town's longstanding tradition of community quilting. Quilting was the way mothers and daughters, sisters and friends connected the past with the present. She'd once loved to quilt, but she hadn't picked up a needle and thread since she'd left. She didn't want those connections anymore. Nor did she particularly want to see anyone she knew now. She was hoping to make her visit short, with as little community contact as possible.

Crossing the street, she kept her head down as she passed Carl's Crab Shack. The line was out to the sidewalk and the delicious smells of clam chowder and fish and chips made her stomach rumble. She'd done the four-hour drive from San Francisco without stopping for food but she couldn't stop now.

As she reached the marina she saw a new sign on her father's bait and tackle shop, now called Brady's instead of Jamison's. The store was closed. She moved down the ramp that led to the boat slips. Luckily the gate had been propped open by a slat of wood, so she didn't need a key. Her father's old trawler had been moored at the second to last slip in the third row since she was a little girl. She hoped it was still there.

The marina was quiet. Most of the action occurred in the early morning or late afternoon, when the sport and commercial fishermen were going out or coming back after a day of work or pleasure. Her pulse quickened as the lights on her father's boat suddenly came on, followed by the sound of an engine. She could see his silhouette in the cabin. What on earth was he doing? He couldn't go out to sea by himself.

"Dad!" she yelled, breaking into a run. She waved her arms as she screamed again, but either he couldn't hear her or he was ignoring her. By the time she reached the slip, her father's boat was chugging toward the middle of the bay. She had to stop him. She needed to call the Coast Guard or find someone to go after him. "Hello! Anyone here?" she called.

A man emerged from a nearby boat and Lauren hurried down the dock.

"What's going on?" he asked.

The familiar voice stopped her dead in her tracks, and as he jumped onto the dock and into the light, her heart skipped a beat.

Shane. Shane Murray.

He moved toward her with the same purposeful, determined step she remembered. She wasn't ready for this—ready for him.

She knew the split second that he recognized her. His step faltered, his shoulders stiffened, and his jaw set in a grim line. He didn't say her name. He just stared at her, waiting. Shane had never been one for words, he'd always believed actions spoke louder than explanations. But sometimes the truth needed to be spoken—not just implied or assumed.

"Shane." She wished her voice didn't sound so husky, so filled with memories. She cleared her throat. "I—I need help. My father just took off in his boat. I don't know if you know, but he has Alzheimer's." She waved her hand toward the *Leonora*, whose lights were fading in the distance. "I need to get him back. Will you help me? There doesn't seem to be anyone else around." When he didn't answer right away, she added, "I guess I could call the Coast Guard."

For a moment she thought he might say no. They weren't friends anymore. If anything, they were enemies.

Finally Shane gave a crisp nod. "Let's go." He headed back to his boat.

The last thing she wanted to do was go with him, but she couldn't stand by while her father sailed off to sea with probably no idea of who he was or where he was going.

Shane's boat was a newer thirty-foot sport fishing boat with all the modern conveniences. There were rod holders in the gunwales, tackle drawers and ice coolers built into the hull. As she stepped on board, Shane released the lines and pulled in the bumpers, then headed toward the center console. He started the engine and pulled out of the slip.

She stood a few feet away, feeling awkward and uncomfortable. How long would it take before he'd actually speak to her? And if he did, what would he say? There was a lot of painful history between them, and while part of her wanted him to break the silence, the other part was afraid of where that might lead.

She'd fallen for Shane just after her seventeenth birthday. He'd been only a year older in age, but a half dozen in experience. She'd been a shy good girl who'd never done anything impulsive in her life, and he'd been the town bad boy, moody, rebellious, and reckless. He'd drawn her to him like a moth to a flame.

Shane definitely wasn't a teenager anymore. In his faded blue jeans, gray T-shirt, and black jacket it was quite apparent that he was all man now. His six-foot frame had filled out with broad shoulders and long legs. His black hair was wavy and windblown, the ends brushing the collar of his jacket, and his skin bore the ruddy tan of a man who spent a lot of time outdoors.

The set of his jaw had always been his "no trespassing" sign, and that hadn't changed a bit. Shane had never let people in easily. She'd had to fight to get past his barriers, but even as close as they'd been, she'd never figured out the mysterious shadows in his dark eyes, or the sudden, sharp flashes of pain there. Shane had always kept a big part of himself under lock and key.

Her gaze dropped to his hands, noting the sureness of his fingers on the wheel. His hands were strong and capable, and she couldn't help but remember the way they'd once felt on her breasts—rough and hungry, the same way his mouth had felt against hers, as if he couldn't wait to have her, couldn't ever get enough.

Her heart thumped against her chest, and she forced herself to look away. She was *not* going back to that place. She'd barely survived the first time. He'd swept her off her feet, into a whirlwind of emotions, then broken her heart.

"It took you long enough to come home," Shane said finally. He glanced at her, his expression unreadable.

"I just came to get my dad. I'm planning to take him back to San Francisco with me."

"Does he know that?"

"He will when we catch him."

Doubt filled Shane's eyes. "Your father has lived in Angel's Bay his entire life. I can't see him moving anywhere else."

"His illness will only get worse. It's the best solution."

"For you or for him?"

"For both of us." Her father might not like the idea of leaving Angel's Bay, but it was the most practical decision. If she moved him closer to her she could take care of him, and perhaps her mother would help. His family was in San Francisco, and that's where he should be.

Her dad hadn't cared to be with his family the

past thirteen years, but she was trying to look beyond that fact. And if the neighbors were right, and her father was rapidly losing touch with the world—would it really matter where he was?

Shane opened a compartment and pulled out a jacket. "You might want to put this on. It will get colder outside the bay."

She accepted with a grateful nod, relieved with both the change in subject and the warm jacket. She'd left San Francisco straight from work, wearing a navy blue skirt, silk blouse, thin sweater, and high-heeled pumps that were perfect for her job but offered no protection against the elements. Shane's big coat enveloped her like a warm hug, reminding her of the way she'd once felt in his arms.

She quickly pushed the thought out of her mind. "So, this is a nice boat," she said into the increasingly awkward silence. "Is it yours? Or is it part of the Murray charter fleet?" Shane's father had run a charter fishing business for as long as Lauren could remember.

"It's mine. I picked it up last year when I came back," he said shortly.

"Came back from where?"

"Everywhere," he said with a vague wave. "Wherever there was water and fish and a boat to run."

"Sounds like you got the life you always wanted."

He shot her a look that she couldn't begin to decipher. "Is that what it sounds like, Lauren?"

Her name rolled off his tongue like a silky caress.

She'd always loved the way he'd said her name, as if she were the most important person in the world. But that wasn't the way he'd said her name now. Now there was anger in the word, and God knew what else.

She sighed. "I don't know what to say to you, Shane. I guess I never did."

His gaze hardened. "You knew what to say, Lauren. You just wouldn't say it."

Thirteen years ago he'd wanted her to say that she believed in him, that she trusted him, that she knew in her heart that he hadn't killed her sister.

All she'd been able to say was good-bye.

"I don't want to talk about the past." The words had barely left her lips when she found herself compelled to speak again. "You lied to me, Shane. I trusted you more than I'd ever trusted anyone, and you lied to me."

He gave a little nod, his eyes dark and unreadable. "Yeah, I did."

"And you're still not going to tell me why, are you?"

"I thought you didn't want to talk about the past."

She debated that. There were so many things she wanted Shane to explain, but what was the point?

"You're right; it won't change anything. In the end, Abby—Abby will still be gone." A chill ran through her, and she glanced at the coastline. It was too dark to see the Ramsay house, where her sister had been found murdered, but she could feel its presence even if she couldn't see it.

"Someone set fire to the house about nine months ago," Shane said, following her gaze. "One wing was destroyed."

"It's too bad the house didn't burn to the ground." She'd never understood how her father could stay in Angel's Bay, could wake up every day and see the house where her sister had spent the last violent minutes of her life. But there were a lot of things she couldn't understand about her dad.

Lauren grabbed hold of the back of the captain's seat as Shane increased their speed. On the open sea, waves slapped against the boat and the wind increased, lifting her hair off the back of her neck. Her nerves began to tingle with fear. She could handle being on the water when the day was sunny and bright and she could see the shoreline, but she'd never liked going out at night, or being hours away from land, where she'd be vulnerable, at the mercy of the unpredictable sea.

"Where is my father?" Panic made her voice rise. "I don't see any lights. How are we going to find him out here? Maybe we should go back." She hated being a coward, especially in front of Shane, who had never felt a fear he didn't want to meet head on.

"Your father didn't disappear. He's just around the bluff." Shane pointed to the GPS on his console. "See that dot—that's him. We'll catch up in a couple of minutes."

"Okay. Good." She gulped in a deep breath of air and wrapped her arms around her waist.

"Are you scared of me?" Shane sent her a speculative look.

"Don't be ridiculous."

"You seem nervous."

"I just want to get this over with."

A few minutes passed, then Shane said, "Your father loves this town. Do you really think you can drop in after all this time and sweep him away without an argument?"

"I have to do *something*. When I arrived at his house tonight, the stove was on. He could have burned the house down. And who knows where he's headed now?" She shook her head in confusion. "This shouldn't be happening. He's only sixty-seven; he's too young to be losing his mind."

"Some days are worse than others," Shane commented. "Other times, he's the same as he always was."

"You talk to my father?" she asked in surprise.

"He's on his boat almost every day. Mort took his key away from him a while ago. I don't know where he got another one."

"My father doesn't—" She broke off the question, realizing she was heading into dangerous territory.

"Blame me for Abby's death?" Shane finished, a hard note in his voice. "Some days he does, some days he doesn't. But he does blame me for your leaving and never coming back."

"That wasn't because of you."

"Wasn't it?" He tilted his head, giving her a considering look. "What's making you so jumpy, Lauren? Don't tell me it's just the water. You don't like being alone with me."

"I got over you a long time ago. It was a teenage crush, that's all. It's not like I'm still attracted to you. I don't think about you at all. I am way, *way* over you. I've moved on."

"Are you done?" he asked when she finally ran out of steam.

"Yes."

He eased up on the throttle so abruptly, she stumbled right into his arms. Her lips had barely parted in protest when his mouth came down on hers, hot, insistent, demanding the truth.

She should break it off, pull away . . . but God, he tasted good. She felt seventeen again, hot, needy, reckless, on the verge of something incredible and exciting and . . .

She had to stop. Finally, she found the strength to push him away. She stared at him in shock, her heart pounding, her breathing ragged.

He gave her a long look in return. "Yeah, I'm over you, too." He put his hands back on the wheel.

Okay, so her body still had a thing for him. That didn't mean her head or her heart intended to go along. Loving Shane had only gotten her a heart full of pain.

"I'm glad we've settled that," she said sharply.

"Me too."

A tense silence fell between them, and the air around them grew thicker, colder, and damp. Her hair started to curl and a fine sheen of moisture

covered her face. As they rounded the point, a sil-
very mist surrounded them. Her father had often
spoken of the angels that danced above the bay, that
watched over and protected them. She'd believed
him with the innocence of a child, but she'd lost her
faith when Abby died. What kind of angel could let
a fifteen-year-old girl be killed?

She felt a wave of panic as the mist enveloped
them in a chilling hug, and had to fight a powerful
desire to fling herself back into Shane's arms.

*Why are you fighting? He's the man you've always
wanted.*

The voice wasn't in her head; it was on the wind.
She certainly hadn't said the words, because they
weren't true. She didn't want Shane—not anymore.

A melodic laugh seemed to bounce off the waves,
as if the ocean found her amusing. She shook her
head, forcing the fanciful thought away. She didn't
believe in angels, or much of anything. Believing in
someone always led to disappointment.

She let out a breath of relief as the fog lifted,
and a beam of light danced off the waves ahead of
them—her father's boat.

Shane's boat was moving faster now. They'd
reach the *Leonora* within minutes. But then what?
"How will we stop him?" she asked.

"We'll pull up next to him. If he doesn't stop on
his own, one of us will have to jump onto his boat
and take over."

"Excuse me? Did you say one of us is going to
jump between the boats while they're *moving*?"

"It's not that difficult."

"Well, it won't be me," she declared.

"Then you can drive."

She didn't like that scenario, either. "I haven't driven a boat in a long time."

"You can do it. Take the wheel now. Get comfortable with it. I'll see if I can get your dad on the radio."

She gripped the wheel with tight hands as Shane tried to raise her father on the radio.

Nothing.

When they neared the *Leonora,* she could see her father standing inside the cabin. The door was closed and he seemed oblivious to their presence. Shane switched frequencies, and the sound of music blasted through. Her father had always loved opera—a strange passion for a simple fisherman, but he found some affinity between the music and the sea.

"I don't think he can hear us," Shane said. "Bring the boat as close as you can."

"Are you sure you don't want to drive it?"

"Just hold her steady, Lauren. I'll jump onto your dad's boat and drive him back. You can follow us."

"You're going to leave me alone on this boat—on the ocean?" It had been a long time since she'd allowed herself to get into a situation she couldn't control, and this was *way* out of her comfort zone. "I don't think I can do this."

He looked her straight in the eye. "You can."

His words, his gaze, reminded her of a conversation from a lifetime ago when he'd handed her a helmet and taught her how to drive his motorcycle. He'd always pushed her beyond her limits, forced her to believe in herself.

"You want your father back or not?" he challenged.

She lifted her chin and drew in a deep breath. "You jump. I'll drive."

"Good. Don't worry, I won't let you out of my sight. It took me a long time to save enough cash to buy this boat. I don't intend to lose it."

"I'm touched by your sentiment." While she was getting dreamy-eyed about their past, he was thinking only of his boat.

"Just stay close, Lauren. I don't feel like going for a swim, even though I'm sure you'd enjoy tossing me into the sea."

She bit down on her lip as Shane went to the side of the boat. She wasn't worried about him, he could take care of himself. Fearlessness was part of his makeup. He wasn't a man to sit on the sidelines and wait for someone else to take charge, and right now she was grateful for that.

Shane stepped over the rail, paused for a second, and then jumped, landing on the fishing platform on her father's boat. He stumbled slightly, then straightened and yanked open the door to the cabin.

Her father finally turned his head. He exchanged a few words with Shane, then Shane took over at the wheel. A moment later his voice came over the radio. "Let's go home, Lauren."

His words brought a bittersweet rush of emotion. Angel's Bay wasn't her home now, and it never would be again.

It took about twenty minutes to get back to the marina. Shane kept in constant contact on the radio and Lauren stayed as close to her father's boat as possible. She breathed a sigh of relief when she drove the boat into the slip. Shane came on board to tie the lines down while she joined her father, who was waiting for her on the dock.

His khaki pants and black windbreaker hung loosely on his thin frame. He'd lost weight in the years since she'd last seen him, and he'd aged quite a bit. His dark hair was all gray now, including the stubble on his cheeks. He stood with his shoulders hunched, but he didn't seem concerned about his jaunt out to sea. She didn't know if that was good or bad.

When he saw her his eyes widened with surprise, followed by what appeared to be teary emotion. He shook his head as if he couldn't believe she was there, and she felt a rush of guilt at all the years she'd let go by. This man was her father. He'd tucked her in at night, scared away the monsters under her bed, been there for her—well, some of the time.

Maybe they hadn't shared a lot of common interests, but they were connected by blood, by love. How could she have let him go? How could she have forgotten what they were to each other?

"Hi, Dad," she said softly.

"Abby." He held out his arms. "My sweet, precious girl. You've come back to me at last. I've missed you so much."

Lauren's heart came to a crashing halt. "I'm Lauren, Dad. I'm not Abby. I'm Lauren," she repeated, seeing disappointment and fear fill his eyes.

"What have you done with Abby?" he asked in confusion, his arms dropping to his sides. "What have you done with your sister?"

Suddenly it was easy to remember why she'd left, and why she'd stayed away so long.

TWO

"Our daughter will need her father, Colin." Kara Lynch gently stroked her husband's hand. His skin was cool, and she wondered if he could feel the chill of fall in the air—if he could feel anything. It had been three months since he had lapsed into a coma after being shot in the head. For those three months she'd talked to him, held his hand, kissed him, played him music, brought in friends and family, and put his hand on her pregnant belly, hoping that something would wake him up and bring him back to her. But Colin remained silent and motionless, his face a mask of calm.

Her gregarious, stubborn Irishman with the sun-kissed blond hair, bright green eyes, and big, generous heart was a ghost of his former self. Colin had always been big and sturdy, built like a football player. He was a natural-born protector and he'd loved being a police officer, keeping the town and the people he cared about safe. But that love had brought him to this, shot down in his patrol car by a madman.

Colin had lost twenty pounds in the past three months. His hair had darkened from the lack of sunlight, and she hadn't seen his eyes open and alert since he'd waved good-bye to her before he'd left on patrol that night.

She felt him slipping further away from her every day, and she was desperate to bring him back. The doctors had warned her that his condition could be permanent, but that wasn't a possibility she could accept. She was going to have a baby soon, and she couldn't do that without him. This was the child they'd spent years trying to conceive. This was their miracle baby.

Kara drew in a sharp breath, worried that she'd already used up her one miracle. But she had to stay positive. Colin would expect that of her. He was the one who believed in the angels, the legends that had surrounded the town of Angel's Bay since its inception a hundred and fifty years ago, when a ship named the *Gabriella* had gone down in a storm outside the bay.

The twenty-four survivors of that wreck had named the bay for their loved ones who had lost their lives, the angels who would forever watch over them and their descendants. Kara was descended from one of those survivors, and the baby she and Colin had created could trace her bloodline back to the original Murray family. If anyone deserved a miracle, it was her daughter, a child who would need her father.

"You have to wake up, honey," she said forcefully. "I know you're tired, and you've been resting a long time. That's okay, because if anyone deserved a break, it was you." She pushed a lock of hair away from his forehead. Colin had always worn his hair short, and he'd probably hate that she'd let it go so long. But his growing hair was one of the few things that reminded her that he was still alive, and some days she desperately needed that reminder.

"I miss you, Colin. I miss your arms around me, the way you laugh, even that awful smacking sound you make when you eat your cereal in the morning. I miss seeing you drink milk out of the carton, your clothes on the end of the bed, the way you hold on to me when you sleep, as if you can't bear to let me go. I miss us." She had to fight to hold back the tears. "I can't do this alone. You've been my best friend since kindergarten. You said we'd always be together. You *have* to come back to me. Please."

Not even the smallest flicker of his eyelid. Could he hear her? The doctors and nurses told her she should keep talking, but who really knew if Colin was listening? Maybe she was just talking to herself. She tried to push away the doubt, but she was tired, and that's when the fear set in—when she wondered if he would ever wake up, or if she would spend the rest of her life talking to a man whose soul had long since departed.

Stretching her arms over her head, she let out a sigh. She should probably go home. It was almost nine o'clock and visiting hours were long over, not that anyone would kick her out. The people who ran the Bayview Care Center were kind and compassionate. Most of the patients at the long-term-care facility were elderly, but there was another woman down the hall who'd been comatose for almost five years after an automobile accident.

Kara didn't like to think about her.

A knock came at the half-open door, and she was surprised to see her older brother, Shane, walk into the room. While everyone in her family had been supportive, their visits to the clinic had dwindled in recent weeks, and she couldn't blame them. Despite her efforts to make Colin's room bright and cheerful, it was still a sterile environment and the disturbing smells of bleach and sickness lingered in the air.

She started to get up, but Shane waved her back down.

"How's it going?" he asked.

His gaze moved to Colin, where it rested for a long minute. Shane was one of the few people who actually looked at him. Most people were either afraid or too uncomfortable to acknowledge his presence. Even Colin's parents had difficulty looking at their son when they came to visit. She was sure that's why they hadn't been back in a few weeks.

"It's all right," she said. "Nothing's changed."

He glanced back at her. "You've been spending a lot of time here."

"I don't know where else to be. If you're going to tell me not to come—"

"I wouldn't dream of it."

"Good, because I've already heard it from Mom and Dad and everyone else who thinks I should be moving on with my life. How can I do that? I can't give up on him, can I?" She paused, shaking her head. "I can't believe I just asked that out loud. I'm more tired than I thought."

"No one would think less of you if you decided not to spend so much time here."

"I'd think less of me. I'd be a horrible wife."

His eyes darkened with compassion. "No, you wouldn't. You've been incredible, Kara. Colin wouldn't want you sitting here day after day."

"He'd do it for me." She looked at her husband and knew that was the absolute truth. Colin had always been devoted to her. His love had never known any bounds.

"He would," Shane agreed, "but I don't think you'd want him to."

Shane might be right, but it was too soon to think about staying away. "So why are you here? Not that I'm not happy to see you, but is there another reason?"

He dug his hands into the pockets of his jeans. "Just checking in."

Something in his eyes belied his words. Though she and Shane were only two years apart, she rarely knew what he was thinking, and never what he was feeling. He was the least forthcoming of her four siblings, a man of few words, and many people in town considered him to be the black sheep of the family—the angry, moody rebel with a quick temper and a penchant for trouble. Some even considered him a murderer. But he was her brother, and she loved him, even if she didn't always understand him.

"Are you sure?" she prodded.

"I didn't come here to talk about me."

"I didn't think you did. But since my life is rather depressing at the moment, I thought you might distract me."

He sat in the chair across from her. "Ned Jamison decided to take his boat out a couple of hours ago. I had to chase him down, bring him back."

"It's so sad what's happening to him. Some decisions will have to be made soon. I don't think he can continue living alone."

"He's not alone tonight." Shane cleared his throat as he stared down at the floor. "Lauren came back."

His words shocked her. "Really? I never thought that would happen. Have you talked to her?" She didn't have to hear his answer to know that he had. That's why he was so edgy. He'd just seen his ex-girlfriend, the one girl he'd never been able to forget.

Shane and Lauren had fallen hard for each other in high school. She'd spied on them kissing in front of the house many times, and they'd always had such a passion for each other. Shane had gone out with a lot of girls, but Lauren had been different. He'd treated her like she was something special. Then their love had come to a crashing, horrifying end with Abby's death. Kara didn't know all that had gone down between them, but they'd both left Angel's Bay for a very long time.

"Lauren went with me to chase down her father," Shane said.

"What's she like now?"

He shrugged.

"Beautiful brunette with dark blue eyes and an incredible smile?" she prodded.

He inclined his head. "You could say that."

"I bet you could say more," she said with a little smile. "You had such a thing for her."

He frowned, his jaw setting in a hard, familiar line. "A long time ago, and it didn't end well."

"Are you sure it ended?"

"Absolutely." He paused. "She's different now. Older, harder . . . she had on business clothes. She looked like a damned lawyer."

"I can't picture Lauren as a lawyer. Do you know what she does for a living?"

"I didn't ask."

Kara sighed. "You are the most frustrating man to get information from. How long will she be in town?"

"As long as it takes to convince her father to move to San Francisco with her."

Kara raised an eyebrow. "That might take forever. Mr. Jamison loves this town."

"That's what I told her. Lauren doesn't know her father at all anymore."

"This could be her opportunity to reconnect. I hope she doesn't waste it. Since Colin has been lying here, I've thought about all the things I wish I'd said to him when I had the chance. If—when he wakes up, I'm going to talk his ears off."

"That won't be anything new," Shane said with a half smile as he got to his feet.

She made a face at him. "Ha ha."

"Can I get you anything before I go?"

"No, I'm fine. So what are you going to do about Lauren?"

"Nothing. I doubt I'll see her again. I'm the last person she wants to spend time with."

"This is a small town."

"Believe me, I won't have to avoid her. She'll be avoiding me."

As Shane left, Kara turned toward Colin and smiled. "Oh, honey, you really need to wake up now. Shane and Lauren are finally in the same place at the same time, and that can only mean trouble."

Lauren's hand shook as she set her father's cup of tea on the kitchen table in front of him. After their first awkward greeting he'd finally recognized her, and they'd returned to the house together. Since then she'd busied herself making him tea while she tried to figure out what to say next.

It had been five years since they'd seen each

other, and that had been a brief evening when he'd stopped in San Francisco during a weeklong fishing trip with his buddies. They'd had dinner, shared some conversation and a hug good-bye, and that had probably been the longest they'd spent together in the past decade.

Her father lifted the cup to his lips and took a long sip. "This is nice and hot. I've been feeling a chill in my bones the last few days. Summer is over, and I never cared much for fall—it means winter isn't far behind."

Another way they were different, Lauren thought. The winter weather hurt her father's fishing business, so she'd grown up hiding the fact that she secretly loved a really good storm—with the wind howling, the rain pounding against the windows, and the air cold enough to bake up sweet, hot desserts that would warm from the inside out.

She watched her father for a moment, noting the little details of age: the sunspots on his hands, the new wrinkles around his eyes and mouth, the weariness of his posture. When she was growing up, he'd been the force around whom they'd all revolved. He had less substance now, like a once-bright picture that was fading around the edges. Had living alone all these years been hard on him? Not that she should care. It had been his choice.

"Dad, do you remember what you did tonight?" she asked.

"I went for a ride with Shane," Ned replied. "He loves the sea as much as I do. It's in his blood."

"Actually, you went out on your boat by yourself. Shane and I followed you, and then Shane jumped onto your boat and brought you back. Do you remember?"

"How's your mother?" he asked, changing the subject. "Is she still married to that accountant? I bet he's a barrel of fun."

"Mom is fine and so is her husband. They live in the wine country now."

"What's David up to?"

"He's starting his senior year at Northwestern. I think he may be headed to law school after graduation." She paused. "Dad, we need to discuss your illness. That's why I'm here."

"I'm fine," he said with a breezy wave of his hand. "I just forgot to take my pills this morning. You don't have to worry about me."

If she hadn't witnessed her father's earlier confused behavior she probably would have believed him, because at the moment he seemed completely rational. But she couldn't let herself forget what she'd seen.

"You're not fine, Dad. You left the stove on. You could have set the house on fire. You're not supposed to take the boat out anymore, and when you saw me on the dock, you didn't even recognize me. You thought I was Abby."

"It was dark." His brows knitted together in a frown. "You're making it sound worse than it was. I was coming back to make my tea. And I know the ocean like I know my own hand; I wasn't in any danger. I was just taking a ride."

"I'm not sure you would have recognized any potential danger."

"I don't want to talk about it anymore. Tell me what's new with you. Are you still baking cookies?"

"No, I work as a corporate event planner at a hotel. I coordinate business meetings."

"You're not cooking?" His eyebrows rose. "I thought you wanted to run your own bakery."

"Well, things changed. I know you don't want to talk about your illness, but some of your neighbors have been in touch with Mom, and they don't think you can continue to live here alone."

"I can take care of myself."

"I've been doing some research, and I found a place three blocks from where I work." She reached for her purse and pulled out the brochure for Bella Mar. "A lot of the rooms have a view of the San Francisco Bay. You'd be able to see the water just the way you do here."

Her father didn't take the brochure. "You want to put me away in some rest home?" His dark eyes filled with disappointment.

"It's an assisted-living facility. You'd have an apartment, not just a room. There's a restaurant downstairs and someone to cook your meals. More important, I would be nearby. I could visit you all the time. When David comes home for vacations, he could stop in, too."

"Neither you nor your brother have visited me once in the last thirteen years. Why would you start now?"

She fought to ignore that pointed comment. She needed to stay on track and not get tangled up in an argument about the past. "Please, just look at the brochure."

"Was this your mother's idea?" he asked suspiciously. "She'd love to see me locked up in some home."

"It was my idea," she replied, unwilling to create any more ill will between her parents. "And you wouldn't be locked up. I want to take care of you, Dad."

"I'm not your responsibility. But if you want to help, you could move back here. This is your home."

She immediately shook her head. "I can't live in Angel's Bay, not after what happened. You know that."

"And I can't live anywhere else." His gaze was direct, determined. "I was born here. My parents were born here, and every generation back for a hundred and fifty years. There has always been a Jamison in Angel's Bay. And besides that, I won't leave Abby here alone."

A painful knot formed in Lauren's throat. She didn't have an argument to that. She hadn't been to her sister's grave since she'd watched them lower the white casket into the ground, and she didn't know if she could ever go back to the cemetery.

Maybe in saving herself, she'd forsaken her sister.

But Abby was dead. And whether or not Lauren or her father was in Angel's Bay wouldn't change that fact.

"Don't you ever miss this town?" Her father's perplexed gaze searched her face. "This is where your memories are, where we were a family. We buried your goldfish in the backyard. You learned how to do cartwheels on the front lawn. We won the award for the best holiday lights the year we put Santa on the roof, remember? You and Abby used to play hopscotch on the front walk, and ride your bikes up and down the hills."

Each reminder cut a little deeper; she almost felt as if she were bleeding. "Please, Dad. Don't do this. Don't try to make me feel bad."

"I want you to remember the good times."

"I don't want to remember—because when I do, all I can see is pain and all I feel is sadness." She drew in a deep shaky breath. "I just want to live where I am now."

"Without a past? Without the memories? You have no idea how much you'll regret that one day."

"I don't think I will."

"You will," he argued. "Because that's exactly where I'm headed. The doctor tells me that one day I'll be a blank slate. I won't know who I am. I won't remember anyone or anything in this town. I'll exist, but I won't be living. You're choosing to forget—and I'm desperate to hang on to my memories as long as I can."

She'd never seen her father afraid, but he was

now. He was moving toward a point that he wouldn't be able to recover from, and it scared her, too. Though their relationship was uncomfortable and complicated, he was her father, and she didn't want to lose him.

"I'll tell you something, Lauren," he added. "While I *can* remember, I'll be here in this town. I'll look at the sun setting over my piece of the ocean, I'll smell the fish frying at the Crab Shack, and get my morning coffee at Dina's Café and listen to Mort tell me about the biggest tuna he never caught. I'll go up to the cemetery and put flowers on your sister's grave and tell her what's happening. And when the day comes that I turn into a zombie, and you want to cart me away and stick me in a closet somewhere, I won't be able to stop you. But not now. Not yet."

"I'm not trying to hurt you, Dad. I don't know what else to do."

Ned got to his feet and carried his teacup to the sink. "There's nothing for you to do. I'm going to bed."

She cringed at the cool note in his voice. She'd never known how to make him happy or proud, and tonight she'd completely failed him. But *he'd* made mistakes, too. Others might applaud him for staying with Abby, but she couldn't forget that he'd just let his wife and his other two children go.

"Dad, we need to continue this discussion."

"Tomorrow. I'm tired. You can sleep in your old room, if you want. I don't expect you'll be staying long." As her father moved away, he knocked a pile of mail off the counter.

Lauren helped him collect the papers, noting the large pile of bills. Some were stamped second or final notice. Did her father know how to write a check anymore? She'd go through them after he went to bed.

As she set the pile on the counter, her gaze caught on two typed pages with a business card attached. It looked like a story outline of some sort. The first few sentences prickled the hairs on the back of her neck. "Dad, what's this?" She skimmed the next paragraph, and her stomach turned over. "Oh, my God, this is about Abby." She lifted her gaze to her father. "Is someone writing a book about her death?"

"It's not a book; it's a movie. A producer came to see me the other day. He's been researching Abby's murder."

Lauren stared at her father in shock. How could he sound so calm? So matter of fact? "Why—why would anyone want to do that?"

"To find the truth and to get justice for your sister. That's all I've ever wanted."

"I want answers, too, but this isn't the way to get them."

"Nothing else has worked. The police haven't done anything in years."

"Because there aren't any leads to follow. This movie won't suddenly create new clues."

"It could. You never know."

She didn't want to kill the hopeful glint in his eyes, but she couldn't stand the idea of someone making money off her sister's death. "Dad, no. Think about it—a movie with actors and actresses playing you, me, and Abby and everyone else?" She shuddered. "Could you handle them recreating the night of her murder? Could you really?"

His expression grew troubled. "That doesn't sound so good, but I want to know who killed her. I want to make him pay."

"Some movie producer can't solve Abby's murder. That's up to the police." She ripped off the business card. "I'm going to call this Mark Devlin and tell him to stop."

"He seems very determined."

"Well, so am I."

"Are you?" her father challenged, a sharp glint in his eyes. "That might require you to stay in Angel's Bay, and you're not willing to do that, are you? Not for me. Not for Abby. You're all fire and righteous indignation now, but when it comes down to it, you'll leave. You'll tell yourself that you did your duty: you came to rescue your father and he refused to go, but you did your best. You even tried to stop them from making a movie about your sister's life, but no one would listen to you. So what could you do but go back to living the life you live, without any memories? Isn't that what's going to happen, Lauren?"

It was the first time he'd used her name since

she'd arrived, but there was no love in his voice—
only disappointment and sarcasm. While she wanted
to tell him he was wrong, she couldn't. She didn't
know how far she was willing to go to help her father, or to protect her sister's memory. And she
wasn't sure she wanted to find out.

THREE

Mark Devlin was becoming a pain in the ass with his slick good looks, styled blond hair, designer clothes, and red Ferrari. He was not only turning women's heads, he was also stirring up trouble in Angel's Bay. And some of that trouble was hitting too close to home for Chief of Police Joe Silveira.

Joe paused inside the door to Murray's Bar, frowning as he caught sight of his wife tipping back beers with Devlin at a corner table. Rachel was laughing at something he'd said, her smile wide and joyous, and a wave of jealousy ran through him. She rarely laughed with him anymore. He was usually the recipient of an annoyed or disappointed glare.

It was his fault things were tense between them—at least according to Rachel. He was the one who'd decided to quit his job as a cop for the LAPD and move north to Angel's Bay. He was the one who'd overlooked the fact that Rachel had a career she loved selling real estate to the rich and famous.

He was the one who had wanted her to change her entire life for him.

Yeah, the move was his idea—but she shared responsibility for some of the other problems in their relationship. And even though his move had strained their marriage, he wouldn't take it back. He'd been losing himself, working as a cop in L.A. If he hadn't gotten out when he had, he didn't know what kind of man he would have become.

Lately he'd begun to think things were changing for the better. Rachel still commuted back and forth to L.A., but she was spending more time here. Angel's Bay was a growing seaside community with new developments going up along the coastline. There was plenty of real estate to be sold right here, and Rachel was beginning to see that—he hoped. They'd been together since they were fifteen years old, and they had a lot of history, a lot invested in their relationship. He needed to make it work.

As he made his way toward her table, he felt a rush of pride. Rachel was one of the prettiest women he'd ever known, with her jet black hair and her dark eyes. She was thinner now than he liked, and she wore too much makeup. She'd also become obsessed with anything designer, which was no surprise, considering how much time she spent in Beverly Hills. He clamped down on the critical thoughts. He couldn't keep focusing on what he didn't like about her. She was changing; so was he; but they were still together—and that was something.

"Joe." Rachel gave him a wave. "There you are.

I was wondering if you were going to stand me up again."

He only stood her up if he couldn't get off duty, but that was an argument he didn't intend to have now. He didn't like Devlin much, nor did he trust him. The guy was too smooth, too quick to tell people what they wanted to hear. Devlin and Rachel had been friends in L.A., and she was the one who'd told him about Angel's Bay, who'd encouraged him to consider shooting a movie here. Joe shouldn't begrudge the fact that she had a friend of her own in town, but he wished it was anyone else.

Sliding into the booth next to Rachel, he gave her a quick kiss on the lips and nodded at Devlin. The man looked like a surfer, with his bleached blond hair and light brown eyes, but his laid-back manner didn't fool Joe. Devlin was a player, a manipulator—the kind of man who always had an agenda.

"Back in town for the weekend?" he asked. "You're spending a lot of time here these days."

Devlin gave him an easy smile. "I have more people to talk to about the Jamison case."

"Yeah, about that." Joe leaned forward, resting his forearms on the table. "I thought you were planning to make a horror flick about a haunted house. When did this movie become about the Jamison girl?"

"When I realized the potential of the story— the unsolved murder of a beautiful teenage girl, in a town where angels and demons lurk side by side. Rachel agrees with me. She thinks it's going to be fantastic, don't you, sweetheart?"

Joe didn't like the casual endearment, or the smile on his wife's face. "Don't you think this movie might hurt the family of that girl?" he asked Rachel. "Her father still lives here."

"Mark will fictionalize the story," Rachel replied. "It will be fine."

"Actually, I'm thinking it would be a good true-crime piece," Devlin said. "I've already got a studio interested in the project."

"This movie could be great for the town, Joe," Rachel added. "Just think of all the revenue that a shoot would bring in—not to mention the tourist dollars after the movie is released. It could put Angel's Bay on the map."

"We're already on the map. We're growing fast."

"And this will speed things along. I can think of half a dozen celebrities who might want to build vacation homes here, if there was more to do in town."

Her words frustrated him. "Why can't you live here without trying to change the town?"

His words drew a pouting frown to her lips. "Sometimes change is good, Joe. Isn't that what you always tell me?"

"And that's my cue to get another beer," Devlin said, sliding out of the booth. "Do you two need anything?"

"Not from you," Joe replied, disliking the cocky smile in Devlin's eyes.

"Well, that was subtle," Rachel said when they were alone. "I'm surprised you didn't just pee to mark your territory."

"Would it make a difference? You're spending a lot of time with him. You know I don't like it."

"Which makes no sense, since you don't know Mark. But it doesn't matter. He's my friend, not yours."

There was a defiant, challenging look in her eyes that disturbed him. "Why would you want to have a friend who makes me uncomfortable?"

"You don't have a reason to feel uncomfortable. There's nothing going on. I haven't been unfaithful to you. Mark and I share mutual friends, common interests. I like that. He's never tried to get between us. If anything, he has encouraged me to spend more time here."

"Because he wants your help to get this movie made. Not because he wants you to be with me."

"The movie would be good for us. I'm still working my way into the local real estate market. If I can have a career here, I won't have to keep commuting to L.A."

Rachel usually avoided making any long-term commitment to a future in Angel's Bay. This was the first time she'd indicated that she'd given the idea some thought.

He wanted to believe her, because he loved Angel's Bay—the brilliant sunsets, fresh sea air, and shocking blue skies. He liked falling asleep to the sound of the waves crashing on the beach. He loved the sense of community, the way people looked out for one another. He'd grown up in a tough working class neighborhood in Los Angeles, where it was dangerous to turn your back on anyone. He felt free here. He just wanted Rachel to love the town as much as he did . . . or maybe even to love him as much as she once had.

"Rachel," he began.

She shook her head, cutting him off with a wary look. "Don't, Joe. It's not a night to be serious. Let's just have some drinks and toast the weekend."

"You don't know what I was going to say."

"Yes, I do," she said, holding his gaze. "I've known you a long time. I'm here. I'm trying. Let's leave it at that for now."

"I'm trying, too."

"Try harder. Be a little nicer to Mark. He's not your enemy."

"I wish he wasn't your friend," Joe grumbled, unable to hide his jealousy. He was hanging on to his marriage by a thread and Mark wasn't helping.

"You have friends, too, Joe. What about that blonde you had over at the house a couple of months ago?"

"Dr. Adams is a colleague." He was more attracted to the pretty blond doctor than he should be, but in the past few months he'd made a point of keeping his distance from her. And Charlotte wasn't the kind of woman to get involved with a married man.

"Mark is my colleague," Rachel said. "So, we're good, right?"

"Yeah, we're good."

Mark set down a beer in front of Joe and resumed his seat. "Thought you could use a drink, Chief."

"Thanks."

"And I need a favor," Devlin continued. "I've read the public records on the Jamison murder, but I'd like to see the police file. One of your officers told me he couldn't release the file because the case was never closed."

"It's an ongoing investigation."

"It hasn't been ongoing in more than a decade. I spoke to Abigail Jamison's father. I have the family's support. And I would think the Angel's Bay police department would welcome any assistance to help solve this crime."

Joe felt Rachel's gaze on him. He needed to show her how much he was willing to try. "I'll consider your request. There may be some information I can release."

"I'd appreciate that." A look of excitement flashed through Mark's eyes as a man entered the bar. "Well, look who just walked in."

"Who is that?" Rachel asked, following Mark's gaze.

"Shane Murray," Joe replied, an uneasy feeling running down his spine. The dark-haired, dark-eyed fisherman had quite the reputation from years past. In the seven months that Joe had been in town, Murray had kept to himself, and he certainly hadn't caused any trouble. But the man had lived a reckless and wild life, fishing some of the most dangerous seas in the world. He wasn't a man to take lightly or to mess with.

"Shane Murray was the prime suspect in Abby Jamison's death," Devlin told Rachel. "He was the boyfriend of Abby's older sister, Lauren."

"He was also never tried, due to lack of evidence," Joe added.

"That doesn't mean he didn't kill her," Devlin said.

"So you intend to ask him if he did?" Joe inquired.

Devlin smiled. "I intend to ask him if he wants to help me find the real killer. Most innocent men would jump at the chance to clear their name."

"What if he's not innocent?" Rachel asked. "You should be careful, Mark. If he did kill that girl, he might not like you asking him about it."

"Maybe I should take the long arm of the law with me," Mark said, grinning at Joe. "What do you say, Chief? Want to be my backup?"

"You're on your own." Was it wrong to hope that Murray would beat the crap out of Devlin? "But if he does kill you, I'll arrest him."

"Joe," Rachel said with a sigh.

"Let's get some chili fries," he said, motioning for the waitress. "Looks like there's going to be a show."

Shane sat on a stool at the end of the bar, watching his younger brother Michael mix drinks. Michael and their cousin Aidan ran Murray's Bar, along with their uncle Tommy. The bar had been in the family for generations and was always crowded on the weekends. Three television screens played sports in the front, while the back room had two pool tables that could be rented for private parties.

Like all of Shane's siblings, Michael was fair, his hair dark blond, a strand of Murray freckles running across his nose and jawbones. Shane had escaped both the fair skin and the freckles—which had always seemed fitting for the black sheep of the family. Michael was the adored baby. Not that he would appreciate being called that at twenty-five, but he still had a youthful innocence that Shane very much wanted to protect.

Michael slid a cold beer down the bar in his direction. Shane grabbed it with a quick hand and took a long swig. He'd felt the need for a drink ever since Lauren had appeared. He'd spent most of the past decade trying not to think about her. He'd seen the world, made some money, and there had been plenty of other women in his life, beautiful, sexy women. He just couldn't remember any of them right now.

He never should have kissed Lauren. That was the damn stupidest idea he'd had in a long time. Now her taste was fresh on his lips, and he could still feel the brush of her soft, full breasts against his chest. But what really stuck in his mind was that she hadn't pushed him away. She'd kissed him back. It would have been a lot easier if she'd slapped his face.

Michael took away the empty bottle, replacing it with another.

"I like the service," Shane said approvingly.

"I figured you'd be in, as soon as I heard Lauren Jamison was back in town. Weren't you doing her back in high school?"

"We went out." Michael was seven years younger and had been in elementary school when Shane and Lauren had been together.

Michael grinned. "Is that what they called it in the old days?"

"I don't want to talk about Lauren. How did you hear she was in town, anyway?"

Michael rolled his eyes. "The gossip was flying as soon as you docked her father's boat. There's already a betting pool as to whether the two of you will get back together. Want to tip me off? I could use some cash."

"Save your money. Lauren is here to deal with her father's living situation. That's it."

"I wonder if she's heard about the movie."

Shane sighed at the reminder. Angel's Bay was buzzing about it. "If she hasn't yet, I'm sure she will."

"The guy who's making it is right over there," Michael continued with a tip of his head. "You meet him yet?"

"Nope."

"It's weird, isn't it? Lauren comes back at exactly the same time that someone wants to make a movie about her sister, and you happen to be here, too. All the players are in town at the same time. It's almost as if the angels are stirring things up again."

"I don't think it's the angels I have to worry about." Shane felt a deep sense of foreboding. He'd waited a long time to come home, for the rumors to die down, for his family to stop being the focus of gossip, for everyone to forget. Now it was all starting up again.

"What are you going to do?" Michael asked.

"I have no idea."

"You'd better come up with one fast. You've got company."

A man slid onto the stool next to Shane's. "Mr. Murray," he said with an easy smile. "I'm Mark Devlin. I'm making a movie based on the death of Abigail Jamison. I'd like to talk to you."

"I have nothing to say," Shane replied, getting to his feet.

Mark stood up as well and put a hand on his arm.

Shane immediately shrugged it off, giving Devlin a small shove at the same time. He had to fight back a reckless urge to take a swing at the guy's arrogant face, but he didn't go off half-cocked anymore. Especially not with the chief of the police sitting a few tables away.

Mark put up both hands. "Sorry. Look, I just want to hear your version of what happened that night. Surely you'd like to clear your name."

"I don't care what people say."

"Well, I don't think you did it," Devlin said quickly.

Shane froze. "Is that so?"

"I have a few other suspects in mind, including one individual who was never interrogated."

Shane couldn't stop the question from slipping out. "Who?"

"The older sister—Lauren. Word on the street is that the two sisters were competitive. Lauren was jealous. Abby was smarter, prettier, more accomplished, and Lauren didn't like the fact that her sister was with you that night."

"You're out of your mind."

"Am I?" Devlin had a troublemaking gleam in his eye. "Are you sure about that? You should talk to me. Together, we might come up with the truth."

"We're done here."

"For now, maybe. But I'm not going anywhere. Just think about it."

Shane strode through the bar, acutely aware that every eye in the place was on him. So much for the past staying in the past. Despite Devlin's claim that Lauren was his number one suspect, Shane knew he wouldn't be far behind. There was no way Devlin was going to make a movie and not include him. He'd been named a person of interest when the murder occurred. He'd been interrogated a dozen times. And even when the police couldn't bring a case against him, half the town had believed him to be guilty. Some still did.

He should have known better than to come

home. And he had a feeling Lauren was going to wish the very same thing.

It was almost midnight before Lauren gathered enough courage to enter the bedroom she'd shared with Abby. As she turned on the light, she felt as if she'd stepped back in time.

Abby's bed was covered by a red polka-dot comforter, a half dozen throw pillows, and Loveylou, the stuffed bunny her younger sister had slept with since she was two years old. Lauren drew in a sharp breath, feeling an overwhelming sense of pain at the sight of the one-eared bunny. She immediately looked away, but everywhere her gaze fell was another memory.

Abby's clothes were in the closet, and her shoes were tossed in a pile on the floor where she'd left them that last day. The bulletin board over Abby's desk boasted her latest straight-A report card, the program from the prom, a photograph of the high school varsity volleyball team, of which Abby had been the star setter, and an unused ticket for a concert the weekend after Abby's death.

Her gaze moved to a photograph on the desk. Her younger sister had been so pretty, with her chestnut hair and big brown eyes. Abby looked like their father, while she and David took after their mother, with dark hair and blue eyes. It was funny that the family had divided along those same lines.

There wasn't one thing of Lauren's left in the

room. Only her bed remained, stripped down to the mattress. When her mother had decided to take her and David away, she'd packed up all their belongings, but Ned had refused to let her touch Abby's things. They'd had a vicious fight that last day, and her mother had cried all the way up the coast. Lauren hadn't understood then or even now how her parents' grief had turned them into bitter enemies, but that's exactly what had happened.

When she'd decided to return home, she'd never anticipated having to confront the past so vividly, to be surrounded by the things that Abby had touched, worn, and slept on. Was it her imagination, or did Abby's perfume still linger in the air?

She closed her eyes, but that only made the memories worse. The day that Abby died had begun so innocently, like any other Monday morning . . .

"Abby, hurry up." Lauren grabbed her lunch off the kitchen counter and stuffed it into her backpack. School started in fifteen minutes, but as usual Abby was running late. "I'm going to leave without you," she added. It was two miles to the high school, and Lauren doubted Abby felt like walking.

When there was no answer from her sister, Lauren stormed down the hall to their room. Abby was sitting at her desk, writing in her journal. She jumped when she saw Lauren and quickly closed her diary, a guilty expression on her face.

"What are you doing?" Lauren asked.

"Nothing."

Lauren hadn't really cared what her sister was up to,

but now that Abby's cheeks were turning red, she was far more interested. "You have a secret. What is it?"

"As if I'd tell you."

"Then I guess I'll have to read about it in your diary."

Abby hastily put her journal into her backpack. "Don't even think about it."

"You like someone," Lauren teased.

"I do not."

"Yes, you do. Who is it? Tell me."

Abby shrugged, an odd look in her eyes. "It doesn't matter. I can't—I can't have him."

"Why not? Does he have a girlfriend?"

"I don't want to talk about it, Lauren. You wanted to go, so let's go." Abby breezed past her, knocking her in the shoulder with her bag.

"Ow," Lauren said, rubbing her arm. "You did that on purpose. You are such a pain in the ass. I should make you walk."

"But you won't, because you love me," Abby tossed out with a knowing smile.

"Not that much," she returned.

The next morning, Abby was dead.

Lauren's eyes flew open, her breathing labored. The last thing she'd said to her sister was that she didn't love her that much. Had Abby known she was just joking? God, she hoped so.

Her gaze traveled back to the desk. She knew the journal wasn't there, because they'd all looked for it after Abby's death, hoping they might learn some secret that might have gotten Abby killed. But Abby's bag had gone missing and had never been located.

What had Abby meant—a boy she couldn't have? The obvious answer had been Shane. That's certainly where everyone had jumped when Lauren had repeated the conversation. The fact that Shane had been seen giving Abby a ride to the high school that night had only reinforced that theory.

Had there been something going on between Shane and Abby? He'd denied it and she'd wanted to believe him, but he'd lied to her that day. He'd told her he was going out on a fishing charter with his father that night, but he'd been in town, with Abby, and he'd never explained why. It hurt to think that Abby and Shane might have betrayed her, and she'd never been able to put the thought away.

But two teenagers cheating was one thing; murder was another.

"Oh, Abby," she said out loud. "I wish we could rewind the clock and replay that conversation, so you could tell me what you were up to that day."

A chill seemed to blow through the room. Although the windows were closed the curtains shimmered with some phantom breeze, and Lauren had the strangest sensation that she wasn't alone. "Abby?" she whispered.

"What are you still doing up?"

She started, whirling around.

Her father stood in the doorway wearing his pajamas and slippers. "It's late, Abigail. You should be asleep. We leave at four. The fish won't wait."

His words shocked Lauren back to the present.

"I don't think we're going fishing tomorrow, Dad," she said slowly, not sure how to talk to him. Was it better to confront him or to go along?

"Of course we are. It's your birthday. We always go fishing on your birthday."

"How old am I going to be?"

"Thirteen. You're a teenager now." His smile turned sad. "You won't be my baby girl for very long. The boys will be knocking on the door soon, but tomorrow will be just for us. Don't tell your mother or Lauren, but I stopped by Martha's and picked up those blueberry muffins you like so much. We'll have them for breakfast. It will be one of our little secrets."

There was something about the way he said the word *secrets* that bothered Lauren even more than the rest of the disjointed conversation. "What are some of our other secrets, Dad?"

He frowned, his gaze narrowing on her face. Uncertainty passed through his eyes. "Lauren?"

He was back to the present.

"Yes, it's me, Dad," she said gently.

"Well, of course it's you. I suppose you think I should have gotten rid of Abby's things by now."

"Doesn't it make it harder for you to see the room like this?"

"I feel closer to Abby in here. I talk to her, and I think she can hear me." He walked across the room and picked up one of several fishing trophies displayed on the dresser. "Abby was only eleven when she won this. She was a natural-born fisherman." He scratched his chin. "Not like you—you hated the waiting. I never could understand how I got a daughter who didn't like the ocean."

"I liked the ocean in the daytime, and for short periods. I just liked other things more—but you didn't really care about those other things."

"Your mom always knew what you liked," he said, as if that excused him from the responsibility.

She took a deep breath, feeling as if she were about to step off a cliff. She'd never discussed anything personal with her father. "I wanted you to know, too."

"I knew. Your mother would tell me." He set down the trophy. "I'm going to bed."

"Dad—in all these years, did you ever find Abby's diary?"

"No. It must have been in her book bag that night."

She nodded as he left the room. That's what they'd always thought. Her sister's secrets had gone with her to the grave.

Lauren couldn't see how the movie producer was going to be able to come up with the name of Abby's killer. There weren't any clues; there never had been. If Mark Devlin was going to name a villain, he would have to make one up.

FOUR

Lauren woke up Saturday morning with a pain in her back and a cramp in her leg. She stretched with a groan, feeling bruised and battered. She doubted the old sofa bed had even been opened in the last decade. But she'd been unable to imagine sleeping in her old bedroom, now a shrine to her sister.

Getting to her feet, she stumbled to the bathroom. The mirror over the sink was not kind. Her dark brown hair was tangled and wild, and there were shadows under her eyes. She smoothed her hair and splashed some cold water on her face. Coffee first, then a shower. She grabbed a sweatshirt out of her suitcase and threw it over her pink camisole and purple pajama bottoms.

She'd make some eggs—maybe French toast with powdered sugar and bacon. It had been years since she'd had bacon, but being home reminded her of the sandwiches her mother used to make, crispy bacon on toast with lots of butter. It was a wonder none of them had had a heart attack.

As she looked at her father's empty shelves, her excitement faded. The only coffee was instant and probably a few years old, which surprised her. Her father had always loved his coffee in the morning. It was one thing they had in common.

She closed the cupboard, suddenly aware of the quiet house. It was nine fifteen; her father should have been up by now. He'd been a fisherman since he could walk, and he'd always talked about the wonder of being on the ocean in the stunning stillness of dawn. She'd never been a big fan of daybreak, but she was a big fan of breakfast. Maybe she'd wake him and they'd go get some pancakes.

But her father wasn't in his room, or anywhere in the house. He was gone again, and she had no idea where. As she considered her options, the doorbell rang. A moment of pure vanity made her hesitate. She looked like hell, and she really hoped it wasn't Shane. She needed her armor on when she talked to him again—or at least some lipstick.

She returned to the living room, glanced through the peephole, and was surprised to see a familiar and attractive blonde on the porch. For the first time since she'd arrived, she was truly happy to see someone. She threw open the door with a smile. "Charlotte Adams. I can't believe it's you."

Charlotte's jaw dropped and her eyes widened in amazement. "Lauren? When did you get back?"

"Yesterday." Charlotte had been her very first best friend. They'd met in kindergarten. Terrified of the big school, they'd held hands at recess and hadn't let go of each other for a long time, not until high school when boys and other problems had gotten in the way. "You haven't changed at all."

Charlotte's golden blond hair was pulled back in a ponytail. Her skin was clear and beautiful, her light blue eyes framed by ridiculously long dark lashes, and she looked fit in her running shoes, black leggings, and T-shirt.

"That is definitely not true. I never thought you'd come back, Lauren."

"I had to. My dad is ill."

"I know." Charlotte gave her a compassionate smile. "You look like you had a rough night."

"I had a battle with the pull-out couch. So what are you doing here?"

"I'm dropping off a casserole and some cookies for your father." Charlotte held up the box in her hands. "Courtesy of my mother."

"That's very thoughtful. Can you come in for a minute, or do you have to work? I hear you've been busy bringing new lives into the world as an ob/gyn."

Charlotte raised an eyebrow. "I guess the Angel's Bay network transmits all the way to San Francisco."

"My mother still keeps in touch with a few people." Lauren led the way into the kitchen. She put the casserole dish in the fridge and the plate of chocolate chip cookies on the table. "These look delicious."

Charlotte grinned as she pulled out a chair and

sat down. "Nowhere near as good as yours, I'm sure. Are you still baking?"

"Not much. Too busy working. I'm a corporate event planner."

"Really? I remember when your mother gave you that miniature oven for Christmas. You made me play restaurant for hours on end," she added with a laugh. "I always thought you'd end up in a bakery somewhere."

"Do you still run?" Lauren asked, eager to change the subject.

"Almost every day. We should go together while you're here. We could take the path that runs along the bluffs. You won't believe how much Angel's Bay has grown. Grand Avenue has completely changed—upscale art galleries, antique stores, and designer clothing boutiques. And there are some mansions going up along the coast. Apparently the rich and famous have decided to make Angel's Bay their new summer escape."

"I noticed a few big houses on my way in," Lauren said. "I guess it's not such a small town anymore. When did you get back? I thought you were practicing in New York."

"I came home several months ago, when my father died. My brother is a marine, stationed in the Middle East. My sister is in San Francisco with her husband and kids, so my mom was here all alone. I was elected to come and take care of her." Charlotte gave a rueful smile. "My mother was thrilled to have her least favorite child move back into the house."

Lauren grinned at her dry comment. She remembered the battles Charlotte had had with her very strict and always opinionated mother. "How's it going?"

"That is too long a story to get into now, and one I should probably save for a therapist. So are you going to make me ask for a cookie?"

"Sorry." Lauren took off the plastic wrap and handed the plate to Charlotte.

"What are you going to do about your father?" Charlotte asked.

Lauren started, suddenly reminded that she didn't know where her father was. "I'm not sure. In fact, I was about to go look for him when you rang the bell."

"He's probably at Dina's Café. He has breakfast there every day."

"Well, I hope that's true. Last night he decided to go for a joyride in his boat." She hesitated, then figured Charlotte would probably hear the story before the day was out. "I saw Shane. He was on the dock when my father took off, and we went after him together."

Charlotte's eyes widened with surprise. "Are you serious? How was that?"

"Uncomfortable, tense." She wasn't going to tell Charlotte about their kiss.

"That good, huh?"

"It's been thirteen years since I saw him, but it felt like five minutes, which scared the hell out of me. The last thing I want to do is go back to that time or place."

Charlotte reached across the table, placing her

hand over Lauren's. "What happened to Abby was unimaginable. And having Shane accused of her murder—I don't know how you got through it." Guilt flitted through her eyes. "I wanted to be there for you, but we hadn't been talking for a while, and I didn't know if you wanted to hear from me."

"I was so wrapped up in my misery, I didn't want to talk to anyone." Lauren paused, thinking about how their friendship had splintered. "What happened between us, Charlie? One minute we were best friends and the next minute we weren't."

Charlotte smiled sadly as she let go of Lauren's hand and sat back in her chair. "We let some boys and mean gossip get in the way."

Lauren tilted her head. "It was more than that. You went through something, but you never told me what. You just pulled away."

"I made a lot of mistakes in high school. I got so tired of being the minister's daughter, the good girl, and I went a little crazy. Thank God I finally grew up. It took me long enough." Charlotte popped the last bite of her cookie into her mouth. "Did you hear about poor Kara?"

"Kara Murray—Shane's sister? What happened?"

"The good news is that she's having a baby in two weeks. The bad news is that her husband, Colin, got shot a few months ago and he's in a coma."

Lauren's jaw dropped. "Oh, my God. That's terrible. How is Kara coping?"

"She's a fighter, but the prognosis isn't good. We're all doing what we can to support her."

"That's tremendously sad. How did Colin get shot?"

"In the line of duty, unfortunately. He's a police officer now," Charlotte said.

"He was always such a good guy. I hope he recovers."

"We all do. And on a happier note, we're having a baby shower for Kara tomorrow at two o'clock at the quilt shop. You should come."

"Oh, no, I don't think so," Lauren said immediately.

"Kara would love to see you, and so would everyone else."

"I'm not part of things anymore."

"That doesn't matter. I was gone for a long time, too. Believe me, a few minutes at the quilt shop and you'll feel like you never left."

That's what Lauren was afraid of. "I don't think Kara would want me there. The Murrays were upset with me for not standing up for Shane."

"The Murrays understood that Abby had just been killed. No one blamed you."

"Shane did," she murmured. "He wanted me to believe in him, stand up for him, but I couldn't. I was so confused and shattered by Abby's death."

Charlotte's gaze met hers. "You don't really think Shane hurt Abby, do you? I know he saw Abby that night, but he was in love with you."

"Then why was he with Abby?"

"He never told you?"

Lauren shook her head. "No. Never. He just asked me to trust that he was innocent."

"Well, I think he *was* innocent, and I'm betting you think so, too."

Lauren gave a small nod. "Yes. But I don't know why I do."

"Because you knew him better than anyone. So come to the shower. Kara doesn't hold grudges, and right now she needs all the friends she can get. Plus, seeing you would take her mind off of her own situation. Think of it as an act of charity."

Lauren waved a warning finger at Charlotte, who had always been very persuasive. "You're not playing fair, Charlie."

"You're going to run into people eventually. You might as well get it over with."

"I don't know if I can face all the questions about Abby and Shane and me. I thought enough time had passed, but now there's a movie producer going around town talking about Abby's murder. I had no idea I would come home and end up right back where I was."

"Another good reason to come to the shower. You're one of us, Lauren. You grew up here. These are your friends, your neighbors. The movie producer is an outsider. You need to remind the women in this town that you're a local girl. They'll circle around you. You'll see." Charlotte got to her feet. "And you don't need to bring a present."

"I'll think about it," Lauren said as she stood up. "It was nice talking to you, Charlotte."

"You too. It's funny how so many of us left Angel's Bay, and now we're all coming back."

"Who else is back?"

"Andrew Schilling," Charlotte said with a mischievous smile.

"Your old boyfriend?" Lauren asked in surprise.

"That's right. He replaced my father as the new minister. How do you like that?"

"How do *you* like that?"

Charlotte laughed as she headed toward the door. "Come to the shower. Maybe I'll tell you."

Kara stood in the doorway of her baby's bedroom. It was almost noon and she'd planned to be at Colin's bedside by now, but she just hadn't gotten up the energy to go. She hadn't slept well, and she felt tired and really, really fat. The baby was getting so big; her abdomen was tight as a drum, which reminded her that time was passing too quickly. The baby's room wasn't done yet. The trim needed to be painted, the curtains hung, and the new bedding had yet to be unpacked. She'd been waiting for Colin to wake up, come home, and finish it, the way they'd planned.

She pressed her hand to her abdomen, feeling the tiny outline of a foot. Her little girl was itching to get out. "Just a little while longer," she told her. "Daddy needs to wake up first."

Tears gathered in her eyes as her daughter kicked. There was a tiny life inside her, a life she and Colin had created. He had been so happy when she got pregnant. He'd watched over her like a hawk and talked about his dreams for the future, all the things they would do with their child. Her big, burly husband had cried when they'd seen the first sonogram. Colin had lost his parents to divorce, and all he'd ever wanted was a family to hold on to.

He has to wake up.

Desperation bubbled through her veins, making her hot and sweaty, and even more anxious by the following thought . . .

What if he doesn't?

She hated herself for going there, but in recent days the doubt had begun to take root. She wanted to be brave and resolute in her optimism, but it had been three months and the clock kept ticking. There was a good chance she would have to raise this baby on her own, and how on earth would she do that?

She drew in a deep breath and shoved the doubts away. She was Colin's wife. If she didn't believe in his recovery, who would?

The door bell rang, and she frowned. She didn't want to see anyone until she had her game face back on, but as the bell rang again, she knew that she had to open the door. Her car was in the driveway. If she didn't answer, someone might think she'd gone into labor, was lying helpless on the floor, and they'd probably call 911 and bring out the whole damn town to save her.

She marched to the front door and flung it open, feeling decidedly grumpy. Jason Marlow stood on the porch. Jason, with his light brown hair, brown eyes, and lazy grin, had grown up with her and Colin, and was also a deputy in the Angel's Bay

Police Department. He was a good guy, but unfortunately he'd come at the wrong time. She was too tired and frustrated to be polite.

"Jason, I do not need any more food." She eyed the paper bag in his hand. "The people in this town must think I'm eating for five. I won't be able to get through the door soon."

"Good thing this doesn't have food in it. Can I come in?"

"Can I stop you?"

He raised an eyebrow. "You're in a mood."

"No, I'm not. I'm the Angel's Bay saint, haven't you heard?" She walked into the living room and sat down on the couch. Jason shut the front door and followed her into the room.

"I've never thought of you as a saint, Red," he drawled.

"Don't call me that." Jason had been mocking her red hair and freckles since junior high school. "So what did you bring me?"

"I'm not sure I should give it to you anymore."

"Fine." She crossed her arms over her enormous stomach. "I didn't ask you here. I didn't ask you or anyone else to bring me anything. God, Jason, when is it going to *stop*?"

His smile faded as he met her eyes. He knew she wasn't talking about the ever-arriving food. "I don't know, Kara."

She drew in a shaky breath as the baby gave her a good strong kick, reminding her to buck up. "I shouldn't have said that."

"You can say anything to me. And I didn't bring food, I brought paint." He pulled the can out to show her. "Colin never got a chance to finish the trim in the baby's room."

"He will when he wakes up," she said for the hundredth time. She'd already refused help from her brothers, her father, and her next-door neighbor.

"When Colin wakes up, he'll be too busy to worry about paint. Let me do it, Kara. Let me finish the room for you."

"You don't think he will wake up, do you?" She could hardly believe she'd said the words, but now they were out there, hanging thick in the air between them. "Do you?" She waited for him to deny it, and saw the conflict in his eyes. When he didn't answer, she said, "You need to go home and take your paint with you."

"It doesn't matter what I think. It doesn't even matter what you think, Kara. Colin's return to the living doesn't depend on your happy, positive thoughts."

"It might. You don't know."

He set the can on the coffee table. "Colin's recovery depends on whether or not the swelling in his brain goes down, and whatever other physiological things have to happen. You don't have the power to bring him back, so stop putting that weight on yourself. It's not good for you, and it's not good for the baby."

"How *dare* you tell me not to believe in my husband's recovery?" She was itching to fight someone and, unfortunately for Jason, he was the closest.

"I didn't say that. And you're not pissed at me, Kara. You're mad at yourself, because you're the one who's having doubts. You're afraid Colin won't wake up, only you can't let yourself say it out loud. So you're putting the words in my mouth instead."

He had a point, but she didn't want to admit it. "That's not true. I don't have any doubts, but if you want to paint the damn trim, then go ahead and do it. And I suppose you could fix the leak in the bathroom sink, too."

"Anything else?"

"I want to hang a picture in the baby's room. My grandmother gave it to me. It's in the garage. And the kitchen floor could use a good scrubbing when you're done with that, not to mention the toilet and the shower."

"Now you're pushing it."

His words drew a reluctant smile from her, then she sighed. "You were right what you said before. I am worried that Colin won't wake up, but I'm terrified that saying it out loud will make it come true."

"Worrying doesn't stop anything, nor does not worrying make something happen. It just makes you feel bad."

She hated his pragmatic attitude, but she knew he was right.

Jason sat in the armchair across from her. It was Colin's favorite chair and she almost asked him to move but managed to stop herself just in time. He'd think she was a complete lunatic.

"I know it's his chair," Jason said, with a gleam in his eyes. "I was with him when he bought it."

"You were the one who convinced him to get the expensive leather version. Thanks for that," she said dryly.

"He was already halfway there; I just gave him a little push. Leather lasts longer."

"You were always there for Colin."

"Not the night he was shot," Jason said darkly. "I called in sick that day. It should have been me who was watching Jenna Davies's house. It should have been me who got shot. I've wanted to tell you that for three months, but I couldn't find the words."

She stared at him, not sure she was happy to have heard his confession. Colin hadn't mentioned he was taking Jason's shift that night. But it wasn't as if the attack on Colin had been directed at him; he'd simply been caught in the line of fire while doing his job.

"Should I blame you for being sick?" she asked Jason.

"I blame myself."

"That's the stupidest thing I've ever heard. You didn't do anything wrong. And Colin was doing his job, a job that he loved."

"You're letting me off the hook that easily?"

"If you want to work off your guilt, Mrs. Marson's dog left some presents in my backyard. Maybe you could take care of them for me." She paused, holding his gaze. "But I don't really need you to do chores around here, Jason. I just need you to be my friend and call me out when I'm being a stupid, emotional girl."

Jason smiled. "The last time I called you a stupid girl, you threw a piece of cake in my face. The icing was coconut, which I'm allergic to, and twenty minutes later I had red welts all over my face, and my throat started closing up. You almost killed me with that damn cake, so if you think I'm dumb enough to call you a stupid girl again, you really are a . . . well, you know what."

She grinned back at him. "I already apologized for that."

"Because your mother made you."

"We were in the fifth grade. You pissed me off."

"Colin made you mad, too, but you kissed him."

"Not until the seventh grade—and that's because he called me a *beautiful* girl." The memory made her smile. "It was my very first kiss. Colin was so nervous his lips only hit the corner of my mouth, but it still gave me a thrill. I think it took him two months to work up enough courage to try it again."

"Yeah, and I think he talked about that kiss for every minute of every hour of every day of those two months," Jason said with a roll of his eyes. "I told him if he didn't hurry up, I was going to kiss you myself. I think that's what made him get off his ass."

"Probably. He was always trying to keep up with you, and you certainly had plenty of girls at your beck and call."

"Not you. You only had eyes for Colin," he said.

There was an odd note in his voice that made her a little uncomfortable. She suspected Jason had had a little crush on her when they were teens, but he'd never said anything, and he'd certainly never done anything. He was loyal to Colin. "Well, it was all a long time ago. Although I wish we could go back to those carefree days."

"You'll have good days ahead."

"I really hope so."

Jason gazed into her eyes. "Kara—for the record—I think Colin is going to wake up."

"Me too," she whispered.

"Then get the hell out of here and let me paint."

FIVE

Lauren hadn't meant to drive to the Ramsay house. After checking in on her father at the café, she'd headed to the market to pick up some food to re-stock the fridge. But on the way to the store she'd found herself driving through town, taking in the sights, and somehow she'd ended up on the narrow road that led to the old house on the bluff where her sister's body had been found.

Before a fire had taken down the east wing of the building, the Ramsay house had been a mansion, three floors, six bedrooms, four baths, and numerous other rooms, including a movie theater. It had been built as a luxurious summer home in the 1950s by a wealthy media mogul named Bert Ramsay, and its owners had had massive parties entertaining celebri-ties who spent weeks in the summer on the beach or on the Ramsay yacht.

After Bert Ramsay died, the house was inher-ited by his children and later his grandchildren, each generation choosing to spend less time at the mansion. Eventually, the Ramsay house was basically a ghost during the winter and an occasional rental property in the summer. Most of the time it sat empty, making it the perfect location for late night teenage party action.

Until Abby's lifeless body was found in the basement.

The Ramsays had sold the property after Abby's murder, and it had gone through several owners since then. Lauren had heard that the house was haunted by her sister's screams. She hated to think that Abby's spirit was trapped in that house, so she chose to believe that people were just imagining sounds based on the fact that someone had died there.

Who'd tried to burn the house down? Local kids playing with matches? A new owner who wanted to collect on the insurance and rebuild a house that wasn't haunted? Someone with a guilty conscience who couldn't stand the constant reminder?

Drawing in a deep breath, she turned off the engine, got out of the car, and began to walk toward the house. It was almost noon, the sun high in the sky, but she still felt spooked by the tall trees that threw dark shadows along the path. Her unease deepened when she reached the front door. It was ajar and as she hesitated for a moment, a breeze made it move slightly on the rusted hinges, as if someone were inviting her in.

She bit her bottom lip, feeling crazy for even

considering going inside. If there had been any clues to Abby's murderer, they were gone by now. Yet something drew her forward. She pushed open the door and stepped into what had once been the grand foyer.

There was no furniture in the entryway or any of the front rooms that she could see, and the wood bore signs of smoke and water damage. A mirror on the wall was broken in several places and part of the carpet had been pulled up from the stairs.

Access to the basement was through the laundry room just off the kitchen. She knew because she'd come to the house once during her senior year in high school to party with Shane and some others. They'd gone down to the basement so no one would see the lights from the road.

Every muscle in her body tightened as she debated her next move. Logically, she knew there was nothing to fear. It had been thirteen years. Abby's killer was long gone.

Or was he?

What if whoever had killed Abby wasn't some drifter, but someone in town, someone who was still nearby?

A gust of wind ripped through the trees and the front door slammed behind her, rattling the windows. Lauren jumped. *Get over it!* The wind was always strong along the bluff; the house was not haunted. It was just old and empty.

Straightening her shoulders, she headed into

the kitchen and then the laundry room. She opened the door that led into the basement. The hairs on the back of her neck stood up as she stepped onto the landing.

Had Abby been afraid that night? Had she felt the same sense of foreboding? Or had she entered the basement with no idea of what was about to happen to her?

Lauren flipped the switch at the top of the stairs, but there was no electricity. A stream of light came through a small window near the ceiling, putting the basement in a shadowy light. She moved slowly down the steps. The room was long and narrow and empty cement planters ran along one wall. An assortment of tools and gardening equipment were heaped in a corner, and a couple of empty beer bottles and cigarette stubs dotted the floor, remnants of a party—but how recent? Did the local kids still come here? Hadn't they learned anything from Abby's murder?

As she reached the bottom of the stairs, she began to shake. This was where Abby had stood in the last moments of her life. Lauren could feel her sister's fear. Her breathing came fast and shallow. The air was too thick, the musty smell suffocating—or maybe it was the knowledge that someone had stood in this spot and pulled a rope around Abby's neck, squeezing the life out of her. How terrified she must have been, looking into the eyes of her killer, knowing that she was dying.

Lauren tried to draw in a breath, but her chest felt tight. She had to get out of here. She needed air. She needed to breathe.

Before she could move, the door above her banged open and she looked up in shock. A man stood in the shadows at the top of the stairs. He wore dark pants and a big coat, but she couldn't see his face.

She'd left her cell phone in the car. *Oh, God!*

Her heart beat in triple time, and adrenaline raced through her body.

He flashed a light on her face, blinding her. She put up a hand in protest. "Who's there?" she demanded, forcing some strength into her voice.

The man turned the light toward the ceiling as he moved down the stairs.

She instinctively backed up, but there was nowhere to go. "Who are you, and what are you doing here?" She grabbed a rake. It wasn't much of a weapon but it was all she had.

"I was going to ask you the same questions." He stopped, his gaze narrowing on her face. Surprise flashed in his eyes. "Are you Lauren Jamison?"

"How did you know that?" she asked quickly. He had blond hair and light eyes, an attractive face, a warming smile. Her tension eased slightly.

"I've seen your picture," he replied. "I'm Mark Devlin."

The movie producer.

"I didn't expect to find you down here," he continued. "In fact, I was just at your house. Your father didn't mention that you were headed this way."

"You need to leave my father alone. You're upsetting him."

"He didn't seem upset. He knows I'm trying to help."

"By making a sensational movie about Abby's death? My entire family was ripped apart by her murder. We can't live through it again. You should drop this project."

He frowned. "I understand it's painful, but don't you want to find out who killed your sister?"

"Of course I do, but if the police couldn't figure it out, what makes you think you can?"

"I have a fresh eye, a different perspective, and the benefit of time. That's the key in cold cases. Over many years, people often remember things. They feel free to speak out. I've already learned something that the police didn't discover."

"What's that?" she scoffed, sure that he was going to throw out some meaningless piece of information just to make her think she should get involved with his movie.

"Two days before the murder, Abby and her friend Lisa were spotted sitting in a car outside their volleyball coach's house around ten o'clock Saturday night."

"So?"

"So their volleyball coach was a young, married man in his early twenties, Tim Sorensen. From what I've gathered, a lot of his female students had crushes on him."

"I knew Mr. Sorensen. He also taught biology, but I don't understand what you're getting at. You think he was involved with my sister?"

"I think you should ask Lisa why she told the police that she and Abby never left her house that night."

"They were probably dropping something off— uniforms or the extra bag of balls or something. Where did you even get this information?" she asked suspiciously.

"Kendra Holt."

"I don't know who that is."

"She's a local woman. At the time of the murder, she was having an affair with the man who lived next door to Sorensen, and she couldn't afford to be placed at the scene. She got divorced a few years ago and now isn't concerned about her reputation or her former husband. Ms. Holt also told me that it wasn't the first time she'd seen the girls on the street." He paused. "I've tried to get in touch with both Lisa Delaney and Mr. Sorensen. Neither one will talk to me. I also passed the information on to the chief of police. I'm not trying to take the police out of this, just to help them along."

"Lisa was Abby's best friend," Lauren said. "She was questioned thoroughly about everything that they'd done in the weeks preceding Abby's death. I'm more inclined to believe her than some woman who was having an affair and thought she saw my sister in a car. Lisa and Abby weren't old enough to drive, so whose car were they in?"

"Good question. Maybe you should ask Lisa."

"I spoke to Lisa several times after Abby died. I asked her to tell me if there was anything that Abby was into that she didn't want my parents to know about, and she said there wasn't." Lauren shook her head, disliking the doubts Mark Devlin was putting in her head. "If you're suggesting that my sister was involved with a married man, who was also her teacher, you're out of your mind. Abby was fifteen. And Lisa would have told me about Mr. Sorensen if there was anything to tell. You're on the wrong track."

"It's possible," he said with a small, conceding nod. "I do have other suspects."

One of those other suspects had to be Shane. "I'm not interested in your theories." She set down the rake and moved toward the stairs.

"Even if one of them involves you?"

She slowly turned. "What are you talking about?"

"You were never really questioned, Lauren."

It took a moment for his words to sink in. Her jaw dropped in shock. "What the hell are you saying? Abby was my little sister! How could you think I had anything to do with her death?"

"She was beautiful, popular, an accomplished athlete, a great student. Some people claim you were in her shadow, that you were jealous of her."

"I was proud of her." Lauren refused to admit to any tinge of envy for her sister's success. Sure, things had come a little easier for Abby, and sometimes that had been frustrating, but she'd loved her sister far more than she'd ever felt jealous of her.

"There's also the question of your alibi—it had a lot of holes in it. The librarian said she saw you enter the library, but she never saw you leave," he said, his gaze never leaving her face. "But even if you had stayed until the library closed at ten, you didn't arrive at your house until eleven twenty-five. That's an hour and twenty-five minutes that were unaccounted for."

Her heart pounded against her chest, but she tried to stay calm. He wanted to get a reaction from her, but she wouldn't give him one. "I went for a walk after I left the library. I got some coffee and then I went home. The police confirmed that I stopped at Dina's to get coffee."

"You were at Dina's for only five minutes. What did you do after that?"

She had gone down to the marina to see if Shane was back from the fishing charter he'd told her he was going to run with his dad. The boat was there, but there was no sign of Shane. She'd gone by his house, but his motorcycle was gone. She'd finally given up and returned home.

She threw back her shoulders. "I don't have to answer your questions. I didn't kill my sister."

"Then who did? Shane Murray?"

"This is just your roundabout way of getting me to implicate him, isn't it?" she challenged.

A small smile crossed his lips. "Maybe. Although

when I mentioned my theory about you to Mr. Murray, he didn't dispute the possibility that you could have been involved."

She stiffened. Devlin was lying. Shane wouldn't throw suspicion on her. Would he?

"The reports that I read indicated that your family was very concerned about Abby's relationship with Shane," Devlin continued.

"Abby didn't have a relationship with him, and in the beginning we were all in shock. We were surprised that Shane and Abby had been seen together, but it was no big deal that he gave her a ride. And there was no evidence to connect Shane to Abby's death." She ran up the stairs, hoping to escape his questions, but he was right on her heels as she reentered the kitchen.

"I realize this is a difficult situation for you, but I'm trying to help," he said as he followed her through the house.

"No, you're trying to make money off my sister's death. Why would you want to put our family through the worst nightmare of our lives a second time?"

"Because your sister deserves justice. I'd rather work with you than against you," Devlin said as they reached the foyer. "But with or without your help, I'm going to pursue the truth."

Before Lauren could answer, a woman came through the front door. She had on a stylish red business suit with a short skirt and very high heels, her black hair pulled back from her face. She gave

Devlin a smile, sending a questioning look in Lauren's direction.

"Hello," she said. "Sorry I'm late, Mark. Am I interrupting something?"

"No, we're done," Lauren said briskly.

"This is Lauren Jamison," Devlin interjected. "Rachel Silveira," he added to Lauren.

"Silveira?" Lauren echoed. "The chief's wife?"

The woman frowned. "In Los Angeles, I never have to introduce myself that way," she grumbled to Devlin.

"The charm of a small town, darling."

"Yes, I'm the chief's wife," Rachel said to Lauren. "I'm also a real estate agent, and an associate of Mr. Devlin's."

"Why are you here?" Lauren asked.

"To help Mark scout the location," she replied.

"I'm going to recreate part of the house, in particular the basement, on a soundstage in L.A.," Devlin interjected. "The exterior scenes will all be shot here."

"You're building a set before you have a script?" Lauren asked. "How can you make a movie if you don't know who the villain is?"

"Everything takes time. I'm just setting the wheels in motion."

He's really going to do this. The truth hit Lauren hard. It wasn't just a vague idea, there was actual progress being made. "This movie is just going to hurt innocent people."

"Or perhaps finally catch the killer," he said. "I *am* going to find out who did it."

She might have found his confidence inspiring if she hadn't just heard some of his half-baked theories, one of them making her the murderer.

"It's not the innocent who need to be afraid," he added. "Just the guilty."

His words ran around in her mind as she walked out of the house. When she reached her car, she slipped behind the wheel, locked the doors, and drew in a deep breath. Mark Devlin had certainly given her a lot to think about. She didn't know what to focus on first: some nebulous relationship with Abby, Lisa, and Coach Sorensen; Shane's involvement with her sister; or her own lack of a concrete alibi. No one had ever doubted her until now. She couldn't wrap her mind around the idea that Mark Devlin could believe she killed her own sister.

And Shane hadn't disputed that possibility, according to Devlin. Well, why would he? He was probably happy to have someone else on the hot seat. But dammit, he should have spoken up for her, not stayed silent.

The way she'd stayed silent all those years ago, when he'd been the one accused.

But that had been different. Shane had lied. Shane had been with Abby. Shane had refused to explain why.

It was past time that he did.

Shane had just returned from a fishing charter and was headed to the Java Hut to pick up some coffee when he saw Lauren striding across the harbor parking lot. She was dressed casually, more like the girl he remembered. Her blue jeans were tight and the white tank top and pink sweater clung to her curves. Her dark brown hair fell loosely around her shoulders and the sway of her hips made his body tighten. He wished to hell he didn't react so strongly to her, but she was pretty and sexy as hell, and he'd had a thing for her since the first moment they'd met. Time and years had done nothing to diminish that attraction. If anything, it was stronger than ever, because Lauren was no longer a shy, uncertain girl, but a beautiful woman—a woman moving toward him with a purpose that did not bode well.

When she reached him, she pushed her sunglasses up on top of her head. Her dark blue eyes had always reminded him of the sea, of the blue water that could only be found miles and miles from shore. He'd once felt like he could drown in her soft, dreamy gaze, but now there was nothing but dark, stormy shadows.

"What do you want?" he asked warily.

"Answers."

"What happened?" Something had clearly set her off.

"I went to the Ramsay house." Her mouth tightened. "I went into the basement."

"Why the hell did you do that?"

"Because I couldn't stop myself. Something drew me there, and the next minute I was walking through that creepy old house and imagining how Abby must have felt when she went down those steps, when she was confronted by her killer, when she realized there was no way out. I could feel her terror, Shane. I could feel that cord tightening around my neck." Her voice faltered as she struggled for composure.

"You shouldn't have put yourself through that, Lauren."

"Well, I did, and I was all alone in that basement when a man came through the door. I almost jumped out of my skin. I thought it was Abby's murderer come back to get me. But it was Mark Devlin. Have you heard who he believes killed Abby?" The angry fire in her eyes burned brighter.

"He has a lot of theories," Shane said neutrally.

"Including one that features me as the murderer, the jealous older sister. The one who was afraid that her boyfriend wanted her sister instead, so she decided to kill her."

"Mark Devlin doesn't believe you killed Abby."

"Really?" she challenged. "Why? Because you told him it was a ridiculous idea? He said you didn't dispute his theory at all."

"He's playing us off each other, Lauren. Can't you see that? Whoever he accuses will try to direct his attention to someone else. It's his way of getting people to talk."

"Is that what you did? Turn his focus to me?"

It pissed him off that she could think he would be such a coward. "That's not what happened."

"So tell me what happened, Shane—and I'm not

talking about your conversation with Mark Devlin. Tell me what happened with Abby—why you were with her that night. Tell me what I don't know, what you should have told me thirteen years ago."

Her demand stole the breath from his chest. He'd known this moment was coming the second she'd stepped back into his life, but he wasn't ready. There were other people involved, innocent people.

But Lauren was innocent, too, he reminded himself. At least she had been before he'd gotten involved with her. He should have stuck with girls who were as wild as he was, because he'd always known Lauren would want more from him than he could give her. If he'd had any sense, he never would have started a relationship that was doomed from the beginning.

"I ran away before, Shane, but I'm not leaving now until I get some answers," she said with determination. "You owe me."

"All right, we'll talk, but not here. There are too many people around." He could see some of the other fishermen looking their way. "Let's take a ride." He waved his hand toward his motorcycle, which was parked nearby.

"Really? The motorcycle?" she asked, obviously not thrilled with the idea.

"We'll leave town, find some open space, some fresh air—"

"Where we can be whoever we want to be," she finished. "It's what you always used to say."

"It's still true."

He saw the indecision in her eyes and was almost sure she'd say no, but then she lifted her chin.

"Fine, let's go," she said.

They walked over to his bike. He handed her a helmet, and she slid onto the seat behind him. As she wrapped her arms around his waist the way she'd done so many years ago, his throat tightened with unexpected emotion. They weren't young, carefree, or crazy in love anymore, and he needed to remember that. When their ride came to an end, Lauren was going to expect some answers. He'd better come up with some, fast.

SIX

She was insane, Lauren decided. No way should she be on the back of Shane's bike, her body pressed against his solid back. But as they sped down the Pacific Coast Highway on a road that twisted and turned high above the ocean, the tension she'd felt since she'd run into Mark Devlin began to ease. With the bright blue sky above and nothing but endless road in front of them, she felt her problems sliding away, along with the years that had passed between her last trip and this one.

The first time she'd gotten on Shane's bike, she'd been sixteen years old and terrified of crashing. She'd never been a risk taker or a thrill seeker. She wasn't impulsive or spontaneous. She made plans. She set goals. She tested the water before she jumped in. Her mother used to say it was the curse of the first-born child to be wary and cautious, and the description had certainly fit her.

Shane had changed all that. He'd swept her off her feet metaphorically and literally when he'd put her on the back of his motorcycle and suggested she take a ride on the wild side with him. Oh, he hadn't used those exact words, but she'd heard them in her head, and she'd been seduced by his sexy smile, the promise in his dark eyes. He'd invited her out of her comfort zone, and she'd thrown her organized calendar to the wind and given in to her emotions. He'd opened her up to a new world. He'd made her feel things she'd never imagined.

She'd never know if she and Shane would have made it if Abby hadn't died, if he hadn't lied, if she hadn't left town . . . There were too many ifs, too many turns they'd both taken, choices they'd made, decisions they couldn't take back. She had no intention of getting involved with him again. She had guys back home who were a lot of fun and fit into her life exactly the way it was. They didn't try to change her, or challenge her to do more than she was comfortable doing. They didn't make her nervous and edgy and in danger of losing control. Who needed all that unsettled emotion? She was thirty years old, a responsible adult, interested in a mature relationship.

But as the wind blew against her face, she felt more like that reckless young girl who had yearned for something she couldn't quite define—something she'd found in Shane's arms.

Racing along the shoreline now, she could feel

Shane's heat, the power in his body. He was a physical man, one who labored in the sun, on the sea, who made his living battling nature. She'd always liked his power, strength, and confidence. And despite his bad-boy reputation, she'd felt safe with him. The only thing that had ever really scared her was her own desire—a reckless, irrational desire that was as strong as it ever had been.

Why hadn't Shane gotten married? Why hadn't she? Why weren't there people between them and reasons to stay apart?

There were reasons, she reminded herself. They were different people now. They didn't trust each other. She was leaving in a few days, and who knew how long Shane would stay? He'd always had one foot out the door, a guy who wanted to keep his options open.

He'd always wanted to travel, and it appeared that he'd fulfilled at least some of his childhood dreams. Her dreams had changed when Abby died. Everything she'd thought she'd wanted for herself had taken a backseat to surviving the grief, being there for her mother and her brother, making it to the next day, hoping to forget the past.

She'd thought she had, but now it was all coming back, and she was caught between the girl she used to be and the woman she'd become. Did Shane feel as rattled as she did, or was she just another girl from his past? He'd never been a saint, and she doubted he'd spent the last decade pining for her.

She was surprised that he'd come back to Angel's

Bay. There'd been a restless fury inside him for as long as she'd known him. He'd always been itching to get out of town, whether it was by motorcycle or by boat. He couldn't breathe in Angel's Bay. He didn't like the fact that everyone knew everyone's business. He'd wanted so much more than she could give him. But now he was home, and so was she . . .

Twenty minutes later, Shane pulled off the highway and drove down a sandy path that ended at a cliff overlooking the water. She'd been enjoying the ride so much, she was almost sorry they'd stopped. It took her a minute to peel her fingers from his waist and slide off the back of the bike. She took off her helmet and shook her hair free.

Shane removed his helmet, then turned and looked out at the ocean. He looked more relaxed now, his anger and rebelliousness had always been tamed by a race down the highway.

She followed his gaze, enjoying the sunbeams dancing off the ocean, the white caps crashing along the beach below, the never-ending pull of the tide. It was beautiful, and Shane was mesmerized. How could he have spent so much time at sea and still look at the ocean with such wonder in his eyes?

"Don't you ever get tired of the water?" she asked. "You see it every day. You go out on your boat each morning. Doesn't it ever get old?"

He turned his head, giving her a half smile that almost undid her. It had been a long, long time since she'd seen that smile.

"Never. The water always looks different, in light,

in dark, in wind, in quiet. Sometimes it acts out like a spoiled child, or a furious monster, and other times like a sweet, seductive lover."

She was stunned by the poetry of his words. Shane had never been one to use two words when one would suffice.

"Let's get a little closer," he suggested.

She started in surprise, thinking for a moment that he meant the two of them.

"Go down to the beach," he added, a knowing gleam in his eyes. "What did you think I meant?"

"Nothing. But I'm fine here. It's a great view, and I don't think we can get down there."

"We can. I've been here before." He held out his hand, his gaze meeting hers. "Come with me, Lauren."

She hesitated for a long moment. Finally she slipped her hand into his, catching her breath at the intense heat of their connection. Shane's eyes locked with hers, and she willed him not to say anything.

He led her toward a steep, rocky path carved out of the bluff. She was grateful for his strong hand when her feet slipped on the loose dirt. Shane seemed to have no problem picking his way down the hillside.

Their journey reminded her of another time. She didn't want to go back there, but the memory had such a strong pull . . .

It was dark, the moon rising high in the sky, the beam from Shane's flashlight bouncing off the rocks as they headed down to the beach. Her pulse raced and not just from the kiss Shane had given her when they'd gotten off of his bike, but from the promise in his eyes.

She was supposed to be at a movie, not headed to a desolate beach with the baddest boy in town, two beers, and a blanket. She was excited, nervous, and breathless by the time they reached the sand.

Shane gave her a smile and spread out the blanket. The waves crashed against the shoreline only thirty feet away. This strip of beach was just a small inlet along miles of wild coastline. They were completely alone, isolated from the rest of the world.

"Do you want a beer?" Shane asked.

She shook her head. "If we're going to do this, I don't want to be drunk." It might be easier if she were, because she'd never had sex before, but she was ready. She wanted to be with him.

"We can do whatever you want, Lauren. You know that, right?"

She did know that. She trusted Shane. She loved him. The emotion put a knot in her throat. "Why me?" she asked, needing the words.

"Why not you?" he countered. He cupped her face with his hands. "You're beautiful."

She wanted him to say "I love you." But Shane was kissing her and her lips were opening under his, and she was done with questions. Blood rushed through her veins, and her heart pounded so loud she couldn't have heard the words, even if he'd said them.

But he hadn't said them, and she hadn't cared. She'd thought she had enough love for both of them.

"Lauren? Are you all right?" Shane asked, jolting her out of the past.

She realized that he'd stopped walking. "I'm fine."

"One last jump." He tipped his head toward the four-foot drop in front of them.

She'd come this far; she might as well go all the way. That thought echoed her earlier memory and made her smile. She was definitely *not* going all the way this time around.

"What's so funny?" Shane asked with a quirk of his eyebrow.

"Nothing. Go on. I'll follow."

While Shane made an easy vault to the ground, she sat down and then slid off the edge. It wasn't particularly graceful, but she made it to the beach without breaking anything. She wiped the dirt off the back of her jeans, then swept her hand toward the ocean. "This is beautiful."

Large boulders rose ten, twenty feet from the sea, and the water crashing against them sent a wet spray high into the air. She felt invigorated by the wind, the energy of the sea.

"It's called Shadow Beach," Shane said.

She could see why. Between the rocks and the jagged cliffs, half the beach was in shadow, the other in dazzling sunlight. The beach reminded her of Shane, who had always had a light and a dark side. It was that dark side she was determined to get to today.

"Let's walk," he suggested, heading down the narrow beach.

"All right." She slipped off her sandals and followed him along the shoreline. Eventually they reached an outcropping of rocks that stretched into the sea, and they could go no farther.

Lauren perched on the edge of a boulder. Shane stood a few feet away. They watched two sea gulls dive in and out of the waves, searching for food. Then the birds squawked and flew away.

"Shane—I need to know what happened the night Abby died," she said abruptly, knowing there was no easy way into the subject.

"You're not really worried that Mark Devlin will turn you into a murderer, are you?" Shane countered. "No one would ever believe you killed Abby."

"No? Apparently Devlin has spoken to people who claimed that I was jealous of Abby's success, her popularity, her good grades, her athleticism, and her beauty."

"What people?" Shane countered.

"He didn't give me names. But I can't deny that Abby had more going for her than I did. She had so much potential, Shane, so much promise." She felt the moisture well in her eyes. "Abby was going to *be* somebody. I was sure of it."

"You didn't kill her, Lauren. You don't have to defend yourself."

"Why aren't *you* worried, Shane? You were the last person to see Abby alive. You have to know you're still a suspect."

"It's nothing new," he said with a shrug. "After I was accused of Abby's murder, people crossed the street when they saw me coming. My parents got death threats. Our house was egged. The *Angel Shark* was sprayed with graffiti calling me a murderer. I can't imagine that Mark Devlin could do anything that would surprise me."

She frowned. "I didn't know it got that bad, that your family was hurt like that."

"You were gone by then. Though I wasn't arrested for Abby's death, this town put me in prison, and when I left, I felt like I'd escaped. I had no intention of ever coming back."

"Why did you?"

He hesitated for a long moment. "I was working a boat up in Alaska last year. It was rough, a lot of bad storms. I lost a couple of friends, and I got tired of being wet, cold, and days from land. Kara sent me a family picture, and I could see that everyone had grown up and changed. I barely recognized Michael. He'd gone from a boy to a man, and I'd missed it all. Kara wanted me to come home, take a break, and I thought why not—it's been thirteen years."

"Where did you go when you left here?" she asked curiously.

"Everywhere. I picked up crew jobs wherever I could find them. I didn't know how to do anything but run boats and catch fish. So I went where I could make enough money to survive. One port blended into the next. One boat turned into another."

"It sounds adventurous. You always wanted to see beyond the horizon—and all I wanted you to see was me."

"You were the only reason I stayed here as long as I did," he said, his eyes serious. "I wanted to leave right after high school, but then we got together, and I wasn't sure I could go at all. You made me want to stay."

"You would have gone. It was just a matter of time. You wouldn't have let me hold you back."

"Maybe, but I don't think you would have left Angel's Bay if Abby hadn't died. You wanted to open a bakery on Ocean Avenue and compete with Martha for the best cookies. Sugar and spice and everything nice," he said with a small smile.

She felt a tug in her heart at the familiar phrase he'd teased her with so many years ago. "I used to hate it when you said that. I didn't want to be the sugar and spice girl. I wanted to be sexy and hot, wickedly irresistible."

"You were that, too. I wanted you from the first second I saw you."

Her heart sped up at the look in his eyes. "I never knew why. I was so not your type. Before me, you went with all the beautiful, wild girls."

"You were different."

She waited for him to elaborate, but he remained silent. "Different how?" she prodded, annoyed with herself because she shouldn't care.

He thought for a moment. "Honest. Genuine. Real."

"You make me sound like a Girl Scout," she complained.

"I don't think what we did together was in any

Girl Scout handbook," he said lightly. "In fact, being on this beach with you reminds me of the night we—"

"Don't go there," she warned.

"Why not?"

"Because I've already been there today," she confessed.

"Really?" His brown eyes sparkled wickedly. "It was a good night."

"Yes, it was," she admitted, meeting his gaze, the delicious heat of their memories dancing between them. Her fingers bit into the hard rock she was sitting on. She forced herself not to get up and fling herself into his arms and see if it was as great as she remembered. "Stop looking at me like that," she ordered.

"You're looking at me the same way. It's still there, Lauren—no matter how much we want to deny it."

She got up and walked to the water's edge. On impulse, she rolled up her jeans and waded into the icy sea. She needed to get rid of the heat between them, to put her memories back into deep freeze.

Then Shane came up behind her, putting his hands on her waist, and she found herself turning into his arms. He gave her plenty of time to move away, but she pressed her palms against his chest and lifted her head to his.

He dipped down, taking her mouth softly in a fleeting caress that left her hungry for more. She slid her hands around his back, bringing him closer, urging him on. His tongue slid across the line of her mouth, finally slipping inside. She tasted the salt air on his lips, the sweet warmth of memories, and blossomed in the heady heat.

His hands moved down to her hips, pressing her against his hard groin, making her feel every inch of him. Her hands found their way under his T-shirt, stroking his warm skin, his ripped muscles, and the gentleness in his kiss turned to a raging hunger.

His mouth moved deeply on hers, his hands restless, their bodies seeking what they'd missed for so long. Her heart pounded, her blood roaring in her ears, as he pulled her down to her knees, down to the sand, down to him. The desire and need she felt were echoed in his eyes.

"Shane." His name left her lips, ran through her heart, tore her apart. She'd loved him. She'd hated him. And now . . .

"Do you want this?" he asked.

"I don't know," she whispered.

"Yes, you do." His fingers slid down the side of her face, cupping her chin, as his questioning eyes met hers.

She did know. She'd always known that she'd never wanted anyone as much as she wanted him. She bent her head toward his mouth, when a sudden rush of water splashed over them. She gasped at the onslaught, wondering what the hell had happened. She was soaked.

Shane jumped to his feet, pulling her up. "Dammit!"

She looked in bemusement as the ocean swirled around her ankles, the pull of the tide digging the sand out from under her feet as it retreated from the beach.

"That was a hell of a cold shower." He scowled at the sea.

"Probably one we needed." She'd drifted far from her original intent. "I wanted to talk to you, not roll around on the beach with you. Let's sit in the sun and dry out."

She headed back toward the rocks and stretched her legs out in front of her, wrapping her arms around her as the breeze made her shiver.

Shane sat on a boulder a few feet from her, his gaze turned toward the sea, his profile hard and unreadable.

For a few moments, they sat in silence. Then she said, "Shane, you need to tell me what happened the night Abby died, why you were with her. I'm not leaving until you give me a straight answer."

He was silent for a moment, then said, "I asked Abby to meet me at the law offices of Harrigan and Miller."

"Where she worked part-time? Why?" Lauren asked in surprise.

He turned to face her. "So she could let me in with her key. I was looking for something. She waited in the hall. Afterward I gave Abby a ride to the high school, just like I told the police. I dropped her off in the parking lot. That's the last time I saw her. There wasn't anything personal between us, Lauren."

She shook her head in confusion. "I don't understand. What were you looking for at the law offices?"

"I can't tell you that, but it didn't have anything to do with you or Abby."

"Why can't you tell me?"

"Because it's not my secret."

She frowned. "What does that mean? Were you in some kind of trouble? Did it have to do with the fight you had with that kid earlier in the week?"

"No, it didn't. After I dropped Abby off that night, I drove down the coast. I had a lot on my mind. I got back around four in the morning and went to bed. The police woke me at eight. They told me that Abby was dead, and she'd been seen getting on my motorcycle just after seven o'clock the night before."

"I left you messages that night," Lauren said, remembering her frantic calls, all of which had gone unanswered.

"I didn't check my messages until the next day, and by then I was locked up in an interrogation room. I called you back as soon as I could, but you didn't want to talk to me anymore."

"Why didn't you tell me before about Abby letting you into the law offices?"

"You were a powder keg about to explode, and I couldn't risk giving you a match. I was afraid you'd tell the police that I'd broken into the law offices, and I couldn't let that happen."

"So you protected yourself," she said with disappointment and anger.

"Not just myself. Look, Lauren. You can be mad, but—"

"You're damn right I can," she said, jumping up. "You withheld evidence."

He jerked to his feet. "No, I didn't. Abby was alive when she was with me. Nothing that we did together contributed to her death. For God's sake—all she did was open a door and stand in a hallway for fifteen minutes."

"But the police tried to recreate where Abby went that night. We made a timeline."

"The timeline was accurate. I gave her a ride from Elm Street to the high school and dropped her off at seven ten. I told the police that, and it was the truth. I don't know what she did before she met me that night, or what happened after I dropped her off. But I was only with her for thirty minutes."

"An important thirty minutes."

"Only for me, not for her," he argued. "Whatever Abby was up to that night had nothing to do with me."

She gave him a suspicious look. "What do you mean? You make it sound like Abby was planning to do something more than study."

"It was the way she was acting. She seemed nervous on the ride to the high school."

"Maybe because you'd asked her to break into her workplace."

"No, it wasn't that. I thought she was meeting a guy. I figured he was in the study group."

Since the alleged study group had never been

located, no one knew who Abby went to meet that night. A lot of people hadn't believed Shane's story; they'd assumed that Abby had meant to meet him all along.

Lauren shook her head, feeling even more confused. "I don't know what to think."

"If what I omitted would have helped the police find Abby's killer, I would have told them," Shane said forcefully. "But it didn't have any bearing on what happened to her."

"I'm not sure you can truly know that," she said, feeling another wave of anger. "Maybe one of the lawyers got mad that she let you into their offices. Maybe you took something and they thought she did it, and one of them killed her."

"I didn't take anything, and no one saw us."

"Mrs. Markham saw you."

"On the street, and the ice cream parlor was right next to the law building. She assumed we were there."

"Did Abby know what you were doing in the law offices?"

"No."

"So why did she do it? She was risking her job. Why would she help you?"

Shane shrugged. "I don't know."

He might not, but Lauren did. "Abby liked you. She had a thing for you. Everyone thought so."

"They were wrong. Even at eighteen, I could tell when a girl wanted me. Abby didn't."

"Abby told me there was someone she liked that

she couldn't have. Who else would it have been but you?"

"I don't know, but there was nothing between Abby and me—not even the most casual flirtation. I was your boyfriend. She was your sister. I wasn't interested in her. Abby didn't betray you."

She wanted to believe that more than anything. "It wasn't up to you to decide what was important and what wasn't. Your first instinct should have been to help me, not protect yourself or whoever it is you care about more than . . ." She stopped, realizing she now had a decision to make. "You took a big chance, confessing to me. It's not too late for me to go to the police."

He nodded, his gaze holding hers. "No, it's not. Was I wrong to tell you, Lauren?"

She hesitated. "I don't know yet."

SEVEN

Two hours later, Lauren walked into the Angel's Bay Police Department and asked to speak to the chief of police. After her trip to the beach, she'd changed into dry clothes and checked in with her dad, who was absorbed in a card game at Dina's Café, and then headed down the street to the police station. She was still debating what she wanted to say when she was ushered into Joe Silveira's office.

Chief Silveira hadn't been in Angel's Bay when she was growing up, and she liked the fact that he was a recent hire. She needed an objective perspective.

"It's nice to meet you, Ms. Jamison." The chief waved her into a chair in front of his desk. "I've heard a lot about you."

That wasn't particularly reassuring. Had Mark Devlin shared his theories with the chief? "Really? From who?"

"Your father. We both like to have our morning coffee at Dina's," he said with an attractive smile.

Joe Silveira was certainly better looking than the last chief of police, with his olive skin, jet black hair, and dark eyes. There was intelligence in those eyes that inspired confidence. Maybe he could help figure out who had killed Abby.

"There's a movie that's going to be made about my sister's murder," she said. "I'd like to know if the police department is planning to release my sister's files to this movie producer, or if you've done so already."

"We're considering what information we might be willing to disseminate."

"What does that mean, exactly?"

"Why don't you tell me what you're concerned about?"

"I'm worried about my father having to relive the worst night of his life, and my sister's reputation being shredded by unfounded speculation. I spoke briefly to Mark Devlin and it's obvious he has a vivid imagination. I want answers, but I want the police to find them—not some Hollywood writer who's willing to make up whatever scenario will sell the most tickets."

"I understand your concerns, but Mr. Devlin can make any movie he wants and call it fiction."

That's what she was afraid of.

"I've read through your sister's case files," Joe continued, "and I spoke with Warren Laughton, who was one of the investigating officers. Unfortunately, the chief of police at the time, Howard Smythe, passed away five years ago."

"Did you learn anything new? Was anything done incorrectly? Were clues overlooked? Were there leads that weren't followed?"

"Not that I've seen so far, but it's never a bad idea to review a cold case. After a period of years, people remember things they didn't think were important at the time, or are simply more willing to talk. Unfortunately, the crime scene provided little forensic evidence. There was no evidence of sexual assault, no DNA, no fingerprints."

She swallowed a knot at the mention of sexual assault. She'd heard that before, but it was nice to have it confirmed. "What about the materials collected at the beach near the Ramsay house?"

"The encampment had remnants of a fire, some food items, no discernible prints, but certainly evidence that someone had camped in the area during the hours related to your sister's death. Apparently that led to the conclusion that a drifter might have been responsible."

"That's what they said, but it never made sense, because Abby wouldn't have gone to that house alone. It was big, isolated, and creepy."

"Yet I understand that the local kids used it as a party venue."

"That's true, but no one ever went there alone."

"Your sister wasn't there alone," the chief said.

Realizing what he meant, Lauren frowned. Her sister's killer had been with her. "If Abby went to the house with someone, then she knew the person who killed her. I have a difficult time believing that anyone who knew Abby would have wanted her dead. She was a young, sweet girl. She had a lot of friends. There was no reason for anyone to kill her."

"What about your boyfriend, Shane Murray? He was the main person of interest in the case. What can you tell me about his relationship with your sister?"

At her hesitation, Silveira's gaze turned speculative. "Is there something you want to tell me about Mr. Murray?"

"No," she said, making an impulsive decision to protect Shane, at least for now. She was probably being a fool, but old habits died hard.

"What about any other male friends your sister might have had?" Joe asked.

"Abby didn't have a boyfriend that I knew about." She didn't like the direction of his questions.

"According to the autopsy report, your sister did not appear to be a virgin."

Her jaw dropped. "Are you sure?"

He picked up a piece of paper and handed it to her. She skimmed through the scientific jargon, pausing over the words "no hymen present." She glanced back at the chief. "She never told me that she had sex. She was only fifteen." She glanced back down at the report, her stomach turning over as she realized just how thoroughly Abby's body had been examined. She set the paper down with a shaky hand. "I didn't need to read that."

"I'm sorry. I should have prepared you." He gave her a compassionate smile. "What can I do to help you, Ms. Jamison?"

"Refuse to help Mr. Devlin make this movie. Can you prevent him from seeing the files?"

"I can, but to be frank, there's little in the case files that Mr. Devlin couldn't find on his own. Your sister's murder was a rare and tragic occurrence in this town. The newspaper covered the story every day for months. People talked about the case, and a lot of those people still live here." He paused. "It's also possible that a reenactment of the crime might provide new leads. Are you sure you want to shut down that possibility?"

She wasn't sure about anything anymore. "I want justice, but I don't want my sister's murder splashed across a movie screen. If you don't give Mr. Devlin the police file, maybe he'll lose interest and go away," she said hopefully. "It would take him twice as long to get the information, and surely there must be easier movies to make."

The chief gave her a wry smile. "Believe me, I'd love for Mark Devlin to leave town, but I doubt that will happen. I'll give him a summary of the information, but not all the interview notes. I will also continue to look into the case myself. In fact . . ." He dug through some papers on his desk. "Something did make me curious."

"What's that?"

"Your father made a cash deposit into your sister's account the day of the murder—eight hundred dollars. I noticed that he did not make a similar deposit in either your account or your brother's." Joe looked back at her with a question in his eyes, a question she couldn't answer.

"I—I didn't know that."

"Did Abby work for your dad?"

"No. She liked to fish with him, but neither one of us worked at the bait shop. And Abby was too busy with school, the volleyball team, her friends. Plus, she had another job."

"That's right—at a law office," Joe said. "They always paid her by check. I asked your dad about the deposit, but he said he didn't remember."

No? Or had he been unwilling to admit he'd been padding Abby's bank account? And why would he have done that?

"Your father did tell me that he was saving money to send Abby to college," Joe continued, "and that if he had put money in her account, it was probably because of that. I guess your sister dreamed of becoming a marine biologist."

"Yes, Abby wanted to study the ocean and save endangered marine life. She was smart. I think she would have made it." Lauren paused. "Why did the police look at the bank accounts?"

"Standard procedure."

"To rule out what?"

"Irregular deposits or withdrawals."

"But at the time, this deposit didn't bother anyone?" she asked.

"Well, it's not unusual for a father to put money into his daughter's account."

"Then why did it make you curious?"

"The timing, the fact that it was cash, and a one-time deposit. I went through the statements from the previous year, and I couldn't find any other deposits to match. It seemed odd."

"Abby must have done something on the side for my dad, or like he said, he just wanted to put some money toward her college." The idea of her father giving Abby money on the sly bothered her. She'd been closer to getting out of high school than Abby. Maybe she hadn't had the big college goals that Abby had had, but she'd had her own dream of attending culinary school. She wasn't going to save the world's sea turtle population, but did that make her goals less worthy?

She saw Joe's speculative gaze deepen. The last thing she needed was for the chief of police to think she was jealous of her sister. That would play right into Mark Devlin's theories. "What difference does it make if my father gave my sister money?" she asked.

"Maybe none. As I said, I'm just reviewing the facts."

She thought for a moment, considering the new information. Joe Silveira wouldn't have brought up the money if he didn't think it meant something.

"I know your parents are divorced now, but I wondered what kind of relationship they had before your sister was killed?" Joe asked, breaching the silence.

"It was good, I think. I never heard them fight. They seemed to get along. It did bother my mother that my dad spent so much time at sea or in the shop. He was often late for dinner and she felt he didn't always put us first, but I don't remember any big problems. After Abby died, they fell apart. They were so angry, and they took it out on each other. My dad refused to leave here. My mom couldn't stand to stay in a place that had stolen her child from her, so she took me and my younger brother away. Abby's death destroyed our family."

"It must have been a difficult time."

"You can't even imagine."

"Was Abby close to your father? Do you think she knew more about his activities than perhaps any of the rest of you did?"

She recalled the conversation from the previous night when her father had thought she was Abby and had referred to *one of their little secrets.* "Activities, as in what?" she asked the chief.

"Something he might have been doing that he didn't want your mother to know about?"

Lauren suddenly realized what he was getting at. "You mean, like an affair?"

"I don't mean anything. I'm just trying to get a feel for the family dynamics."

"What do our family dynamics have to do with Abby's murder?"

"Probably nothing."

The *probably* part bothered her. "It sounds like you have doubts about my father."

"I have doubts about everyone. That's the only way I know how to investigate."

"Would those doubts also involve me?"

"Do you have something to hide?" Joe asked.

"No."

"Then we're good."

She got to her feet. "Thanks for your time, Chief. You've given me a lot to think about."

"No problem. Do you know how long you'll be staying in Angel's Bay?"

That seemed to be the question of the day. She just wished she had an answer. "I don't. I thought this would be a quick trip home to assess my father's illness, but it's turning out to be a lot more complicated."

Charlotte had never imagined that she'd one day have to pack up her childhood home and move on. As she looked at her bedroom, she felt a little sad. The twin beds where she and Doreen had slept throughout their childhoods had been stripped. The dresser, closets, and bookshelves had been emptied. Even the carpet had been pulled up to reveal a hardwood floor she'd never known existed. There was only one thing left to do.

She moved toward the closet. Along the door trim were ink marks that represented every year of her life from the age of five up to fourteen. By fourteen she'd begun to rebel, to throw off the yoke of responsibility, of being the perfect minister's daughter. Her parents, especially her mother, had set the bar high, and Charlotte had always fallen short. She might be a doctor now and respected by her patients, but in her mother's eyes, she was still the not-so-great screw-up of a daughter. She doubted that would ever change.

Charlotte dipped her brush into the paint and applied it to the trim. It took several swipes to cover the marks, and each swipe made her feel a bit more melancholy. It was ridiculous to care about a house that she'd spent most of her childhood wanting to get out of. But she did care, and the emotion surprised her.

Her parents had lived in this house for thirty-four years. She'd been born here, and every big event of her childhood had been celebrated within these walls. But life was changing. Her father had died almost a year ago, and soon her childhood home would belong to someone else. It was ironic that that someone was her high school boyfriend, but Andrew was the new minister, and the house belonged to the church.

Andrew Schilling had generously given her mother three months to find a new home. After a thorough search, her mother had decided to buy a house on Ravenswood Lane, a few blocks away. Charlotte had agreed to move there with her for the foreseeable future. They didn't make the best of roommates, but since she'd talked her mother into taking in a pregnant teenager, she could hardly leave her mother and Annie to fend for themselves. So the three of them would live together. She hoped they wouldn't kill each other.

"Hey Charlotte," Annie said as she walked into the room. "Your mom said to tell you that she'll meet you at the new house."

Annie was a pretty eighteen-year-old who was seven months pregnant. Three months earlier, she'd left home, desperate to get away from her father, a disabled veteran with psychological problems. Carl Dupont had abused Annie, and in confusion and despair, she had thrown herself into the bay. Fortunately, she'd been rescued and had immediately regretted her momentary insanity. Charlotte had met Annie in the emergency room, and upon learning of Annie's situation, she'd convinced her mother to allow Annie to live with them until she had the baby and could find a way to support herself.

"Is there anything else I can do?" Annie asked. "Otherwise, I'll walk over to the new house and help your mom start unpacking."

"No, you've been a great help." What had surprised Charlotte most about Annie coming to live with them was how well her mother and Annie got along. Monica Adams had taken Annie under her wing like a mother hen, and had never offered the slightest criticism or judgment about how Annie had foolishly gotten herself pregnant. Apparently *other* people's daughters could make mistakes.

"I really appreciate your letting me stay with you in the new house," Annie said.

"It's no problem. We're happy to have you."

"Your brother sent another email today. His note was so sweet, it made your mom cry. He said that he dreams about her barbecue chicken and potato salad, and that he never thought he would miss her so much."

How like Jamie to remember to compliment their mother. She really should take a page out of her brother's book once in a while.

"He sounds really nice," Annie said quietly. "I didn't think he would be."

Annie had been terrified to sleep in Jamie's room when she'd first moved in and realized he was a soldier. Annie's father still lived up in the mountains, roaming the woods with a shotgun, fighting the war in his own head. But since Annie and Charlotte's mother had started reading Jamie's letters together, Annie had begun to see that not all soldiers were crazy.

"Jamie also wrote me a little note welcoming me to the family. Not that I'm in your family or anything," Annie added. "You know I don't think that." She gave Charlotte a worried look.

"You *are* part of our family, Annie. My mother has practically adopted you."

"Well, just till the baby comes, right?"

"Don't worry, no one will be kicking you out anytime soon. My mom loves having you around. And she'll adore having a baby in the house."

"But I need to go to work and make some money after the baby comes."

"You have time, Annie—really. My mother doesn't need rent money, and she loves to cook for you. You make her feel needed, and that's a tremendous gift."

"I need her more than she needs me."

"I wouldn't be so sure of that." After her husband's death, her mother had needed someone to take care of, and Charlotte was too busy defending her independence to be that person. "Oh, and don't forget there's a baby shower tomorrow for my friend Kara. I'd love for you to come."

"I can't go, Charlotte. I'm sorry."

"Are you sure? It will be fun. You can't hide forever."

"All those ladies will be looking at me and gossiping."

"The easiest way to stop the gossip is to name the father of your baby."

Annie frowned. "You know I won't do that."

Charlotte did know, since she and her mother had been trying to convince Annie that the father bore some financial responsibility, but Annie had refused to give a name. She'd worked for a cleaning service in town prior to her pregnancy, and rumors were flying that one of the clients might be the father of her baby.

"I'll see you at the house." Annie moved toward the door, clearly eager to avoid further discussion.

Charlotte put another coat of paint on the trim, then took her paintbrush into the kitchen and ran

some water through it. She was just drying it out
when she heard the front door open.

"Anyone here?" Andrew called.

"In the kitchen," she yelled back.

He walked in and set a bag of food on the counter, giving her a smile. "I hope you're hungry. I got
Chinese food for two."

"I can't stay. I need to help my mother." While
Andrew seemed interested in pursuing a relationship
with her, she wasn't sure she wanted that. They'd had
a brief romance in high school, but that was years
ago, and the fact that Andrew was a minister now
didn't play well in her mind. She certainly couldn't
see herself as the minister's girlfriend, or the minister's wife.

"You can stay for a few minutes, Charlie," Andrew said firmly.

"Well, maybe a few." She leaned against the
counter as Andrew pulled out cartons of food. He
was dressed in casual tan slacks and a button-down
blue shirt tucked in at the waist. His blond hair was
cut short and with a little gel flowed back in perfect waves. He always had a freshly shaved look and
a scent of cologne about him, and she had to admit
that his smile still had the ability to make her heart
beat a little faster.

"You left the plates behind," Andrew said in surprise as he opened the cupboard. "I thought we were
going to have to eat out of the cartons."

"Those are new plates. My mother bought them
for you, along with some glasses and silverware for

four. She didn't want you to walk in and have nothing to eat on."

"That was very generous. I'll reimburse her."

"You can try," she said with a smile.

He smiled back. "Okay, I'll just say thank you."

"Good call."

"So how do you feel about all this, now that moving day is here?"

"Weird. Strangely sad." She gave a little laugh. "I hated this house for most of my teenage years. It was prison, and my mother was the warden."

"But there were some good times, too."

"Yes, there's a lot of history in these walls. The new house will never be home. Christmas won't be the same without the tree in the corner of the living room by the fireplace. It's ridiculous. I'm a grown-up—I shouldn't care."

"You don't have to give up this place entirely. You can always visit me. Help me buy furniture, decorate."

"I'm not good at any of those things. That's my mother's area. I'm sure she'd be happy to help you."

He heaved a dramatic sigh. "When are you going to give me a break, Charlie?"

"A break from what?"

"From me asking you out, and you saying no."

"We can't recreate the past, Andrew."

"I don't want to do that. I'm talking about the future." He moved toward her and put his hands on her waist. "I like who you are now. I like who I am. We could be good together."

Maybe they could be. But if she ever got seriously involved with Andrew, she'd have to get seriously honest with him, and there were some things in her past she didn't want to bring up. "It wouldn't work. You have a reputation to maintain. I know what it takes to be the minister in this town and to be the woman at his side. That woman could never be me."

"You don't have to be your mother. There are all kinds of minister's wives, but I'm not talking about marriage," he added quickly. "Just dinner—you and me—where we go to a restaurant and sit down and maybe have some wine."

"Let's start with *this* dinner and see how we do." She stepped away from him and started dishing out the rice.

Andrew pulled out a chair and sat down. "Is there someone else?"

Joe Silveira's face flashed through her mind. He was not *someone else*. He was the chief of police. He was married. But he sent her blood pressure soaring, a fact she tried very much to deny. "No," she said, realizing Andrew was still waiting for an answer.

"That took you a while," he said with a contemplative expression.

"I'm concentrating on my career and my mother right now. That's all I can handle at the moment."

"How is Annie doing?"

"Good. She's getting along great with my mother. And I must say I'm surprised that my mom can be so open-minded about Annie's teenage pregnancy, when she was so . . ." She bit off the rest of her sentence, realizing she was getting into dangerous territory.

"So what?" Andrew prodded.

"So rigid with me. Remember my curfew? It was ten o'clock when I was sixteen years old. Talk about embarrassing—everyone made fun of me."

"We still managed to have some fun," he said with a mischievous smile.

She gave him a warning look. "I can't imagine how you're going to counsel the teenagers in this town, having done what you did."

"I think it will help me." His expression grew serious. "I know what they're feeling."

"So you'd tell them to wait?"

"I would," he said, meeting her gaze.

"Do you regret that we didn't?"

He thought for a moment. "I think I do. Not because it wasn't great, but because if we hadn't crossed that line back then, maybe you'd be more willing to give me a chance now."

"You think I won't go out with you because you took my virginity?" she asked in amazement. "I'm not holding that against you."

"What about the fact that I slept with someone else three days later? Not my finest days."

"True, but those weren't my finest days, either." And she wasn't talking about what had happened with him. "Let's eat before this gets cold."

"All right. When we're done, I'll practice my sermon on you. That way if you fall asleep during the service tomorrow, you won't miss anything."

She made a face at him. "That was just once, and I was up all night delivering a baby. As I recall, you were talking endlessly about apples."

"I was talking about temptation," he corrected.

"Well, you tempted me to fall asleep."

"That's why you need your own personal minister: to keep you on the straight and narrow."

"I tried to walk that line for eighteen years, Andrew. I failed." She put up a hand to ward off any pep talk. "Enough about us. What gossip have you heard lately?"

"I can't tell you what I hear in confidence."

"How about what you hear at the café?"

He grinned. "Well, this morning I overheard Mary Harper tell Lucy Schmidt that you got a boob job. And how it was so sad, because men didn't marry women with fake breasts."

Her jaw dropped, and she felt even more uncomfortable when Andrew's gaze fell to her chest. "They're real. You *know* they're real. Mary Harper said that so you'd overhear her. She has her eyes on you, so watch out."

"I'm not worried—because I have my eyes on you." His gaze moved once again to her chest. "They *are* a little bigger, Charlie."

She threw her napkin at him. "Okay, dinner is officially over."

EIGHT

When Lauren returned from the police station, she found her father dozing in his favorite recliner. She shut the door softly, watching him thoughtfully. It was no secret that he'd favored Abby with his attention, but his money—that surprised her.

She'd been surprised a lot in the past few days. She'd thought she knew the people she lived with, the people she loved. But they were showing new sides of themselves, making her doubt that she'd known them at all. She hated the idea of Mark Devlin's movie, but she had to admit he was stirring things up.

She set her purse on the table, and her dad started. He opened his eyes, blinking against the light, as he stretched his arms over his head. "Lauren," he murmured with a yawn. "You're back."

Thank God he knew who she was.

"Where have you been?" he asked as he brought his chair back up into a sitting position.

"The police station." She sat on the couch. "I met with the chief of police, Joe Silveira. He's reviewing Abby's case."

Her father looked pleased. Would he be so happy if he had something to hide? She might as well find out.

"Chief Silveira mentioned a bank deposit that you made the day Abby died," she continued. "You put eight hundred dollars into her account."

"He asked me about that the other day. I was starting to save for her college education. She had a couple of years of high school left, and I wanted to put some money aside."

His answer seemed truthful. And he wasn't acting as if he'd done something wrong, which disturbed her on another level. "Why weren't you putting money aside for my college?"

Surprise flashed in his eyes. "You wanted to go to the community college and work at Martha's Bakery."

"I wanted to go the Culinary Academy, but I didn't think we could afford it."

His mouth turned down. "You're angry about the money."

"I know you and Abby were close, but why was her education more important than mine?"

"It wasn't more important. I don't remember ever hearing that you wanted to go to the Culinary Academy. But Abby and I used to talk a lot about her dreams. I wanted to be a marine biologist when I was young, too, but there wasn't enough money for me to go to school. I wanted to give Abby what I missed out on. It's not that I didn't want to help you, Lauren. I thought you had what you needed. You seemed happy." He gave a little shrug, as if he'd never understand her or get it right.

She had been happy that year. She'd been falling in love with Shane, and she'd spent less and less time at home. Was she wrong to blame her father for not knowing her dreams? Had she even tried to share them with him? Or had she just gotten so used to his disinterest that she'd given up?

"Your mother gave me hell for putting that money in Abby's account," her father continued. "It was one more reason for her to hate me."

"So Mom didn't know about the money until later?" It was nice to know that her mother hadn't been conspiring behind her back.

"No. She liked to keep her eye on the money, along with everything else in the house," he grumbled.

"Were you and Mom happy together, before Abby died?" Lauren asked, wondering what else she didn't know. "Mom always said that Abby's death killed the marriage, but it sounds like you had some issues."

"Every marriage has problems, but I thought things were good. Life was busy. We had three kids. My business took up a lot of time that your mother didn't always appreciate. I don't know. I suppose we both could have done some things differently. No one is perfect."

"That's true." Lauren settled back against the cushions. "So how are you feeling tonight? Do you want some dinner?"

"I had stew at the café with Mort. You know, Mort, Rita, and your mom and I were quite a foursome back in the day. We'd barbecue every weekend, go out on the boat, spend Christmas Eve at each other's houses. You and Leslie were good friends for a long time, and Rita and your mother loved to quilt together. I bet your mother doesn't quilt anymore, does she?"

Lauren was sure her mother had left her needle and thread in Angel's Bay, along with everything else. "She's into wine tasting. She lives near a couple of vineyards."

"She used to like beer." His lips tightened. "I guess she couldn't allow herself to like anything that she cared about before she left."

Lauren saw sadness in his eyes, as well as anger. She'd always been on her mother's side in the divorce; she'd never considered her father's point of view. Maybe she hadn't been completely fair. But when only one person spoke, it was difficult to understand the other side of the argument.

Her father picked up the newspaper in his lap and handed it over to her. "You might want to take a look at this."

"What is it?"

"Some gold coins from the *Gabriella* washed ashore yesterday on Refuge Beach. The ship's bell was discovered three months ago, and now these coins. I think that wreck may finally be ready to show itself."

Lauren skimmed through the article. The ship had been sailing south from San Francisco filled with what was rumored to be Gold Rush spoils, when it had gone down in a ferocious storm in 1850. After several bodies and the initial items of the wreck washed ashore, nothing was ever seen again. Treasure hunters speculated that the *Gabriella* was hidden in one of the deep underground canyons off the central coast, which were only revealed during certain tidal conditions, but to this day no one had been able to find the wreck.

"I'd love to see that ship raised," Ned said with a sparkle in his eyes. "I wonder what story it would tell—if we'd finally know what happened to the crew, the passengers, and the gold."

"Don't we already know most of it?" she asked, setting the paper aside. "I remember when you used to read to me from Leonora's diary. It was such a romantically tragic story."

"It was. She and Tommy met when they were kids, but Leonora was promised to another man. She married Clark Jamison, they had a son, Jeremy, and a few years later, Clark died. Then Tommy suddenly reappeared. He sailed into San Francisco, the captain of the *Gabriella,* and when he saw Leonora on the docks, he was amazed and struck by her beauty, just as he'd been at sixteen. It had been twenty years since they'd seen each other but Leonora said it felt like only a few minutes."

The phrase hit home. Lauren had thought the same thing when she'd seen Shane again after thirteen years.

"Tommy was a widower, too," her father continued. "His daughter was living in San Diego with his mother while he was away at sea. He had to sail the *Gabriella* back down the coast, and he asked Leonora and Jeremy to go with him. They married the night before the ship sailed south. They only had a short time together before the storm hit and the *Gabriella* broke apart. The ship had taken on more than its normal number of passengers, because people were leaving the Gold Rush by them, and there weren't enough lifeboats. Leonora wanted Tommy to come with her and Jeremy on the lifeboat, but he was the captain. He would be the last to go." Her father paused, his eyes distant, as if he could almost see that moment in his mind. "That was the last time Leonora saw Tommy, and his body never washed ashore."

"And Leonora made a life for herself and Jeremy here in Angel's Bay. And that's where our family started," Lauren finished.

"First love is a powerful thing. It's hard to get over," her father said.

"Mom was your first love, wasn't she?"

"Oh, yes. She came to visit her cousin one summer, and we fell instantly in love. We got married after four months. It was probably too fast. I was ten years older than her and should have given her more time to grow up. But I wanted her, and at the time she wanted me."

"I wish you had fought harder to stay together after Abby died," Lauren said quietly. "I know Mom tried to comfort you, but you wouldn't let any of us in. You shut down emotionally. You went out to sea for days at a time. Every night that you weren't here, Mom would cry herself to sleep. I couldn't stand the sound of her sobs." She drew in a shaky breath. "You think Mom ran away with me and David, but you left *us* first."

The bleakness in her father's eyes reminded her of how he'd looked in the weeks after Abby's death. "I didn't know what to do back then—how to handle things. I tried to talk to your mother, but she wouldn't let me speak of Abby. All she wanted to do was throw things away. Every time I left to go to work, I was afraid I'd come back and discover that your mother had erased Abby's life from the house. And when your mother announced she was leaving, there was no discussion. She didn't ask me to go with her, with you and David."

"You shouldn't have waited for her to ask. You should have insisted that we all stay together, either here in Angel's Bay or somewhere else. We were a family, Dad. Even with Abby gone, we were still a family. Why didn't you fight for us?"

He swallowed hard. "I knew you'd go with your mother. You were always her champion. And David was too young to be without her."

"You should have come with us."

"I couldn't leave Angel's Bay. I couldn't leave Abby behind."

"But you had two other children who still needed you."

"You weren't alone," he argued. "You had your mother and David. The three of you had each other."

"We didn't have *you.*" She blinked back an unexpected tear. "You were my hero when I was a little girl. I loved you. I needed you. When we left, I cried all the way up the coast." She wiped her eyes. "I would have been your champion, too, if you'd given me a chance."

Her father stared down at the carpet. The minutes ticked away. Finally, he lifted his head. "I'm sorry, Lauren."

She'd wanted to hear the words for a long time. Now that she had, it didn't change anything. It didn't make up for the fact that she'd lost her father at the same time she'd lost her sister.

"I never meant to hurt you and David," he continued. "I couldn't leave, and your mother couldn't stay. Part of the reason I didn't fight to keep you here was because I wasn't sure I could be a good father anymore. I hadn't protected Abby, kept her safe. I thought you were better off with your mom."

"You should have found out if I was better off. At the very least, you should have come to visit, written me letters, and called. But you didn't do any of those, except for a few holidays and birthdays."

"You're right. I could have done better." He paused, his gaze direct and clear. "So what do you want from me now?"

That was the toughest question he'd ever asked her. What *did* she want? She wanted her family to be the way it was. She wanted Abby to be alive. She wanted to turn back the clock. But none of that was possible.

"I want you to be happy, and I want you to be safe," she said. "If you won't come to San Francisco with me, then what's your plan?"

"I'm not your problem, Lauren."

"I can't just close my eyes to your medical condition. You're my father. I'm your daughter. That's the way it is. So let's figure something out."

"I do understand that my brain is shutting down," he said slowly. "It scares me, not always knowing what I'm doing. Sometimes I wind up places and I don't understand how I got there."

She was shocked to hear his admission. He'd been brushing his illness aside since she'd arrived.

"But here in Angel's Bay, I have landmarks," he said. "I know where I am, and I can find my way home. I couldn't move to a strange city; I need things to be familiar."

His fear tugged at her heart. "All right, Dad. So how can we make it work? What if I hired someone to move into this house with you?"

"I couldn't live with a stranger."

"What about someone who comes in during the day, cleans up and makes sure you have food?"

"I guess I could use a little help, but I don't have much money."

"I can help pay for it."

"You got a lot of money, do you?" he asked with a quirk of his eyebrow.

"I wouldn't call it a lot, but I'll share what I have."

He tilted his head, giving her a thoughtful look. "Why would you want to? I think we just established I'm a rotten father. I don't want to be your duty."

"I don't want you to be, either, but you are."

"Well, at least you're honest."

"It's time for that, don't you think?"

"If you want to know what I *really* think—I think you should move back here. We haven't had a bakery in town since Martha retired two years ago. Sam at the café makes some cookies and pies, but that's about it. And the supermarket brings in pre-packaged sweets from who knows where. Angel's Bay could use a good bakery. You could open one, the way you always said you would."

She was shocked by his suggestion, especially since it appeared he'd actually thought about it. And he was right. Opening a bakery had been her dream once, but not anymore. "I don't want the same things now. I've moved on."

"Move back."

"No."

"It could be good for you."

"It wouldn't be."

"How do you know?"

"Because I do," she said in frustration, feeling as if she'd just gotten on a runaway train. Her father had never cared about what she was doing. The fact that he did now was unsettling.

"Just think about it," he said. "Spend the week here, get reacquainted. You might discover something."

"Like what?"

He smiled. "That there's no place like home."

Shane had grown up in a two-story house at the end of a cul-de-sac in one of the older neighborhoods of Angel's Bay. With five kids in the family as well as an assortment of pets, home had never been a quiet place. Tonight was no exception. As he parked his motorcycle at the curb, he could see a crowd of people in the living room. His mother had gone all out for his father's sixty-fifth birthday.

It was strange to think that his father and Ned Jamison were almost the same age, yet there was a world of difference in the state of their health. John Murray was a robust man with a healthy appetite, a few extra pounds of girth, a hearty laugh, and an energetic spirit. He'd always had a personality that was bigger than life. Shane had been close to his father in childhood, but high school had been a different matter.

He got off his motorcycle as his sister Kara parked her car in front of the house. She got out with an exaggerated groan, weighted down not only by her very pregnant belly but also by an enormous gift.

He walked over to take it from her. "What's this? Trying to outshine me?"

"Would that be difficult? Your hands appear to be empty."

He grinned. "Can I put my name on this present?"

"You certainly can—if you want to cough up forty bucks."

"You bought him an eighty-dollar present? Very generous. What is it?"

"It's a new radio. And it wasn't eighty, it was a hundred and twenty. Dee and I bought it together, but I'm happy to take your money and call it thirds. I'm also happy you're here. I didn't think you were coming."

"It *is* the old man's birthday," he said.

"And you've missed the last twelve. So why are you standing out here? Are you worried about all the Lauren and Abby questions?"

"Among other things."

Kara gave him a speculative look. "What is up with you and our parents? You're all very polite, but there's an underlying tension. I thought maybe it was because you were gone for so long and it was awkward being back, but you've been home for a while now."

"Everything is fine," he assured her. "Don't worry about me."

She glanced at the house. "I don't really want to go in, either. It's bad enough that my baby shower is tomorrow. Now I have to face everyone twice. It's not the questions I mind, it's the looks—the pitying, sad, she's living in a world of denial looks." She turned back to him. "I know that's what people think. I'm not stupid."

"No one said you were."

"Oh, they do behind my back. But they'll see—they'll see when Colin wakes up." She sighed. "Well, the sooner we go inside, the sooner we can leave." She threw back her shoulders and headed down the path.

They were greeted with hugs and kisses by family and friends. Shane escaped as quickly as possible, putting the present on a side table, then heading to the kitchen where the bar had been set up. He poured himself a shot of Jack Daniel's and downed it in one gulp. Although he liked being back in Angel's Bay, being in this house was another story. Every time he walked through the door, he was hit by a blast of painful memories.

He could still remember the day when his life had changed. He'd been fifteen. He'd come home early from football practice with a sprained knee. He'd hobbled into the kitchen to grab an ice pack and overheard a very disturbing conversation.

He poured another shot of alcohol and tossed it down as his dad came over.

John Murray's eyes lit up with pleasure. "Shane. Good to see you, son." John gave him a slap on the back. "I'm glad you came."

"Happy birthday, Dad." He tried not to let any

emotion show on his face. It was the only way he knew how to deal with his parents.

"Help yourself to some food. Your mother outdid herself tonight."

"I will," he promised, but when his dad moved away, he poured himself another drink. He saw two women watching him from across the room with scowling, judgmental looks—Nancy Whittaker and Michelle Holmes, friends of his mother. He raised his glass as if to toast them. Michelle's frown deepened, she whispered something to Nancy, and then the two walked away.

After setting down the shot glass, Shane headed through the house and out to the back porch, where it was dark and quiet. A wide expanse of lawn greeted his gaze, along with several tall trees that ran along the edge of the property. One of them held the treehouse that he'd built with his father and older brother, Patrick. They'd needed a place to get away from the younger kids, especially pesky Kara, who always wanted in on their action. Not that the treehouse had kept her out. In fact, it had become a popular meeting place for everyone in the neighborhood.

He crossed the lawn and tested out the boards nailed into the tree. He had no idea if the old steps would hold his weight, but he had an irresistible urge to find out. He scaled the tree and crawled through what now seemed like a midget-sized door. There were a few newish toys in the treehouse, probably left behind by Patrick's kids. A new generation was enjoying the hideaway.

He sat on the floor and gazed up at the roof. There were large open slats where the moon and the stars showed through.

He'd seen the night sky a million times. Out in the middle of the ocean the stars could be something special, but this sight took him back to high school, to another night a very long time ago.

He'd had a bad day, another fight, and being in the house was too much, so he'd come here to escape. Someday he would leave Angel's Bay. He just needed enough cash and then he'd be gone.

"Shane, are you there?" *Lauren's sweet voice washed over him like a warm caress.*

He'd been avoiding her all day. He never should have gotten involved with her. She made him want to stay in this town, and he couldn't do that.

"I'm coming up," *she said.*

He watched as Lauren juggled a plastic container in one hand while she climbed up the ladder. She had on jeans and a long-sleeve top that clung to her breasts. Her long brown hair curled around her face, her skin lit by the moonlight. God, she was pretty. Beautiful and perfect and innocent, and he should leave her that way.

"You shouldn't have come," *he told her roughly.*

She sat down across from him, worry in her eyes. "What's wrong? I've been calling you all day. Why didn't you call me back?"

"I didn't want to talk to you."

She looked startled by his blunt response but immediately shook her head. "I don't believe that."

"Then you're a fool."

"And you're a liar. What is going on with you? Why were you fighting Marty? He's one of your best friends."

"I just like to fight."

Lauren held out the plastic container she'd brought with her. *"I baked you some double chocolate nut brownies. Chocolate always cheers me up."*

He wanted to yell at her that she was crazy if she thought a brownie could make him feel better, but there was something about the sweet affection in her eyes that prevented him from lashing out at her. This wasn't her fault. He didn't want to hurt her, but dammit, couldn't she take a hint?

"Shane," she began.

"If you're staying, let's make out." He yanked the container out of her hand and set it down. Then he put his hand behind her neck and pulled her to him. He saw the surprise in her eyes and he waited for the fear, the anger. But all he saw was trust, and he froze. What the hell was he doing? He let her go.

"What's wrong now?" she asked in confusion. *"You can talk to me. You can tell me anything. I won't judge you."*

"Go home, Lauren."

"Stop trying to scare me away. I know you, Shane,"

"You don't know everything," he whispered.

"You'll tell me one day," she said confidently. She put her fingers against his mouth as he started to protest. *"Let's not talk anymore."* She covered his mouth with hers and pressed her breasts against his chest, and drove everything else out of his mind.

Shane opened his eyes and stared up at the sky.

Lauren had always wanted to see the good in people, especially him, but so much had changed since that night. So many things had happened that couldn't be taken back or undone. The past was gone, and he was far too old to be hiding out in the treehouse.

He swung his leg over the side and climbed down to the ground. He was thinking about slipping through the side yard when his father came out the back door.

"Shane? Is that you?" his dad asked, squinting into the darkness.

"Yeah." He walked over to the deck. "I'm here."

"Hiding out?" John asked with a speculative gleam in his eye. "I know things are heating up for you around here, but you have to ride it out, son. You can't run away again; it will only make you look guilty."

"I am guilty. I didn't kill Abby, but I left her alone at the high school that night. I should have made sure someone was there to meet her." It was a regret he would never get over. "If I'd waited . . ."

His father put a hand on his arm. "Life is full of should haves, Shane. You can't look back; you just gotta move forward. It's not your fault, what happened to Abby." John smiled. "Kara told me that you might need to hear that again."

"Kara should butt out."

"No, she was right. I want you to know you'll always have my support. Now come back to the party. Take your mind off your problems."

"Thanks, but I'll pass. Some people in there aren't nearly as happy to have me here as you are."

"Screw 'em. You're my son and you're always welcome here. Who don't you like? I'll throw them out."

Shane grinned at his father's offer. "Thanks, but I can't see you tossing Nancy and Michelle out on their asses."

"Don't tempt me. Those women have been driving me crazy for thirty years."

"John," his mother interrupted, sticking her head out the door. She gave them a quizzical look. "What are you two doing out here? We have a house full of guests."

"Just talking," his father said.

Moira stepped onto the deck. "About what? Is something wrong, Shane?"

Something had been wrong for a long, long time. "Everything is fine," he said. "You should go inside, Dad. You're the guest of honor."

"We'll talk later," John promised.

"Talk about what later?" his mother asked as John led her back into the house.

Moira shot Shane a worried look over her shoulder, a look he knew all too well. She'd been trying to stop him from talking to his father for a very long time.

NINE

Charlotte slipped into the back of the church during Andrew's Sunday sermon. She was late, but Donna March's newborn daughter had decided to come a week early. She still felt a little giddy from the delivery. No matter how many babies she'd helped come into the world, there was nothing better than hearing a child's first cry and seeing the look of wonder on the parents' faces. It was truly the miracle of life.

As she shifted in her seat, she saw her mother and Annie in the first row. Andrew's mother was sitting in the first pew on the other side. The two women had been in competition for a long time, and Charlotte felt sorry for Andrew's future wife, who would have to battle for a seat up front—which reminded her that she really needed to tell Andrew that she wasn't interested in dating him. It was fun to flirt, and it was flattering to be pursued, especially since, once upon a time, she'd been the one running after him.

Andrew had grown up well. He seemed to genuinely care about ministering to the community, and he was gaining more confidence in his role as a spiritual leader. Although some of the older members of the congregation still muttered about him being too young to know what was best, most people had come around. Andrew certainly had a plethora of single women attending church now. With his good looks and heavenly aura, he was pretty damn irresistible. So why was she resisting?

Her gaze moved to a man sitting a few rows in front of her, Joe Silveira. Joe, with his dark hair and dark eyes, was night to Andrew's day. The chief was rugged and physical, with rough edges that were always apparent despite his polite and professional manner. She'd seen him in action and off duty, and she found him more than a little intriguing, which was completely inappropriate, because Joe was married.

His wife sat next to him in the pew. Rachel had the brittle sophistication of an L.A. transplant and didn't quite fit into Angel's Bay, unlike Joe, who seemed happy to have ditched his big-city cop days for life in the picturesque seaside town. Rachel seemed to have more in common with the man who sat on her other side, Mark Devlin. He also gave off that slick L.A. vibe, and Charlotte didn't trust him one bit. He'd left her a couple of messages, wanting to talk about the past. She hadn't returned them. She didn't know who killed Abby, and she certainly didn't want to help anyone railroad Shane or one of her other friends.

As the congregation rose to its feet, she started. The service was over, and she hadn't heard one word of it.

When she made her way out of the church, she found Andrew on the steps surrounded by women. He sent her a silent plea for rescue, but she simply smiled. She didn't want to give anyone ideas about her and Andrew—at least any more ideas than they already had.

But Andrew wasn't about to let her get away that easily. "Charlotte," he called. "Excuse me, ladies. I have to speak to Dr. Adams."

The women looked like they wanted to shoot her.

"Hey," Andrew said as he drew near.

"Hey, yourself. You just made all those women want to kill me."

He grinned. "You used to like it when I singled you out."

"I used to like a lot of things, and then I grew up."

"You're not still mad at me about the fake boobs comment, are you?"

"No, but if you keep looking at my breasts, I think God might strike you down."

His smile broadened. "I like talking to you, Charlie. I can be myself. I don't have to live up to anyone's expectations."

Judging by the weary note in his voice, maybe everything wasn't going as well for him as she'd imagined. "You're doing fine. Don't worry about what people think of you."

"I'm still figuring out what *I* think of me," he said with a rueful expression. "By the way, my mother is hosting a lunch today, and she's having at least five eligible women over to meet me. She's decided that since I'm settled in a job, I should be thinking about marriage and children."

"Well, you're not getting any younger," she said lightly, wondering who some of the women were. Not that she cared. She should be happy that he was mixing with other people.

"I want you to come, stake your claim." He gave her a hopeful smile.

"I don't have a claim."

"Yes, you do." He moved in closer. "Seriously, Charlotte."

"Andrew, we can't talk about this now. People are waiting to speak to you." Out of the corner of her eye, she could see a half dozen interested gazes focused on them.

"Why do you keep pushing me away?"

"Because I'm not interested." There, she'd said it.

"Ouch."

"You asked." She refused to weaken in the face of his disappointment.

"I'm not taking that as your final answer. But I'll go—for now." He moved away, joining an older couple and their grandchildren.

Charlotte let out a breath. She wasn't getting through to Andrew at all. Now that she didn't want him, he wanted her even more. She should have played harder to get in high school.

Turning to go in search of her mother, she stumbled right into Joe.

"Careful," he said, grabbing her arm to steady her.

"Sorry. I didn't see you there." Heat ran through her body, and she fought back the urge to hold on to him.

"You were in deep conversation with the minister," Joe said, letting go of her arm. "The two of you are close, aren't you?"

There was an odd note in his voice. She wished she could read his expression, but his eyes were hidden by dark sunglasses.

"We grew up together," she said.

"High school boyfriend, right?"

"You're up to date on the rumor mill. It was a long time ago."

"He doesn't act like it was that long ago."

"How does he act?"

"Like he wants you."

Joe's words were warm and husky, and she felt herself melting, until she reminded herself that Joe was talking about Andrew, not about himself. She straightened. "It's not like that. We're friends."

"Maybe you should tell him that."

"I have. So, where did Rachel go? I saw her in church earlier."

"She went with Devlin to talk to someone," he said shortly.

She frowned. "Can't you get rid of him, Joe? He's

talking all kinds of nonsense. This morning at the hospital, someone told me that Mr. Devlin thinks there's a possibility Mr. Jamison killed his own daughter. It's not right. He's making everyone suspicious of each other. You have to stop him."

"I'd love to do just that, but he's not breaking any laws." Joe tilted his head, giving her a curious look. "You were in town back then. Who do you think killed Abby?"

"I have no idea. But it wasn't Shane. He had a bad rep in high school because he was reckless and short-tempered, but he had a good heart. He helped me out of a bad situation once, and I know he wouldn't have hurt Abby."

"What happened to you, Charlotte?" Joe asked curiously. "That's not the first time you've mentioned a problem in your past."

"It's not important. We all have our baggage. I'm sure you do, too. You should go find your wife."

"Yes, I should," he said heavily. "Although there was a time when I didn't always have to go looking for her. The good old days."

As Joe left, Charlotte's gaze returned to Andrew. He was part of her good old days—and some of the bad ones, too.

Sunday afternoon Lauren opened the door to the Angel Heart Quilt Shop with a tingle of anticipation. She'd loved the quilt shop growing up, and as she stepped inside and breathed in the heady scent of fabric, she felt a delicious high. It wasn't the same high she felt when she walked into a bakery, but it was a close second.

She stopped to take it all in: the colorful bolts of material; the hanging quilts on every available wall space; the shelves of threads, rulers, tissue paper, and quilting books. She hadn't quilted since high school, but she could still remember the thrill of picking out the perfect fabric, making that first square, watching the design come to life. Quilting was a lot like cooking—starting with nothing and finishing with something amazing.

There was a teenage girl sitting behind the counter reading a magazine, probably bored without any customers to attend to. Everyone was upstairs in the big loft for Kara's baby shower.

As she headed toward the steps, Lauren paused to take a look at the glass case that held the original Angel's Bay story quilt. The quilt had been made by the twenty-four survivors to honor their families and those who had died. Leonora's square was in the bottom right-hand corner, the design two gold rings with a butterfly in the center. The fabric had come from the light blue dress she'd worn the day she'd reunited with Thomas. The rings symbolized the intertwining of their hearts, and the butterfly referred to Tommy's pet name for her.

Lauren smiled. The romantic tale had always captivated her, and she'd stitched that family square many times in her life. Did her father still have some of those old quilts up in the attic?

The sound of laughter drew her out of the past, and she climbed the stairs with some trepidation. Despite Charlotte's warm invitation, Lauren wasn't sure how well she'd be received. It had been a long time since she'd been a friend to any of the women, and she was fairly sure some of the older ones would judge her harshly for not having come back to visit her father before now.

Her steps slowed as she reached the top. There were at least thirty women milling about the big room. The tables, usually covered with quilting fabrics, now boasted pink tablecloths and vases of flowers. The sewing machines had been pushed against a wall and a large of tower of presents filled one corner.

"I'm so glad you came," Charlotte said, greeting her with a smile. Charlotte wore a pretty floral dress with a light sweater, and her blond hair hung loosely around her shoulders. "I was afraid you'd chicken out."

"I was tempted. There are a lot of people here." Baby showers, like so many other events in Angel's Bay, were a community affair.

"Let's find Kara," Charlotte said, grabbing Lauren's hand.

The warm contact felt both familiar and right. Just like when they were in kindergarten, Charlotte was taking her hand and telling her it would be fine. And just like before, Lauren wanted to believe her.

Kara broke away from a trio of women when she saw Charlotte and Lauren approaching. Her brown eyes sparkled with what appeared to be genuine delight. "Lauren, you came! Charlotte told me she invited you, and I'm so happy you're here." She gave Lauren a hug.

Lauren felt a little awkward as she hugged her back. She and Kara had gotten close when she'd begun seeing Shane, but after everything that had happened, Lauren wasn't sure how Kara felt about her.

"I'll get you some punch, Lauren," Charlotte said. "Can I spike it for you?"

"Absolutely." She had a feeling she was going to need some alcohol before the afternoon was out. When Charlotte moved away, Lauren smiled at Kara. "You look great."

"Liar. I look like hell," Kara said, resting her hands lightly on her enormous belly. "But I appreciate the effort."

"I was so sorry to hear about Colin."

Kara gave her a small nod. "Thanks." She glanced down at the package in Lauren's hands. "You didn't have to bring me a present. You just got into town."

Lauren handed her the small box that she'd decorated with a yellow bow. "It's the music box that your mother gave mine at her baby shower for me thirty years ago. I always liked listening to it when I went to sleep, and I thought it might be nice to return it to your family."

Kara opened the music box, revealing a ballerina spinning to a soft melody. "This is so sweet. My mother loved the ballet. It was her greatest disappointment when I hung up my tutu. And God knows Dee would never put one on," she added with a laugh. "Maybe my daughter will take to dance." She smiled at Lauren. "Colin will love this. He likes things that connect to the past, to our circle of friends and family. I can't wait to show it to him."

"I'm glad you like it."

"I do. So, do you know everyone here?"

Lauren glanced at the crowd, many of whom were casting interested looks in her direction. "There are some familiar faces, but definitely some new ones. I seem to be drawing a lot of attention. I really don't have to stay."

"Are you kidding? I was *not* looking forward to being the focus today. It's been a long three months, with every action being constantly analyzed and judged. Now everyone will be talking about you instead of me. It's a welcome relief."

"I'm glad I can help," Lauren said dryly. "But I'm sure people aren't judging you."

"The people who believe Colin will recover want me to stay strong and positive, and the people who think I'm crazy for believing that my husband will ever get better want to see signs that I'm cracking. The truth is, sometimes I feel optimistic and other days the doubts overwhelm me, and then I feel guilty, because I can't lose faith." She paused and drew in a deep breath. "But today it will be about you, and quite frankly, Lauren, that is the best present you could have given me. I do feel a little sorry for you, though."

"Yeah, I can tell."

Kara grinned. "So before everyone descends on us, what's going on with you and Shane?"

"Nothing," Lauren said, trying to quell the hopeful gleam in Kara's eyes.

"Shane told me he saw you. Any old sparks still lingering?"

"Did he say there were?" She mentally kicked herself for asking such a thing. She felt like she was back in high school again.

"Shane doesn't say much, but I know you meant a lot to him."

"At one time, but there's nothing between us now." She tried not to think about how they'd almost made love on the beach the day before.

"That's too bad. I always thought you were good for each other. You softened him up, and he brought you out of your shell." Kara gave Lauren a speculative look. "Maybe you should give him another chance. Fate has brought you back together again, and you're both single, right?"

"I am," she admitted, "but fate didn't bring me back here. I came home to help my father." Lauren was relieved when Charlotte returned with her punch, interrupting their conversation. Charlotte was accompanied by a slender brunette Lauren didn't recognize.

"This is Jenna Davies," Charlotte introduced, as

she handed Lauren a glass of punch. "Jenna has only been in Angel's Bay a few months, but she's related to Gabriella, the baby discovered after the shipwreck."

"Really?" Lauren echoed in surprise. "That means you're related to Rose Littleton, too. She was a descendant of Gabriella."

"She was my grandmother," Jenna replied. "Unfortunately, I never met her. She passed away before I came to Angel's Bay. Apparently Rose gave my mother up for adoption, so I wasn't aware of her existence until a few months ago. But I'm slowly getting caught up with the Angel's Bay history, and it's kind of fun to be tied to one of the original settlers of the town."

"I remember Rose and my father poring over old family journals," Lauren said. "My great-great-great-grandmother Leonora was on the ship, and my dad was obsessed with the family history."

"We're going to teach Jenna how to make the Gabriella quilt square so she can take over as the official descendant," Charlotte interjected.

Lauren smiled. It was a tradition that the Angel's Bay story quilt be reconstructed by the descendants of the survivors whenever possible. "That's great. Are you a quilter, Jenna?"

"Not even close. I've taken two classes and I'm all thumbs." She paused as her cell phone rang. "Excuse me, I need to take this. I'll talk to you later."

Lauren took a sip of her punch, feeling the kick

of bourbon. She met Charlotte's smiling eyes. "You are a very bad girl, Charlie."

"You'll thank me later." Charlotte turned away from Lauren as two older women engaged her and Kara in conversation.

Lauren glanced across the room, recognizing Dina from the café, Dina's daughter Liz, Mrs. Stevens and Mrs. Hooper, who had both been friends with her mother, Mort's daughter, Leslie, and . . . her heart skipped a beat as she saw Lisa Delaney.

Lisa had auburn hair and dark eyes that stood out against her pale, freckled complexion. She was dressed in black, which accentuated her extremely thin body and the lines around her eyes and mouth. She looked so much older now, not at all like the young girl who had spent so many hours sitting on Abby's bed that Lauren had considered her a second little sister.

Lisa's parents had split when she was five, and she'd ended up with a mother who was more interested in finding a second husband than taking care of her daughter, so Lisa had spent most of her free time with Abby.

Lisa looked up and caught Lauren staring. Her smile faded and she looked somewhat torn, as if she knew she had to say hello but didn't really want to. Lauren could understand her ambivalence. After Abby died, Lauren and her parents had shut Lisa out; she'd reminded them of the girl they'd lost. It wasn't fair, but it had happened.

Lisa squared her shoulders, excused herself from her conversation, and headed over to her. "Lauren, I heard you were back. How are you?"

"I'm good. How are you?" Lauren inquired.

"Great. How's your father?"

"His health is slipping, as you probably know."

"Yes, I'm so sorry."

Lisa didn't sound sorry. She sounded uncomfortable and looked like she'd rather be anywhere else than engaged in this particular conversation.

"I'm glad you're here," Lauren said. "I was looking through some of Abby's things last night, and remembering how much time you used to spend at our house. I thought you might want something to—"

"I really don't want to talk about Abby," Lisa interrupted. "It's still so painful. I miss her every day. She was like my sister."

"I know." In the face of Lisa's comment Lauren was hesitant to bring up Devlin's suspicions, but she didn't know how long she'd be in town, or when she'd have another opportunity to speak to Lisa. "Mark Devlin told me about the movie he's making based on Abby's death. He mentioned something to me, and I'm sure it doesn't mean anything, but it got me wondering."

"That man is making up lies," Lisa said abruptly. "You shouldn't believe anything he says, Lauren."

"I'm not inclined to believe him, but he told me that you and Abby were seen sitting in a car outside Coach Sorensen's house the Saturday night before Abby was killed. It didn't make sense to me, because you told the police that you and Abby stayed in that night. And if you were out, I wondered whose car you were in, since neither of you could drive."

Lisa hesitated, shifting her weight from one foot to the other as she crossed her arms. "We were in Jason Marlow's car. We were just driving around town; we weren't spying on anyone. I don't know what that woman was talking about."

"Jason Marlow?" She had a vague recollection of the guy. He'd been a year younger than her and very close to Colin and Kara. "I don't remember you mentioning his name."

"Really? I'm pretty sure I gave the police the name of just about every boy we'd ever spoken to."

Was that true? It had been a long time since the investigation, and Lauren certainly hadn't been privy to all the details. "I know you didn't mention that you left your house that night."

Lisa shrugged. "It wasn't important."

"Do you know that for sure?"

"Good grief, Lauren. Why are you grilling me?"

"I'm just trying to understand what was going on."

Anger simmered in Lisa's eyes. "Nothing was going on. Look, I had promised my mom that we'd stay in the house that night, but we snuck out for a while. I didn't say anything back then because I didn't want to get in trouble. It was two nights before Abby died. It didn't have anything to do with anything."

Lisa's words reminded Lauren of what Shane

had said when he'd claimed that his errand at the lawyer's office hadn't been relevant to Abby's death. And the woman who had spoken to Mark Devlin had suddenly come forward now because she was divorced and she could speak freely.

How many people were holding on to information they didn't deem important? Or that they hadn't revealed because they were afraid whatever they had seen would get them into personal trouble? Was it possible that Mark Devlin's movie *was* actually bringing new evidence to light?

"You should have told the police, Lisa. You should tell them now."

"Why would I need to tell them? Jason Marlow is a police officer. He knows what we were doing that night."

Lauren was surprised. "Jason Marlow is a cop in town?"

"He has been for years. Mr. Devlin is just stirring up trouble, Lauren. We weren't spying on the coach. Why would we? We were riding around town that night, like we did a million other nights, like you and Shane used to do, and all the other kids in this town. I don't know why you're bringing this up now."

"I hadn't realized there was anything I didn't know about that night."

"Abby was a good girl, Lauren. She didn't drink much. She didn't do drugs or hook up with random guys. She certainly didn't get into the kind of trouble you did when you hopped on the back of Shane Murray's motorcycle," Lisa added. "I still think

Shane is the most likely suspect. I know you don't want to hear that, but most people believe he did it."

Lauren shook her head. "He didn't."

"He offered Abby a ride on his bike, but he didn't take her to the high school. He took her to the Ramsay house. He tried to hit on her, and she said no, because she wouldn't betray you. Shane got so angry he killed her. Everybody knew about his temper. He was always getting into fights at school. That's what happened, Lauren. Shane Murray killed Abby. And he should have paid for it a long time ago."

A shiver ran down Lauren's spine at Lisa's forceful words. It was the exact scenario that the cops had painted all those years ago, the one that made her doubt him. But she'd known Shane better than anyone. She never should have given in to her doubts.

"Shane did *not* kill my sister," she said firmly. "He's innocent and he always has been, and I should have said that a long time ago."

As Lauren finished speaking, she realized a hush had come over the room. At some point she and Lisa had become the center of attention.

"Lisa, you need to go," Kara said, as she and the other Murray women stepped forward with blood in their eyes. They wouldn't stand for anyone talking bad about Shane in their presence.

Guilt flashed in Lisa's eyes. "I'm truly sorry you overheard that, Kara. I spoke without thinking." She set down her glass of punch and left.

"Maybe I should go, too," Lauren suggested.

"No, you're staying," Kara said firmly. She glanced at her mother and grandmother. "I think it's time to open presents. Don't you?"

A murmur of approval broke out and the group began to chatter again as Kara's mother and grandmother headed toward the gift table.

Kara turned to Lauren with gratitude in her eyes. "Thank you for saying that about Shane."

"It was the truth, and long overdue."

As Kara left to open her presents, Charlotte moved to Lauren's side. "It looks like you're the life of the party."

"I told you that you shouldn't have invited me."

"Every baby shower needs a little drama. I can't believe Lisa said that to you about Shane. She was certainly worked up."

"She thought I was attacking her, because I asked her what she was doing the Saturday night before Abby died."

"Why would you ask her that?"

"That movie producer made some comments to me, and I wanted to follow up on them." Lauren paused. "Do you remember Coach Sorensen?"

"Of course. Half the girls in school were in love with him. Why do you ask?"

Lauren shrugged, not wanting to create any further speculation.

"You're making me really curious," Charlotte said.

"Is Mr. Sorensen still teaching at the high school?"

"Yes, in fact I'm doing a health lecture in his biology class on Tuesday. He's still very good looking and very married. Erica had their third child about four months ago." Charlotte paused. "You're really getting pulled into the past, aren't you? Are you sure you're prepared to deal with all that again?"

"I don't think I have a choice. I'm just afraid . . ."

"Of what?" Charlotte prodded.

"That I'll find out I didn't know Abby at all."

"You knew your sister. Don't let someone else's doubts become yours."

"It's hard not to. I'd accepted that we were never going to have answers. But now everything has changed. Now I have to know what happened."

"That may not be possible, Lauren. The case went cold because there weren't any clues."

"That's what I thought, until Mark Devlin came up with something the police didn't. Now I wonder what else got missed—what other secrets people are keeping."

"Then start mingling," Charlotte said. "Because if there's one thing the ladies in this town do well, it's gossip about other people's business."

TEN

The baby shower yielded no secrets, which was a relief, since Lauren was still trying to absorb the new information she'd learned. She'd enjoyed reconnecting with old friends and being part of the community again, though. It surprised her how easily she'd fit right back in.

Upon returning home, she'd spent several hours cleaning out her father's kitchen, restocking the cupboards, and getting rid of all the expired food items. She'd washed the floor, scrubbed the inside of the refrigerator, and made a nice dinner. Her father had seemed to enjoy the fresh grilled halibut, green salad, and vegetables. He'd taught her how to clean and cook fish when she was a small girl, and for some insane reason she'd wanted to impress him with her cooking skills.

Of course, the best part of her meal had been the fresh berry tart with lemon cream that she'd whipped up. Lightly dusted with sugar, it had been pretty as a picture.

Smiling to herself, Lauren started the dishwasher, then went into the living room. In his bedroom, her father was singing along to one of his Italian opera CDs and seemed in a great mood. She'd decided to table his medical issues and living situation for one night, and it had been a good decision. It had been nice to spend time with him without being in conflict.

She picked up the Sunday newspaper and organized it on the coffee table. This room needed a good cleaning, too. Maybe she'd do one room a day until the house was sparkling and reorganized. Then she'd hire a cleaning service to keep it up and find someone to cook for her dad.

Heading down the hall, she stopped at the linen closet to grab some sheets and blankets. She was tired of sleeping on the pull-out couch. It was time to brave the memories and make up her old bed.

Stepping inside the bedroom drove the upbeat feeling right out of her. She dumped the sheets on the mattress, already having second thoughts.

She sat on her bed, thinking about all the times she and Abby had talked after the lights went out. They'd speak in whispers, hoping their parents wouldn't hear them. But eventually someone would say something funny, and they'd start giggling. Then her mother would come down the hall and tell them to be quiet. The silence would last five minutes after the door shut, then they'd break into laughter again.

When Abby got scared, she'd crawl into bed with Lauren, and Lauren felt a wave of sadness as she thought about all those times she'd told Abby it would be fine. There weren't any monsters, there weren't any bad guys. They were safe. Everything would be okay. And Abby had believed her. But Lauren had been wrong about the monsters.

What else had she been wrong about?

Lisa had assured her that Abby hadn't been up to anything, but perhaps Lisa hadn't known everything, either.

If Abby had had a secret, she would have written about it in her journal—the journal no one had ever found. Had it been in her book bag that day? Or had Abby hidden it as she had done so many times before? After Abby had caught Lauren peeking in her diary, she'd made a game of hiding it all over the house: at the bottom of the laundry hamper, in the back of the linen closet, under their parents' bed, on a shelf in the garage.

But if Abby had hidden it somewhere, wouldn't her father have found it in the past thirteen years?

He'd never touched this room, though—and the rest of the rooms were piled high with clutter. Could the diary still be somewhere in the house?

Lauren went to Abby's desk, where she went through the drawers, then tackled the dresser. Her parents and the police had searched the room after the murder, so it was ridiculous to think she'd find anything now. But she felt the need to do something. After looking in all the obvious places, she found herself slowing down, studying the photos, reading the birthday cards and progress reports.

For the first time, Lauren was starting to remember the good years they'd had together. Abby had been far more than just a tragic victim.

Lauren pulled a yearbook off the shelf and flipped it open. The first few pages were completely blank, which surprised her. Where were all the notes from Abby's friends? Then she realized the yearbook had come out after Abby died. This yearbook was the one that Abby had most looked forward to seeing, because she'd spent all year working as a yearbook staff photographer.

As Lauren skimmed through the book, she wondered which photos Abby had taken. There weren't any credits and she knew her sister had taken hundreds of shots at every event, hoping one or two might make the cut.

Hundreds of photos . . . The thought teased at her mind. Abby and the two other staff photographers had loved catching people in candid, often embarrassing moments. It was high school, so the more humiliating the photo, the more fun it was.

Where had all those photos ended up? They would tell the story of the last year of Abby's life. If Abby had had a secret, a boyfriend no one knew about, was it possible she'd captured him on film? The police might have looked through the yearbooks, but would they have looked through every picture that had been taken?

She'd go down to the school tomorrow and find out if there were any photo archives. It was a long shot, but Mark Devlin's comments had rattled her, and Lisa's explanations had given her even more to think about.

She turned to the junior class section and ran down the class photos until she reached Jason Marlow. His face rang a distant bell. He was definitely attractive, with light brown wavy hair, brown eyes, and a flirty smile. Her sister might have had a crush on him, and he was still in town. Perhaps she should pay him a visit, as well. She'd been a fool to think she could come home to so much unfinished business and not want to finish it.

She closed the yearbook and rolled her neck, trying to ease her tight muscles. It was getting late; maybe she'd spend one more night on the couch. There was only so much of the past she could take.

She left the room, shutting the door. The opera music had stopped, and she heard her father bustling around in the kitchen.

When she entered the room, she was stunned by the mess. Her father stood at the stove, whipping eggs in a frying pan. There were bowls all over the counter as well as milk, eggs, flour, and butter. Pieces of bread were sticking out of the toaster. A pot of water was boiling over. Her dad moved to the sink, took out a glass, filled it with water, then put it back in the cupboard.

"Dad, what are you doing?" she asked.

"It's time for dinner. I'm hungry."

"We ate two hours ago. I made you halibut."

Her father laughed. "You haven't made me fish in years. I bet you don't even remember how."

"I made it tonight," she reminded him. "You said you liked it."

"How do you want your eggs? Sunny side up or scrambled?" He moved back to the stove and started to whip the eggs. "Do you know the trick to the best scrambled eggs?"

"What's that?"

"Water, not milk." He set down the whisk and walked out of the room. She waited a second, then finished scrambling the eggs. When he didn't return, she turned off the burners and went searching for him. He was in his bedroom and had put on his pajamas. He was fiddling with the TV channels.

"Dad, aren't you going to eat your eggs?" she asked, feeling a heavy weight in her heart.

He looked at her in confusion. "Who are you? What are you doing in my house?" He jumped to his feet and backed toward the far wall, his eyes growing wide with fear.

"I'm Lauren, your daughter."

"Lauren doesn't live here anymore. She hates me. She won't come home."

"Dad, it's me. I'm Lauren," she repeated, desperate to bring him back from wherever he'd gone.

"Go away. Get out. I'll call the police."

It was clear that he had no idea who she was. He

was scared of her, and she was terrified by what was happening to him. "Dad," she said. "Please, try to focus on my face. I need you to remember who I am. I'm your daughter, Lauren. I've come home to take care of you."

Her father looked at her for a long moment. He blinked his eyes rapidly and pressed his hand to his temple, as if he had a terrible headache.

"Dad? Are you all right? Do you want me to call the doctor?"

"Doctor," he echoed. "What—what are you talking about, sweetheart? What are you doing in here? Did you need something? I was just about to go to bed."

Did "sweetheart" mean her, Abby, her mother? Who the hell knew? Frustrated tears welled in her eyes.

"Lauren?" he questioned.

The reality of his condition hit her hard. Despite his clear, lucid moments, he was slipping away from her. Someday he wouldn't come back. Someday he wouldn't know who she was. Someday she'd lose him forever.

She'd told herself for years that she didn't need a father. She'd stopped crying when he didn't call on her birthday or on Christmas, pretending it was fine. But he'd always been alive and well; she could go see him if she really wanted to. But now he was disappearing right in front of her, and it was the most frightening thing she'd ever seen.

"Turn off the light when you go, Lauren," her father said as he got into bed. "I'll see you in the morning."

She watched him settle into the pillows, then she hit the light switch and closed his door.

She walked into the kitchen and picked up the frying pan, dumped the eggs into the trash. She put the milk, butter, and remaining eggs back in the fridge. Looking around, she saw not just the mess in the kitchen, but the mess in her life. Her well-controlled existence was in complete chaos, and she had no idea how to fix any of it.

She couldn't stay in this house. She needed air. She needed to walk off the adrenaline coursing through her body. She needed—something.

Grabbing her coat off the rack, she headed out the back door.

Shane had spent so much time on the water in the past ten years that he'd become accustomed to the roll of the waves under his feet, the slap of water against the boat, the smell of salt in the air, and the moonlight dancing off the ocean. He sat down in a deck chair and opened up a beer, propping his feet on the rail of his boat. He could see Ned Jamison's boat, dark and empty. Had Lauren managed to convince her father to leave town yet?

He drank his beer, enjoying the cool slide of the liquid down his throat. Lauren had been on his mind all day. Had she gone to the police and told them that he'd broken into the law offices the night Abby was killed? He didn't know why he'd told her that after keeping it a secret for so many years. Maybe it was the sadness in her blue eyes when she spoke of Abby, or the fear he'd heard in her voice when she wondered if he and Abby had hooked up. Maybe it was just that he'd *wanted* to tell her.

He'd always wanted to tell her—not just about that, but about everything that had led to that moment. He'd made a promise, though, and too many people would be hurt. There was nothing to be gained by confessing now. It was too late to take back the pain he'd given her. It wouldn't change anything.

At the sound of footsteps, he looked up. For a moment he thought it was Lauren, but then he realized the woman walking down the dock was his mother. He jumped to his feet. Moira Murray never came to the marina. She was usually found at home, the quilt shop, or chatting with her friends at Dina's Café. Her red hair gleamed under the light, and she gave him a nervous smile as she asked if she could come aboard.

He offered her a hand, and she got on with a nimble step. Sixty-three years old, she still had the beauty, energy, and athleticism of a much younger woman. Moira had always been a driving force in their family. She ran everything: her husband, her five kids, her home, and whatever else she was involved in. Most people had a great deal of respect for her. Not everyone knew her as well as he did.

Since he'd returned to Angel's Bay, they'd shared only conversations in the earshot of others in the family, and that's the way he preferred it. His mother and he shared a history that was not for public consumption.

Moira sat down on the bench. "I went to your sister's baby shower today."

"Oh?" He resumed his seat. Maybe this visit had to do with Kara. He could handle that.

"Lauren Jamison was there."

He stiffened.

"She got into a heated discussion with Lisa Delaney about Abby's death. Lisa said some very negative things about you."

He shrugged. "She's not the first, and I doubt she'll be the last."

His mother's lips drew into a tight line, a battle raging in her eyes. Whatever she wanted to say wasn't coming easy, which made him sure he didn't want to hear it.

"Lauren stood up for you," his mother said finally. "She told everyone in the room that you were innocent, that you didn't kill her sister—but as far as I'm concerned, it's too little, too late. She should have stood by you in the beginning."

"She was seventeen years old. Her sister was dead. She was shattered."

"And she was willing to let you go to prison. Don't forget that. Just because she's standing up for you now doesn't mean she won't throw you to the

wolves again, especially if this movie gets going."
Moira got to her feet. "I'm worried, Shane. Questions are being asked. Suspects are being lined up. I don't know where it's going, but I don't think it will end well, and I'm afraid for you."

"I didn't kill Abby. Mark Devlin can't prove that I did."

"He can make his case. It will be hard on you."

"Don't you mean it will be hard on *you?*" he asked cynically.

She ignored that. "Maybe you should leave for a while. If you're here you'll be questioned again. I don't want anyone to twist your words. Just think about it. I have to get back before your father realizes I'm gone."

"You didn't tell him you were coming here?" he asked, though he already knew the answer.

"He wouldn't want you to leave. But I'm looking out for the family, the way I've always done."

His mother had *never* looked out for him, and he was damn tired of being her partner in crime. "I told Lauren that Abby let me into the law offices that night," he said abruptly.

Shock whitened her face. "Oh, Shane, how could you?"

"Lauren thought I was involved with Abby, and that we'd betrayed her. She didn't deserve to live with that for the rest of her life."

"Did you tell her why you went there?"

"No."

"She'll keep asking now that she knows this much. You need to *go*, Shane. Pull up the anchor and sail out of this harbor, and don't come back until everyone is gone. I know you think that I'm worried about myself, but that's not true. Kara's husband is in a coma—don't we have enough to deal with? Promise me you won't say anything else to Lauren."

He remained silent.

"Shane?"

"I don't know."

She flashed him a disappointed look. "You're not thinking about getting back together with Lauren, are you? She told everyone at the shower that she's not staying here. You can't go back in time. You can't re-create what you had."

"You should get home. Dad is probably wondering where you are."

"Fine. I'll go." She rose, then paused. "I hurt you, Shane. It was never my intention. Things just spun out of control."

"I know. I was just collateral damage," he said pragmatically.

"You were much more than that. You were my son, and I loved you. I still do." She drew in a deep breath. "Good night, Shane."

He raised the beer to his lips and drained it. She hadn't told him she loved him in years, and was no doubt playing that card to keep him quiet.

Love—a ridiculous ideal that no one could ever live up to, an illusion that people were fools to believe in. He'd learned that a long time ago.

For a while he'd had the crazy thought that he could beat the odds, that things might be different with Lauren. But he'd crashed and burned that relationship. *Like mother, like son.* Her lies had become his—and there was no changing that.

ELEVEN

Lauren knew she'd end up down on the docks where Shane's boat was moored. It was almost eleven, far too late to claim she was just passing by. She couldn't even say she was looking for her father. She was still trying to think of a good excuse when Shane came up the stairs from below deck and saw her. He was barefoot, wearing jeans and a plaid shirt with the top two buttons undone. Butterflies danced in her stomach.

Shane stiffened. "What do you want?"

He did not look happy to see her, and a sudden thought occurred to her. Shane might have a woman in his cabin—talk about embarrassing. "I shouldn't have come," she said hastily.

"Probably not, but you're here."

"Are you alone?"

"At the moment."

"Are you expecting someone?"

"Lauren, get on board or go home."

She hesitated another second, then climbed aboard. "I wasn't sure if you were living on this boat or staying at your parents' house. Or maybe you have your own place?"

"I live here."

"You've always felt more comfortable on water than on land, haven't you?"

He crossed his arms. "Why are you here, Lauren? You didn't come to chat about my living conditions."

It had been years since she'd run to him for anything, years since he'd been close enough to run to. Yet here she was. "I need a friend."

"A friend?" he echoed in surprise. "And you came here?"

"You were once the best friend I ever had."

"All right. I can be a friend, I guess," he said somewhat grimly. "What's on your mind?"

"Nothing is going the way I planned—my father, the movie—I don't know how to fix things."

"Who said you had to be the fixer?"

"There isn't anyone else. I made dinner for my dad tonight, and he was normal. We talked, connecting in a way that we hadn't done in a long time. I thought everything might work out—I could just get him some help to come in during the day. Then two hours later, he was back in the kitchen making eggs and saying that he hadn't eaten. He looked right at me, and he didn't know me. He put up his hand as if I was going to hit him. I'd never seen such fear on his face." She shook her head in despair. "I've been kidding myself, Shane. My father is going to need real help. He's slipping away, and I don't know what to do. Tell me what to do."

He ran a hand through his hair, his expression troubled. "I don't know, Lauren. I don't think anyone does."

"I can't move back here, it's not home anymore. I keep telling everyone that, but no one believes me."

"Maybe you're the one who can't believe it."

"There's too much pain, too much sadness for me in this town. Everywhere I look there's a memory. In San Francisco, I don't see Abby in store windows or skipping down the street. I don't see you—or anyone else." She'd almost admitted that some of her memories involved him.

"That would change with time. You once loved Angel's Bay, Lauren. You used to get up every morning at five to work at Martha's Bakery. I'd pick you up to give you a ride to school, and you'd have flour on your face, along with the happiest smile I'd ever seen."

"Those days are long gone."

"But you still feel the draw," he said, his gaze clinging to hers.

"I don't want to feel it." She wasn't just being pulled back to the town, but to him. He stepped forward, putting his hands on her shoulders. She stiffened, then relaxed as he began to work the tight muscles in her neck. She was walking a dangerous line, but she couldn't seem to get off of it.

"When we were young, you always smelled like cinnamon," Shane mused. "I got high just smelling your hair."

"And here I thought it was me."

He smiled and her heart beat a little faster. The moonlight danced off his face, highlighting his beautiful eyes, his strong jaw, and his full lips. She really shouldn't have come here. She'd never been good at saying no to Shane.

Shane tucked a strand of hair behind her ear, then his finger slipped down the side of her face in a gentle caress. "It was always you, Lauren. You got under my skin, and I've never been able to get you out."

She put a hand against his chest as he moved closer.

"It's just a kiss."

"It's never 'just' a kiss where you're concerned." She licked her lips and saw his gaze follow the motion.

"Now you're not playing fair," he whispered.

She didn't want to be fair or responsible or practical. She'd had a hell of a day—make that a week—make that the last thirteen years when she'd had to grow up overnight. She'd tried to forget Shane, locking the memories away, but now they were clamoring to get out.

Maybe she needed to get him out of her system, to confront her past.

"Oh, to hell with it." She pressed her lips against his. The heat of his mouth sent her pulse into overdrive. It had always been that way. No slow buildup; one touch and she went up in flames.

She slid her hands up his arms, feeling the power in his biceps. He was bigger, stronger than she remembered, and so deliciously male. She wrapped her arms around his neck, pulling him even closer. She loved the way his mouth moved on hers. She loved the way he tasted like salt and beer, the way her body wanted to melt into his. She felt tight, achy, desperate for him, for his hands all over her body, for his bare skin rubbing against hers. And she was tired of fighting it.

Shane's hands slid under her jacket, his fingers flirting with the undercurve of her breasts. His touch was warm, and she shivered.

Shane broke away, his breathing rough. "If you're planning to say no, you might want to do it now."

She should say no. She should run like hell. But her feet didn't want to move. This moment had been coming since she'd driven into town. It had been inevitable. She wanted Shane just one more time . . .

"Why don't you show me the cabin?" she suggested.

She held out her hand and he took it, his fingers squeezing tightly around hers, as if he were afraid she'd change her mind. Then he led her down the stairs.

The cabin was intimate and dimly lit with one small lamp by the bed. The galley came first, then a double-size bed that was tucked into the walls beyond. "It's cozy."

"Do you want something to drink?"

She shook her head, seeing the question in his eyes. He was giving her time to call things off, but that was the last thing she wanted to do. She slipped off her jacket and tossed it on the bench, then she drew her knit top up over her head. Shane's gaze ran down her face to her breasts, barely covered by her lacy bra. She flushed a little, wondering what he thought of her now. She wasn't a teenager anymore. She had a few more curves than he probably remembered.

"So beautiful," he murmured.

Her heart flipped over. She moved forward and undid the buttons on his shirt, helping him off with it, then she ran her hands over the solid planes of his body. He was hard and tan. She loved the smattering of dark hair that ran down the center of his chest, the ripple of his abdominal muscles, the strength of his arms. Shane smelled like soap and the sea, a heady mixture that made her head spin. She stood on tiptoes, her mouth searching for his once again.

Shane's hands moved from her shoulders to her back, caressing her bare skin. With one quick flick, he opened the back clasp of her bra and slipped it off. His hands palmed her breasts and a jolt of fire ran from her chest to her thighs. His mouth roamed across her lips, her cheek, his tongue tracing the line of her collarbone, dropping lower . . . swirling around her nipples until she gave a cry of pleasure.

She dropped her hands to the snap on his jeans.

He returned the favor. They kicked off their pants, coming together skin to skin in delicious abandon. His hands ran up and down her back, cupping her buttocks, pulling her against his hard groin.

"Lauren," he whispered harshly, his mouth coming next to hers. "I want to go slow, but I don't think I can."

The same fire burned in her. "We'll go slow the next time."

Her words unleashed a passionate fury. His kiss was hot, hard, demanding, the kiss of a man, not a boy. And she was no longer that shy, hesitant girl. She was a woman who knew what she wanted.

She pulled him down on the bed, feeling sizzling heat everywhere their bodies touched. His mouth roamed across her breasts, down her belly. His hand slid between her legs, making her tremble. Then his mouth followed, sending her over the edge. She cried out his name, fisting her hands in his hair as he loved her. But it wasn't enough. She wanted to get closer, wanted that connection she'd been missing for so long.

When Shane reached for the drawer by the bed and pulled out a condom, she helped him roll it on. Then he was on top of her, inside her, moving the way she remembered, only much, much better. There was no past causing her pain, no future making her worry, just the present. She had Shane and he had her—and she didn't want it to end.

*   *   *

It took Shane a long time to catch his breath, to slow his pounding pulse, to absorb what the hell had just happened. He would have thought it was a dream, but Lauren's head was on his chest, her arm around his waist, her leg entwined with his. It was very, very real, wonderfully real. He breathed in the scent of her hair and tightened his arm around her.

She'd been pretty at seventeen, but she was beautiful now. He liked how she'd grown up, how she'd come into her own. He wanted to spend months exploring every inch of her body, showing her what he couldn't give her with words.

But Lauren wasn't going to stay. This wasn't the beginning of something. Hell, maybe it was the end. Maybe Lauren had just wanted one last fling, one last memory to finish it off.

"Your heart is beating really fast," Lauren said, her fingers playing through the hair on his chest.

"That's because you almost gave me a heart attack."

She lifted her head and smiled. Her eyes were a deep, dark blue, languid and filled with sweet satisfaction. "I could say the same about you. That was even better than I remembered." She turned on her side, pulling the pillow under her head. "You've learned a few things."

He rolled over to face her. "So have you."

"We were so young. Do you know this is the first time we've had sex in a bed? The first time, we made love on the beach; then we did it in the treehouse; and then we went back to the beach the night before . . ." She paused, her smile fading. "We can't do this again, you know."

"Why not?" His fingers slid down her arm, drawing a line of goose bumps along her skin.

"Because there's nowhere for us to go. I'm not staying . . . and who knows what your plans are. I just wanted to know what it would be like to be with you again."

"I wanted to know, too," he admitted. "It was good."

"We have a chemistry that I've never had with anyone else."

"No one else?" he asked, surprised. But Lauren had never been able to lie to him. She'd always worn her heart on her sleeve; she'd never played games. It was one of the many things he liked about her.

"No," she said, not looking too happy about her admission. "But I'm not done looking."

He wanted her to be done looking. He wanted her to be with him—which scared the hell out of him. They weren't kids anymore, dreaming of happily ever after. And he'd never believed in the one woman, long marriage, white-picket-fence kind of life. At least, that's what he'd told himself. The truth was that Lauren had always made him want things he knew weren't possible to have.

He rolled onto his back, staring up at the ceiling.

"What did I say?" Lauren asked, her eyes solemn as she propped her head up on one elbow. "You've gone to that dark place again."

"I'm just tired."

"I don't think so. I've seen this look before,

Shane. When I was young I thought you were mad at me—but I think you're angry with yourself, and I don't know why."

"I'm not mad at anyone. I don't know why women always have to analyze men."

"It's our calling," she said lightly. "You're not going to tell me what you're thinking, are you?"

"Nope."

"Then I'll talk. I went to see Joe Silveira yesterday after I left you."

He tensed, waiting for her to go on.

"I didn't tell him you were at the law offices with Abby, though I still might. It depends on what else comes out."

"It's up to you."

"It would make it easier if you would just tell me why you went there, what you were looking for and who you're protecting."

"I can't, Lauren."

She let out a sigh of frustration. "Why can't you trust me?"

"It's not about you."

"This secret that you keep—it's what puts the shadows in your eyes, isn't it?"

"You sure talk more than you used to," he grumbled, wishing he could get her off the subject.

"Because when I was young, your scowl used to make me nervous. Now I'm just curious." She paused. "Will you ever let me all the way in?"

"Why would you want me to? You just told me this was a one-night thing."

She frowned. "I hate it when you're right."

He smiled. "Then you must hate me a lot."

She punched him on the arm.

"Ow, that hurt."

"Good. So, if we're not going to talk and share our feelings," she added with a mischievous grin, "I have another idea."

"What's that?" he asked, turning to catch the wicked sparkle in her eyes.

"We could do some of the things we never did as teenagers."

"Really? Feel like showing me?"

"Absolutely."

She flung one leg over his waist and straddled him, her beautiful hair swirling around her equally beautiful breasts, and he was lost again.

Lauren woke up to the light of early dawn. She could hear the boats heading out for the morning run. It was Monday, the start of the work week, and she wondered if Shane had a fishing charter. He didn't seem to be in any hurry to get up. He was snuggled behind her, his face buried in her neck, one of his legs pinning hers down. He was deliciously warm and when his fingers stroked her abdomen, she felt the same jolt of electricity that had kept them up half the night. She'd told herself she'd get her fill of him and then it would be done, her curiosity satisfied.

Ha! Now she remembered exactly how well their

bodies fit together, how much she loved his touch, how much she loved him . . . She put the brakes on that thought. It wasn't love—it was lust. There couldn't be anything more. Even if she weren't leaving, how could she be with a man who kept secrets from her—a man who always had one foot out the door himself?

"Stop thinking. You're getting tense," Shane murmured.

"I have to go." She slipped out of bed before she could change her mind and dressed as quickly as she could, aware of Shane's intense gaze on her the whole time. She glanced over at him and then wished she hadn't. He looked endearingly handsome with the dark stubble on his jaw, the sexy waves of his hair, the fullness of his lips, his incredibly wonderful mouth . . . She swallowed hard. Why the hell did he have to be so good looking?

"What's your hurry?" Shane asked. "It's not even six."

"I want to get home before my dad wakes up." She pulled on her shirt. "I'm sure you need to get on with your day. Don't you have some fish to catch or something?" In the moonlight, it had been easier to lose herself in the fantasy of her and Shane. The morning sun reminded her that the fantasy was over.

Shane got out of bed, pulled on his boxers and jeans, and came toward her. "You don't have to run out, Lauren. Let me make you some coffee."

"I'll get some at home."

"What are you afraid I'm going to say?"

She was more afraid of what *she* would say. "I'm not very good with morning-after conversation. We both know that last night was just a fling for old times' sake."

"Are you sure that's all it was?"

"Yes. We blew it. We hurt each other. And now we want different things, different lives."

"Are you sure you know what you want, Lauren?"

"I am. And it's not you," she said, then she ran.

TWELVE

To the most beautiful girl in the world: these reminded me of you. Call me. Andrew.

Charlotte set down the card and stared at the bouquet of yellow daisies Andrew had sent to her office. The man was definitely making the effort to get her back. He'd never had to work this hard to get her the first time around. Was she a fool to keep pushing him away? Her mother would say she was, but her mother didn't know the whole story of their love affair.

She picked up the phone, then hesitated and set it back down. She didn't have time for this today. She had a full schedule of patients to see, especially since her associate, Harriet Landon, had just gone home sick for the day.

She stuck the card in her drawer and headed down the hall to the first examination room. She grabbed the file off the door, gave a knock, and entered. The woman sitting on the edge of the examination table in a paper robe was none other than Erica Sorensen, the coach's wife. Erica was an attractive but tired-looking woman in her late thirties, who'd just given birth to her third child a few months earlier. She was officially Harriet Landon's patient, and Charlotte had only seen her once for a brief blood pressure check.

Erica didn't appear at all happy to see her. "Where's Dr. Landon?"

"She just went home. She wasn't feeling well."

"I should reschedule, then." Erica frowned.

"I'm happy to do the examination, if you like. Is there anything in particular that's bothering you today? Or is this just a checkup?"

"I can't talk to you—you know too many people."

"I can assure you that anything we discuss in this room is confidential," Charlotte said.

Erica gave her a long, hard look. Finally, she said, "I'm concerned I might have an STD."

"What kind of symptoms are you experiencing?"

"I'm not sure. It's just that . . . I was pregnant, then the baby came, and I haven't been getting any sleep. So I haven't felt very much like having sex, and—and I'm afraid my husband might have had an affair."

Charlotte remained calm, though inwardly she was reeling. "Well, let's check it out." She washed her hands and put on her gloves. "Lie back on the table."

Erica didn't move. "I know that girl, Annie, is staying with you. She used to clean my house. She was supposed to come once a week, while my husband and I were at work, but once I came home early and she was talking to Tim. They were having tea. He made her tea! He never makes *me* tea."

Charlotte sensed where Erica was going, but she didn't intend to help her get there, so she remained silent.

"Has Annie told you who the father of her baby is?" Erica asked.

"I can't answer that question."

"A lot of men would find it hard to resist a girl like her, especially if their wife wasn't available. It's difficult for a wife to compete with a beautiful young girl who has a perfect body and hasn't had kids, hasn't had to juggle a house, a job, and a marriage. Do you know how hard that is? No, you're not married. Of course you can't understand."

Charlotte *was* beginning to understand that Erica was very much on edge. She was jittery and anxious, and her eyes were a little too bright. While Erica rambled on, Charlotte read Dr. Landon's notes from the last visit. Dr. Landon had broached the subject of postpartum depression but Erica had refused to see a psychiatrist, saying she was fine, just exhausted and overwhelmed.

"I'm afraid the father of Annie's baby might be my husband," Erica finished in a rush.

"Did you ask your husband about it?" Charlotte asked quietly.

"Of course not. How could I?" Erica slipped off the table. "I want to wait for Dr. Landon to examine me. You won't say anything, will you? I shouldn't have talked to you. I was stupid."

Erica's breath came in quick, short gasps, and she put out a hand toward the table to steady herself.

"Breathe," Charlotte ordered, helping her into a nearby chair. "Are you feeling dizzy?"

"I'm just scared," Erica said. "I don't know how to handle all this."

Charlotte squatted down in front of her. "You should talk to a psychiatrist. Dr. Raymond is excellent; she could be very helpful to you."

"You think I'm crazy."

"I think you're very stressed. You've had a baby recently and your hormones are still settling down. You're not sleeping. Sometimes problems seem bigger than they are when you're feeling overwhelmed."

"I *am* tired. That's probably all this is. Tim is a good husband. He takes care of us. I just feel guilty that I haven't been much of a wife lately. I'll think about seeing Dr. Raymond, but I want to go home now."

"All right. And please, Erica, don't worry about what you've told me. Our conversation is completely confidential."

"Thank you."

"If you feel you need some tests, don't wait too long before you see Dr. Landon." Charlotte took off her gloves and left the room. Out in the hall, she stopped to catch her breath. *Was* Tim Sorensen the father of Annie's baby? Had Erica just implied that her husband had a thing for young girls?

Lauren had questioned her about Coach Sorensen at the shower, something to do with Abby. Had he had a thing for Abby, too? Or was she jumping to a crazy conclusion? Either way, there wasn't a damn thing she could say or do about it.

The only way she'd ever been able to work off frustration and anger was to bake, but around one o'clock on Monday afternoon, Lauren realized she'd gone overboard. She'd started out making a few cookies, which had segued into banana bread, blueberry muffins, and strawberry tarts. The counter was now loaded down with desserts and she had no idea what on earth she would do with it all.

The timer went off, and she took out the last tray of cookies and turned off the oven. She blew a wisp of hair off her hot face as her father came through the back door.

"What do we have here?" Ned asked in amazement.

"I thought you could take cookies and muffins to Mort and your other friends, to pay people back for all the casseroles they've been bringing you."

"That was thoughtful of you. But I'm not sure I have enough friends to eat all this," he said with a grin.

Her father seemed in good spirits, with no trace of his forgetful paranoia from the night before. That was the problem with this disease. It was easy to get lulled into thinking things weren't that bad, because between episodes her father acted perfectly normal.

"Have you been at the café all this time?" Her father's routine included a trip to Dina's Café every morning for breakfast and cards with the boys.

"I stopped by my old shop. Walter Brady's grandson is going to run it into the ground if he's not careful, selling things for half price for no good reason." Ned paused as a knock came at the back door. "Can you get that? I need to use the bathroom."

Lauren opened the door, surprised to see Shane on the step. A little thrill ran through her, and as his dark gaze swept across her body she felt heat rise within her. One look and she remembered everything—the way he'd kissed her, touched her, moved inside of her. She pulled in a sharp breath. "What are you doing here?"

"Picking up your father," he said tersely. "He asked me to take him out on the water for a few hours. Don't worry, I didn't come here to see you."

"I wasn't worried." She didn't like the cold awkwardness between them now, but she could hardly blame Shane for not being happy to see her. She'd flat-out told him she didn't want him in her life only a few hours earlier.

Shane's jaw dropped as he walked into the kitchen. "Are you getting ready for a bake sale?"

"I thought I'd pay back some of the people who've been kind enough to bring my father food the past few months. When did you and he make your plans? You didn't say anything this morning."

"I ran into him an hour ago. It was a spur of the moment invitation. I know how he likes to get out on the water, and I'd rather take him than chase him down again."

"That's generous of you."

"It's not a hardship. I like your dad."

"You have more in common with him than I do," she said, realizing how true that was.

Shane shrugged as he grabbed a peanut butter cookie off a plate on the counter. He popped it in his mouth and finished it in two bites. "These are great. I'd forgotten how good you were at making cookies."

"It's not that difficult."

"What's with the sudden modesty? You used to brag that you could be the best baker in town."

"That wasn't much of an ambition, was it?"

His gaze narrowed. "What does that mean?"

She shrugged. "It's not saving the world, or doing something important. I forgot to tell you yesterday that I found out my father had put some money away for Abby. He wanted to fund her dream of becoming a marine biologist."

"Sometimes your father is an ass."

"You just said you liked him."

"I can't believe he told you that he gave Abby money."

"He didn't tell me, Chief Silveira did. He found the one-time cash deposit on the day of Abby's murder to be interesting in some way."

There was an odd gleam in Shane's eyes. "The day of her death, your dad put money in her account?"

"For college. He didn't want my mother to know about it."

"The timing *is* a little odd."

"I think it's just a coincidence. It makes sense he'd do it, though. My dad and Abby were super close. They loved the same things and he wanted her to have the education his parents couldn't afford. And she deserved it. At her funeral, every person who spoke talked about how much promise she had, how it was so wrong that someone with all of her potential could die so young, and I kept thinking, they're right. It shouldn't have been Abby."

"If you say it should have been you—"

"I wasn't going to go that far, but Abby was special, and I don't think I fully appreciated her. She was my often annoying little sister who shared my room and took my stuff, and used up all the hot water in the bathroom every morning."

"And that's the truth, too. People are not one-dimensional. Abby had her faults."

"It's hard to remember what they were now." She paused. "Neither Chief Silveira nor Mark Devlin thinks that Abby was killed by a transient. They believe someone in town murdered her, someone she knew." She shook her head. "I can't imagine who that would be."

"I heard what you said about me at the shower yesterday," Shane said. "My mother told me you stood up for me."

"It was long overdue."

"Still appreciated."

Her father reentered the room, looking happy. The eagerness in his eyes took ten years off his age. "I'm ready to go."

"We should take some cookies with us." Shane sent Lauren a hopeful look.

"I'll put some in a plastic container for you," she agreed.

"Why don't you come with us, Lauren?" her father suggested. "I bet you haven't been on a boat in a while."

She'd been on one the night she'd arrived, to chase him down, but she didn't feel like putting a damper on the day by reminding him. "You two don't need me." She glanced at Shane, wondering what he thought of the invitation.

"You can come if you want," he said, as if he didn't care either way.

"Come," her father urged. "It will be good for you to get some fresh air."

Only a few hours ago she'd decided that she wouldn't see Shane again, yet here she was, considering another invitation. But her father would be there, and maybe it would be good to spend some time with him in his element.

"All right," she said. "Just let me put the food away and I'll be ready."

*   *   *

It was a perfect day for a cruise, Lauren thought. The sun was out, the wind was down, and the waves were gentle. Her father sat on the bench, his gaze fixed on the horizon, pure joy in his expression. When he lifted his face to the sun, closed his eyes, and took a deep breath, he seemed completely at peace with his world.

"You made his day," she told Shane, who stood at the helm, his hands light on the wheel.

"I'm glad I could help."

"You've taken him out before, haven't you?"

"A few times," he replied with a casual shrug. "We've done a little fishing together since I came back to Angel's Bay."

"Did you talk about me?"

He gave her a lazy smile. "We mostly talked about catching fish, what kind of bait to use—fascinating stuff."

She slid into the chair next to his. They were passing around the point now, and she couldn't help noticing the odd markings on the rock wall, as well as a group of spectators gathered above. "What's going on at the cliff?"

"A few months ago, Henry Milton's grandson took a video of what looked like angels flying around the point, carving symbols or some kind of map into the rock face. People have been going there ever since, to see the angels or say a prayer or figure out if the rocks are trying to tell them something."

She tilted her head, studying the cliff face. "I

see a woman with long hair flowing out behind her." Abby's face flashed through her mind, but that wasn't Abby's picture on the wall. "I guess angel sightings will always be a part of this town."

"I don't believe in angels," Shane said.

"Or much else." Shane had been a cynic as long as she'd known him. "It's funny how different you and Kara are. She seems to have endless faith."

Shane didn't reply, but she didn't really expect him to. He'd been willing to share his body with her, but heart and soul, definitely not.

She turned her gaze toward the horizon as they headed farther away from shore. They sailed for almost ten minutes without saying a word. The waves grew a little rougher, and she put out a hand to steady herself. Her hand came down on Shane's arm rather than the chair next to her, and she quickly removed it. "Sorry."

"You never have to apologize for touching me," he said, his hand reaching out for hers.

She wanted to resist, but his fingers squeezed hers in a reassuring grip. His warm smile caressed her face, and she couldn't pull away.

"I feel like a fish," she said abruptly. "Your smile, your hand, your touch—it's the bait, and I keep taking it, and I keep getting reeled in."

"Not very easily. You're putting up a damn good fight."

"If that were true, I wouldn't be here so soon after my declaration of independence this morning."

She paused, her gaze meeting his. "But I don't think you really want to catch me."

"Why do you say that?"

"Because long-term, intimate relationships scare the hell out of you."

"That's a sweeping statement."

"Has there been a long-term relationship in the past decade?"

"Hard to have one, when I wasn't in one place for more than a few months at a time."

"It was your choice to move around. If you wanted a different kind of life, you could have had one." She gave him a thoughtful look. "Are you really going to stay in Angel's Bay? How could it possibly be enough for you?"

"Maybe it won't be," he said shortly. "My plans are—fluid."

"So you're leaving your options open. That doesn't surprise me." Shane had never been one to commit. She could give him everything he wanted, and he still might leave. She'd known that at seventeen, and it was still true. She pulled her hand away from his. "I'm going to sit with my dad."

She made her way to the stern and sat next to her father on the bench seat.

He opened his eyes and gave her a joyous smile. "There's nothing better than this, Lauren."

"It is nice," she agreed. "Reality feels a million miles away."

"If I could choose my own way to leave this

world, it would be to get in my boat and head out to sea. I'd find the perfect, bluest-blue water, miles from land, where the fish practically jump out of the ocean, and I'd just stay there—drift away."

It was a nice fantasy, but she didn't think it would work that way. "You'd have to deal with storms, illness, lack of food and water. You'd be alone, too."

"I don't feel alone on the sea. Nature is my company—the birds, the fish, the wind, the clouds, even the rain."

She couldn't imagine sailing anywhere by herself. She'd be terrified.

"It's okay, Lauren. You don't have to get it." He patted her hand. "You have your mother in you. She always felt better on land. Now Shane, he gets it. The sea runs through his soul." He nodded his head toward Shane, who stood with his back to them.

"Why don't you still dislike him?" Lauren asked. "You once thought he had something to do with Abby's death. What changed?"

"I was blinded by rage. I regret that."

"So you don't believe he could have hurt Abby?"

"No. Because he loved you," Ned said, his gaze meeting hers.

"We were kids back then. We didn't know what love was," she said, dismissing his words.

"What about now?" her father asked quietly. "You're not kids anymore. And when you have a second chance at love, you should take it. Think of Leonora and Tommy."

She smiled. "You're such a romantic."

He smiled back. "So are you, deep down. Abby hated reading through those old journals. She wasn't much of a history buff."

"No, she wasn't," Lauren said. Maybe she and her father did have something in common, after all.

Shane called her name, interrupting their conversation, and she walked back to the helm. He slowed the boat down and pointed out several dolphins sliding through the water with grace and speed.

"Beautiful," she breathed.

"Yes," he agreed. But he wasn't looking at the dolphins, he was looking at her.

And with that smile, he reeled her in just a little bit more.

THIRTEEN

It was almost five o'clock when Lauren and her father returned home, although her dad wasn't staying there long. Lauren had begun to realize that despite his declining mental condition her father led an active social life. He had a circle of male friends, most of whom were either widowed or divorced, and they spent a great deal of time together. Tonight he was meeting his gang at Murray's Bar for dinner, beers, and a football game on the big screen.

She, on the other hand, was at loose ends. She needed to keep herself too busy to go looking for Shane again, so before her father left, she broached a difficult subject.

"Dad, I was thinking I might do some cleaning and organizing around here," she said. "I could pack up some of your older clothes and give them away to charity. I could also go through Abby's clothes."

Her father's happy smile faded. "Thought you'd just throw that in there, did you?"

"Just the clothes and shoes—nothing personal, no mementos. It has to be done at some point, and if I'm not here, who will do it? Wouldn't it be better if I did just a little now? I won't change the room. I'll just go through the closet."

Her father hesitated for a long minute. "All right, but don't touch her desk or her bed."

"Okay, good." She felt relieved with the small victory. As her father walked into the living room, she grabbed a roll of trash bags out of the closet and headed down the hall.

A few minutes later, the doorbell rang. She heard her father say he'd get it and then he was leaving.

Her ears perked up at the sound of a female voice, followed by footsteps coming down the hall. She expected Charlotte or Kara, and was surprised to see Lisa Delaney in the doorway. Their last conversation hadn't been particularly friendly.

Lisa stepped into the bedroom and the blood drained out of her face. She put a hand on the wall to steady herself. "Oh, my God! I—I didn't know that the room was still the same. I thought your parents cleaned it out long ago. It's like Abby never left."

Her gaze moved to Abby's bed. Her bottom lip trembled and her eyes grew misty. "I can almost see Abby sitting there, holding that stupid bunny, and talking a mile a minute." Lisa walked across the room to the bulletin board and touched the concert ticket there. "We were supposed to go to this together." She turned and looked at Lauren, at the trash bags in her hand. "Are you clearing the room out?"

"I'm going to start with the closet."

"Can I talk to you in the other room? I can't stay in here."

"Sure." Lauren followed Lisa down the hall and into the living room. "Are you all right?"

"Not really. How can you stand to be in that room?"

"I'm getting used to it. Do you want to sit down?"

"No, I just wanted to apologize for being so abrupt yesterday and for what I said about Shane, even though I still think it's true. But I didn't mean to snap at you when you asked about that Saturday night." Lisa glanced toward the hall, as if she were afraid Abby's ghost would suddenly appear. "Maybe we could talk on the porch."

Lauren opened the front door and ushered her outside. "Better?" She felt far more sympathetic to Lisa than she had the day before. This was the girl she remembered, the one who'd been Abby's best friend, who'd cried buckets of tears when Abby died.

"Yes, thanks. I didn't expect to see Abby's room looking exactly the same. It's like she's just out for a walk and will be right back."

"It shook me up, too," Lauren admitted. "My father couldn't let go of her things. I'm going to try to get a little organization done while I'm here."

"How long will that be?"

"I'm not sure yet." Lauren leaned against the

porch railing. "I never thought you'd stay here, Lisa. You always said this town felt too small to you."

"It still does, but I'm too lazy to make any big changes. My mom moved a couple of years ago and left me the house. I work at the Blue Pelican, and I have a boyfriend. He runs the bar. We're thinking about getting married."

"That's great. I'm happy for you."

"Thanks. Anyway, I just wanted to reassure you that Abby wasn't doing anything wrong before she died. I know that movie producer wants to make it seem like she had some big, dark secret, but she didn't."

"I'm really happy to hear that." Lauren hesitated, not sure if she should ask, but this might be her only chance. "Did Abby have a crush on someone?"

"She had crushes on lots of boys. She was fifteen. It was a new guy every week. You remember high school, don't you?"

"Do you know who she had sex with?" The question had been nagging at her ever since Joe Silveira had told her Abby wasn't a virgin.

Lisa's eyes widened in surprise. "How do you know she had sex?"

"They looked for signs of sexual assault during the autopsy. They didn't find any, but it didn't appear that Abby was a virgin."

"Really? Are you sure?" Lisa asked in surprise. "I can't believe Abby wouldn't have told me. Who would she have slept with?"

"What about Jason Marlow? What kind of relationship did you two have with him?"

"We just drove around one night and had some drinks. He was a cool kid, but he had a thing for Kara Murray."

Lauren frowned. "But Jason was best friends with Colin."

Lisa shrugged. "He still had a thing for her."

"It's funny that the woman who saw you didn't mention seeing a guy in the car."

"Who knows if she really saw us? Maybe she just wants to be in the movie." Lisa paused. "Let's have a drink one night before you leave. You were the closest thing I had to a big sister and it would be nice to catch up." She took a breath. "It would be difficult, but if you want me to help you go through Abby's room, I will."

Lauren raised an eyebrow. "Seriously? You almost passed out in there."

"Well, it must be even harder on you."

"Thanks for the offer, but I can handle it."

"Okay," she said with a relieved smile. "I wish I could be of more help, Lauren, but obviously I didn't know everything about Abby, since I never knew she had sex." Her smile dimmed. "I guess you never know anyone as well as you think you do."

"I don't have to do this today," Kara told Jason as he escorted her up the steps to the Redwood Medical Clinic. Her natural childbirth class was due to start in five minutes but Colin was supposed to be her coach, and the idea of anyone else helping her through the labor was unthinkable.

"You have to do it. You're going to have a baby in two weeks," Jason reminded her.

"But if it's natural, why do I need to take a class for it? Shouldn't it come naturally?"

He smiled. "I don't know. This is not my area."

"Then why are you dragging me here?"

"Because your mother is sick, and you need a coach."

She frowned. She hadn't wanted to do the class with her mother, either, but she'd been railroaded into it. When her mom had called to say she wasn't feeling well, Kara thought she'd been given a reprieve. Unfortunately, Jason had overheard the conversation and insisted that she go to the class.

He opened the door for her and she reluctantly stepped inside. As they headed toward the elevator, she felt guilty about her mixed feelings. She wasn't looking forward to the class or to the birth of her daughter. She'd wanted this baby forever, but not like this, not without her husband.

When they arrived the room was crowded with at least six pregnant women and their husbands. The women all looked happy and glowing, the men doting and supportive. Kara felt sick to her stomach.

"Come on." Jason took her hand and pulled her through the doorway.

She saw one of the men rub his wife's pregnant belly. Then he leaned over and kissed her on the lips, his hand still resting on their baby. "I can't do this," she muttered. "It's too hard."

"Kara, I'll help you."

She knew he wanted to. She could see the worry in his eyes, the earnest determination. "It's not supposed to be like this, Jason."

"But it is," he said solemnly. "Your baby is going to come and you need to be as ready as you can be."

"I'll do the next class. It's quilt night at the shop. I'm supposed to help my grandmother set up. They have a guest speaker."

"The speaker doesn't start until eight o'clock. You'll have plenty of time to get there."

Kara frowned. "How do you know when quilting night starts? Did you talk to my mother? I bet that's why you were at my house when she called—she gave you the heads-up."

"Someone has to give you a kick in the ass. I know you think that Colin will wake up and be at your side when labor comes, and I hope to hell that happens. But if it doesn't, you need to be prepared."

The instructor interrupted them with a warm welcoming smile.

"Hello, I'm Deborah Cummings," she said. "I'm a registered midwife, and I'll be running the class today. You are . . ."

"Kara Lynch," she replied grumpily. "And this is Jason Marlow. He's just my coach. My husband can't be here today."

"All right," Deborah said easily. "Come on in and get comfortable. We'll begin in a few moments."

Kara knew two of the other women, and she gave them a brief smile, then sat on the floor mat. Jason squatted down next to her as the teacher conferred with one of the other women.

"I thought you usually worked Mondays nights," Kara said to distract herself from the other happy couples.

"I've got the graveyard shift tonight."

"And this is how you wanted to spend your time off?"

"It wouldn't have been my first choice."

She smiled at his uncomfortable expression. He'd been gung-ho to get her here, but now, surrounded by pregnant bellies, he seemed a little rattled. "Wait until you have to watch the movie. I hear the birthing experience is quite something to see."

"Great. Just great."

"You wanted to come," she pointed out.

"Anything for you, Kara."

She knew he was serious, and she was touched by his friendship. She also felt a little ashamed. "Sorry I'm being such a brat. You've been incredible, Jason. This is above and beyond the call of duty."

"Nothing is too much for you—and for Colin."

"I feel guilty taking up so much of your time. What happened to that girl you were seeing a few months ago?"

He shrugged. "I don't remember."

She raised an eyebrow. "What? There are so many women in your life, you can't keep track?"

"They come, they go," he said easily.

That was true. Jason rarely introduced her to the same woman twice. She wished he would find someone he really cared about and settle down, but she didn't know if that would happen. Jason didn't let people get close to him, aside from her and Colin. They'd been the three musketeers for as long as she could remember.

Sometimes she thought Jason used them as an excuse not to go out and make his own family. He and Colin had bonded when they were little kids. Both coming from broken homes, they had found brotherhood with each other. Jason probably felt almost as lost without Colin as she did. Maybe that's why he was spending so much time with her.

"You should find a woman who wants to stay," she said. "You're a good guy. Anyone would feel lucky to have you."

"I doubt that. Especially not these days."

Hearing the anger in his voice, she gave him a thoughtful look. "What does that mean?"

"That Hollywood scriptwriter came to the station the other day. He wanted to know if I dated Abby back in high school, making it sound like I was up to something with her. I wouldn't be surprised if I end up the villain in this movie by some wild stretch of his imagination."

"That's crazy. Why would he even suggest that you and Abby had a relationship?"

"Lisa Delaney is spreading shit about me."

Now Kara was extremely curious. She hadn't heard Lisa and Lauren's conversation at the shower, but they'd obviously been discussing the murder. "What has Lisa been saying?"

"Don't worry about it."

"Did you ever date Abby?" she asked, sensing there was something he wasn't telling her.

"The class is starting."

And that wasn't an answer. "Jason, if you were involved with Abby, how come you never said anything?"

"It wasn't a big deal. We hung out at a few parties, but that was it."

He wasn't looking her straight in the eye, which surprised her. "Why are you so pissed off?"

"I'm fine."

"You're not acting fine."

"Just breathe, Kara. That's all you have to worry about right now."

She wished that were true. But breathing was the least of her worries, and probably his, too.

FOURTEEN

Lauren filled two large plastic bags with Abby's clothes and shoes, which she'd donate to charity tomorrow. Now nothing but wire hangers remained on the old wooden rod in the closet. She tucked a strand of sweaty hair behind her ear as she stared at the emptiness.

It hadn't been easy to go through Abby's clothes. She kept seeing her sister in her favorite T-shirt or worn jeans or the big bunny slippers she'd gotten one Christmas. One of her own sweaters was mixed in with Abby's clothes, and she remembered that Abby had taken it without asking. But that was what sisters did: they shared things. Just not everything.

As she'd gone through Abby's clothes, she'd searched every pocket for something that might give her a clue to Abby's life, but she'd found nothing. She still didn't know who Abby had liked, or who she'd had sex with.

They'd always promised to tell each other when

they had sex for the first time, but, to be fair, she hadn't been open about her own experience, either. Maybe she would have talked to Abby eventually, but it had been too new at the time. And she hardly saw Abby in the weeks preceding her death. They'd been on different tracks, going in different directions. If she'd paid more attention, maybe she could have prevented Abby from going to the Ramsay house that night. Maybe her sister would still be alive.

With a sigh, she wrapped the tie around the plastic bag and shoved it against the wall. She reached for the light switch, then paused. On impulse she ran her hands over the floorboards, wondering if any were loose, if any offered a hiding place, but nothing budged. The walls were stucco, and the shelf that ran along the top was empty. There was certainly no diary in the closet.

She turned off the light. As she left the room, she thought how quiet the house was. Growing up, there had always been so many people around: her parents, her brother and sister, neighbors, friends. Now it was a ghost house. Perhaps that's why her father spent so much time away from home. He couldn't bear to leave, yet he couldn't stand to stay.

As she walked into the kitchen, she heard a crash followed by the sudden barking of the dog next door. Looking out the kitchen window, she didn't see anything out of the ordinary in the shadowed yard. A brisk breeze blew through the trees, rustling the flower bushes along the fence. Something must have fallen in the yard next door.

She had just moved away from the window when the doorbell rang and she started in surprise. Why was she so jumpy? Probably because she'd spent half the night thinking about the murder and wondering whether that person was still in Angel's Bay.

When she looked through the peephole on the front door, her tension eased at the sight of Charlotte on the porch. She opened the door with relief.

"I'm kidnapping you," Charlotte declared. "Get your purse and your coat."

"Excuse me?"

"You heard me. I'm not taking no for an answer. I know your father's at the bar, and Mort assured me that he will see that your dad gets home safely. And I don't see Shane hovering in the background, so I'm guessing you're alone."

"I'm not dressed to go out," Lauren protested. "I've been cleaning."

"Jeans work fine for this outing." Charlotte tapped her watch. "I'm waiting."

"You are *so* bossy."

Charlotte grinned. "I had to learn something from my mother."

Lauren grabbed her coat and purse and stepped onto the porch, pulling the door shut. She was grateful for the interruption; the eerie quiet of the house was playing on her nerves.

"Why can't you tell me where we're going?" she asked as they walked down the street.

"Because you'd say no. But you'll have fun, I promise." Charlotte gave Lauren a happy smile.

"This feels like old times, you and me together. I'm glad you decided to stick around for a few days. How are things going with your father?"

"It's up and down. Some moments he's fine, and then he's completely out of it."

"You should talk to your father's doctor. Does he still see Harry Meyers?"

"Yes. I called Dr. Meyers, but he told me that unless my father gave permission, he couldn't discuss his medical condition with me."

"Won't your father allow you to talk to his doctor?"

"Not at the moment. He's afraid that if I learn how serious it is, I'll push to get power of attorney and force him to leave. He wants to live here until he dies. I don't know what to do."

"Alzheimer's can be more difficult for the family than for the person going through it. At some point, your father won't know his condition or his surroundings, but you will. That will be hard for you."

"I know. I can't see a winning scenario anywhere. If I take him away, I'll know that somewhere inside his head he hates me for forcing him from the only home he's ever known. But what's the alternative? And don't say I could move back here," she added quickly. "Although I guess you *could* say that, since you did it for your mother. Maybe I'm being selfish, putting my life before his."

"My situation is completely different, and it's not necessarily permanent. Besides that, I don't have the same feelings about this town as you do. I didn't go through the nightmare of losing my sister, seeing my boyfriend accused of murder, watching my family split apart. It's harder for you to be here than it is for me. I would never judge your decision, Lauren."

"Thanks. That means a lot."

They walked the next few blocks in easy quiet. As the marina came into view, Charlotte said, "So, how is Shane?"

"We're not talking about him."

Charlotte laughed. "Maybe not yet. The night is young."

Lauren let out a groan as they turned the corner and it became apparent where they were heading. "Not the quilt shop again. Didn't I see enough people yesterday at the shower?"

"It's quilting night. You used to love it, remember? But don't worry, it's almost over. They're having a speaker, a woman from Los Angeles who's an expert at appliqué."

"I can't believe you, of all people, are taking me to quilting night. You always said how many quilts does one person need?" Lauren teased her.

"Well, I'm glad I took the classes. The sewing techniques came in handy when I got to medical school. Now I get to stitch people up." She laughed at Lauren's expression. "It's fun."

"It sounds disgusting," she said with a shudder. "How do you stick a needle in someone's skin?"

"Believe me, I do more disgusting things than that," Charlotte said with a laugh. "But it's the best job I've ever had. I love being a doctor."

"You always liked taking care of people and animals, anyone in pain. You get that from your mother, too."

"Oh, please, do *not* say that."

Lauren smiled. "Is your mom going to be here?"

"No, she has a cold, so she's staying home tonight."

"What about that pregnant girl you have living with you?" Lauren asked. "Mrs. Jenkins stopped by my house earlier to drop off a casserole, and she couldn't wait to fill me in on Annie and the mystery of her baby's father. I heard that the mayor is now the front runner."

"Who knows?" Charlotte said.

There was an odd note in Charlotte's voice, and Lauren stopped abruptly. "You know something. *Is* it the mayor?"

"I have no idea," Charlotte said. "Annie won't tell me. I don't know why she's protecting the father—if she's scared, or if she believes it will ruin his life. I think he should be involved or at least informed, but I can't force it."

Lauren had a feeling Charlotte knew a lot more than she was saying. But while she'd always been happy to gossip about little things, she could be trusted with the big secrets.

"I wish everyone would stop talking about her," Charlotte continued. "She's just a mixed-up teenager who had a terrible childhood. Her father is a mentally disabled war veteran who's fighting his own private war up in the mountains, and she has no other family support. Someone needed to step in and help, so I did."

That was Charlotte, Lauren thought—always willing to step in. Even now she was dragging Lauren out of the house, intent on making sure she felt a part of the town again.

A minute later they entered the quilt shop. A group of younger girls was sewing in the first-floor classroom, but the rest of the action was on the second floor. The room had been set up like a classroom tonight, with tables and sewing machines and a demonstration going on at the front of the room. They paused in the back to listen.

Nina Stamish, a middle-aged brunette dressed in a bright green dress with a colorfully embroidered vest, was discussing the latest technique in embroidery stitching using a computer software program.

"As you can see on the screen," Nina said, motioning toward the screen behind her, "this program can help you design your stitching before you get near the fabric. The appliqué pieces are displayed and then the embroidery design is placed within the shape. The computer makes it easy for you to mirror the images throughout the piece. Once you're satisfied, you save it on your USB stick or hook up your computer directly to your sewing machine. The software will then tell your sewing machine what to stitch."

"Wow, things have changed a lot since we used to handstitch," Lauren muttered to Charlotte. The quilt that Nina was creating was a piece of art.

As Nina finished her presentation, Fiona Murray, the eighty-five-year-old owner of the quilt shop, and Shane's grandmother, stepped forward. Fiona still had the fiery red hair of her youth and was the grand dame of quilting in Angel's Bay.

"Nina will stay and answer questions," she said. "Those of you who are going to work on the Angel's Bay quilt can gather around the table in the back. Otherwise, we'll see the rest of you next week."

"Who's working on the Angel's Bay quilt?" Lauren asked suspiciously. "And you'd better not say us."

"Not us—you," Charlotte replied with a grin. "I'm not related to the original twenty-four."

"I haven't quilted in years. I don't even remember how."

"Sure you do." Charlotte headed toward the table where a dozen women had gathered. Fabric blocks in varying stages of construction were spread across the top, all replicas of the original Angel's Bay story quilt.

"I can't believe Charlotte got you here," Kara said, disbelief in her eyes. "I was sure you'd say no."

"She didn't tell me we were coming here, or that we were sewing," Lauren replied.

Kara motioned to the chair next to her. "Have a seat. You can work on the Jamison block." She pushed a scrap of fabric in Lauren's direction.

Lauren stared down at the design. She'd done this before a hundred times, usually assisting her mother. Along with the butterfly soaring through two gold rings, the letters L and T were entwined, standing for Leonora and Tommy and their endless love. She'd enjoyed quilting in the past, imagining Tommy and Leonora's love affair as she stitched their letters.

She *did* have a soft spot for their romantic story, and she was the one who'd wanted to carry on the family tradition. Abby had only worked on the quilt a few times, most of them under duress from their mother.

"It will be fun, Lauren," Charlotte said with encouragement.

Kara gave her a sympathetic look. "You don't have to if you don't want to, Lauren."

"Of course she wants to," Fiona Murray interrupted. The matriarch of the Murray family had an iron will, and no one crossed her. Her blue eyes glinted with steel as she gazed down at Lauren. "It's your duty, dear. You must carry on the family tradition. Your father would be very proud if you did."

"I'm not sure I remember how," she prevaricated, knowing that her hesitation was futile.

"You will, once you pick the needle up," Fiona said. Her eyes softened briefly. "How is your mother, dear? We miss her around here."

"She's well."

"And happy?"

"Yes," Lauren said.

"She deserves to be, after the terrible tragedy that befell your family. It's nice to have you back. Your father has been lonely these past years."

"His choice," Lauren said shortly, unwilling to allow her father to be the victim.

"One I suspect he regrets," Fiona said.

"I'm not sure that he does, but it's done."

"Yes, we can only look forward, not backward." Fiona drew in a breath and looked at her assembled workers. "All right, ladies, let's get to work."

"What are you going to do?" Lauren asked Charlotte, who was leaning against the counter next to them.

"I'm going to have a drink." Charlotte pulled a bottle of red wine out of her bag. "And supervise."

"Charlotte, put that wine away," Fiona Murray said sharply, her eagle eye not missing a thing. "No liquids near this quilt. You can help Jenna with her square. We don't need idle hands at this table."

Charlotte put the wine away. "Yes, ma'am," she said meekly.

Lauren smiled. They were all in their thirties, but Fiona still treated them like they were teenagers. Charlotte sat down next to Jenna Davies and soon they were all involved with the task at hand.

It was amazing how quickly the quilting came back to her. Threading the newer sewing machines took a little time to learn, but within minutes she was on her way. There was a certain peace that came with quilting, and as the conversation flowed around her, Lauren relaxed, taking pleasure in the work and enjoying the camaraderie of working on a shared project.

The quilt had brought the original survivors together, had given them a chance to connect, to grieve, to start over, and through the quilt to tell the stories of their loved ones, their shattered families. The quilting had helped them to move on and today, some hundred and fifty years after that first quilt had been sewn, it was helping Lauren to heal. She'd turned her back on Angel's Bay and everything and everyone in it. She'd been filled with so much hate and rage that she couldn't see anything good, but there was a lot of good here. There always had been.

She was the last to finish. "Does it look horrible?" Lauren asked Kara. "Am I a disgrace to the Jamison women who have come before me?"

Kara inspected the square. "It's great. The stitching is very even. You did a wonderful job. You haven't forgotten a thing."

"I hope it passes your grandmother's inspection. She demands perfection," Lauren said.

"Actually, when it comes to quilting, my grandmother prefers handstitching and a lot of love over machine sewing. She brings the modern techniques to the town because the business has to keep growing, but the fact that you made this square and that you're a Jamison means everything to her."

"So now we celebrate," Charlotte said, pouring Lauren a glass of wine. Everyone else had left, including Fiona, who'd told Kara to lock up when they were ready to go.

"I'm so jealous," Kara said with a yearning glance.

"Apple cider is not doing it for me tonight. And by the way, Charlotte, I'm mad at you."

"What did I do?" Charlotte asked in surprise.

"You did not tell me how horrible childbirth is. I went to the birthing class tonight, and the movie was quite an eye-opener. I don't want to have this baby anymore."

Charlotte grinned. "Too late for that kind of thinking."

"It was horrifying. I thought Jason was going to pass out," Kara added.

"Jason?" Lauren cut in, surprised to hear his name again. "Jason Marlow?"

"Yes, he stood in for my mother. She's supposed to be my coach until Colin wakes up. But she got sick, and I wasn't going to go, but Jason pushed me to do it," Kara explained. "I think he's sorry now. Childbirth is a little on the disgusting side, I have to say."

"Wait until you have that beautiful baby in your arms," Charlotte said. "It will all be worth it."

"You have to say that; you're the doctor."

"You and Jason have been friends for a long time, haven't you?" Lauren asked.

Kara nodded. "He was Colin's best friend growing up. Mine, too." Her brows knit together in a frown. "Jason said that there are some rumors going around about him and Abby."

"Did he have a relationship with my sister?" Lauren asked.

"He said they were friends. Wouldn't Abby have

told you if she liked him, Lauren? You were close. You shared a room."

"We weren't that close in the months before her death. I was thinking about graduation, and I got caught up in my own romance. I didn't pay much attention to her. She was always with Lisa, and they were two years younger. They had their own friends." Lauren shook her head. "You don't know how many times I wish I'd done things differently that year."

"I know you blame yourself, but you can't," Kara said quietly. "Sometimes bad things just happen."

Lauren knew Kara wasn't talking just about Abby, but also about Colin, and she felt a little guilty for being so absorbed in her own problems. "You're right, of course. So how are you feeling tonight?"

Kara sighed. "Tired, but happy to be with old friends. The birthing class was tough to get through, and not just because of the gross movie. Doing it with Jason and not Colin felt so wrong. But this was a rehearsal, not the real thing. Colin will be there when the baby comes. I'm sure of that." She cleared her throat. "And getting back to Jason, I think he would have told me if he was involved with Abby in high school. Although I must admit my attention at the time was mostly on Colin."

"That's for sure. You two were attached at the hip." Charlotte's eyes sparkled with mischief as she refilled Lauren's glass as well as her own. "So, here's a question, Kara, since we're taking a trip down memory lane. Did you have sex with Colin in high school?"

"Hey, that's a little personal," Kara protested.

"And I'm a little buzzed, so answer the question."

Kara looked around the room as if she were afraid her mother or grandmother might be lurking somewhere, but they were alone.

"Is it really that big of a secret now?" Charlotte asked. "You're almost thirty years old, and you *did* marry the guy."

"You first, Charlie," Kara said. "You and Andrew? Did you do the wild thing?"

Charlotte's smile widened. "Yes, but only once. Three days later, Andrew did it with Pamela the Slut—at the beach—at a party I was at."

"I hope you didn't actually see them," Lauren interjected.

"I caught the previews."

"That sucks," Kara said. "I didn't know he was such a jerk."

"He was a teenage boy," Charlotte said. "And he was hot. I was mad for him."

"Now he's a minister," Lauren put in. "Who would have thought?"

"Certainly not me," Charlotte replied. "He's good, too. I think he's found his purpose in life."

Lauren wondered if Charlotte still had a thing for Andrew. First love was tough to shake, as she knew only too well. "You're making light of it now, but you must have been hurt when Andrew cheated on you."

"I was devastated," Charlotte admitted. "That beach party is one big painful blur in my mind. I was drunk. I was angry. I was stupid."

"What does that mean?" Kara asked curiously. "Did something else happen?"

"As if I could remember? I had tequila amnesia."

"What about now?" Lauren asked. "Are you going to give Andrew another chance? Obviously he's cleaned up his act."

"I don't think so, and not because of Pamela. There are other reasons."

"Like what?" Lauren prodded.

"Yeah, like what?" Kara echoed.

Charlotte frowned. "I can't see myself as the girl-friend or the wife of the minister. It's not just that, though. I'm flattered by Andrew's attention, but I think it's because I'm easy." She stopped short. "Whoa, that didn't come out right. I meant I'm easy for him to be with, because I know his past. He feels comfortable with me, and deep down he's still inse-cure about being the spiritual leader of a town that remembers him as a kid. With me, he doesn't have to be anyone but himself."

"All that seems like stuff you could work out," Kara interjected. "If you still like him?"

Charlotte ran her finger around the edge of her wineglass, her expression pensive. "I do like him, but I don't know."

"Maybe you should find out," Lauren suggested. "Don't write him off without giving him a chance."

"Is that what you're going to do, Lauren?" Charlotte asked, lifting her gaze to Lauren. "Give your old high school boyfriend a second chance?"

"Damn, I walked right into that one," she replied. "No comment."

"No way—you don't get off that easily," Charlotte said.

"What are you thinking, Lauren?" Kara asked, her gaze curious and a bit concerned. "Shane is my brother, and I love him. I don't want either of you to get hurt."

"I know you slept with Shane in high school," Charlotte cut in. "There's no way you didn't. He was way too hot to resist. Those dark, moody eyes, that ripped body."

"I might have," Lauren admitted, thinking it was easier to confess to sex thirteen years ago than sex last night.

Kara winced and put her hands over her ears. "Please, I don't want to hear any details. That's my brother you're talking about."

"Don't worry, I wasn't going to give you any," Lauren said, feeling a blush warm her cheeks.

"Well, you can give them to me on the way home," Charlotte said with a laugh. Then she turned back to Kara. "So that leaves you, Kara. Were we all bad girls back in high school? Or just Lauren and me?"

Kara hesitated, then gave a sheepish smile. "Colin and I did not have sex in high school. We made out a lot, but we waited until we were twenty-one."

"Really," Charlotte murmured.

"Interesting," Lauren said.

"It wasn't easy, but I'm glad we held off, because I think we might have ruined it if we'd had sex too early."

"Maybe," Charlotte said thoughtfully.

"Maybe," Lauren echoed.

Kara looked from one to the other and laughed. "You two look like you just got called into the principal's office for bad behavior. Believe me, you had a lot more fun in high school than I did. And who knows what might happen now? Your men are still single and available and right here in town."

Silence fell between them for a moment. "I slept with Shane last night," Lauren said abruptly, not sure why she'd felt the need to confess, but there it was. "I shouldn't have, and I don't know why I did. It can't go anywhere." She glanced at Charlotte, who seemed to be having trouble keeping a straight face. "What?"

"Lauren, you need to stop pretending that Shane wasn't important to you."

"He was important, but we were kids back then."

"You weren't kids last night," Charlotte reminded her.

"I felt like one," she confessed. "Young, reckless, and wild, like the girl who got on the back of Shane's motorcycle all those years ago and threw caution to the wind. But it's over. It was just one last fling for old times' sake. I'm not going to sleep with him again."

"Because it was horrible?" Charlotte asked.

Lauren made a face at her. "No, because it was

incredible, and I can't let myself fall for him again. We've both moved on." She looked at Kara, who was giving her a thoughtful look. "Sorry, you probably didn't want to hear all this."

"Just—be careful, Lauren. I don't want either one of you to get hurt. Shane acts tough, and it's hard to get a handle on what he's thinking or feeling, but he cared about you in high school and I think he still does."

"Does he know that last night was just a fling?" Charlotte asked.

"I told him," Lauren said, drinking the last of her wine. "But I'm not sure he believed me."

"Why not?" Charlotte persisted.

"Because I have a hard time keeping my hands off of him."

"Then it sounds like I'd better walk you all the way home just to make sure you don't take any side trips," Charlotte said.

"Good idea," Lauren said, as Charlotte helped Kara to her feet.

They rinsed out their wineglasses, turned off the lights, and left the store, locking the doors behind them. The streets were quiet, just the distant sound of music coming from one of the bars. Angel's Bay had grown a lot since she'd left, but it still had the feel of a small town. They left Kara at her car and then continued on to Lauren's house.

"What about you, Charlie?" Lauren asked as they turned down her street. "Who's going to walk you home?"

"I'll be fine, it's only three blocks. And I'm in no danger of wandering down to the marina and stopping by a certain sexy someone's boat."

Lauren frowned. "I do have *some* self-control."

"Then go in the house and stay there," Charlotte said with a grin. "It was fun tonight. I'm glad you came. It was like old times."

"Yeah, it was." She had girlfriends in San Francisco, but not women who'd known her as a child. There was a certain honesty she shared with Charlotte, and even Kara, that she didn't share with anyone else. That was her fault. She'd shut her current friends out of her past life. She'd wanted to keep the two separate, and that had come with a price.

"Looks like your dad is home," Charlotte said. "The lights are on."

"That could mean anything, but I hope he's tucked safely in bed."

"Do you want me to wait, in case you have to hunt him down?"

"No, I'm sure it's fine." She paused as her gaze caught on a stack of bricks under a side window—a window that was now open, the edge of a curtain blowing through the space. "That's odd," she muttered.

"What?" Charlotte asked, following her across the yard.

"It looks like someone stacked these bricks so they could get up to the window."

"You think someone broke into your house?"

"I don't know." She remembered the sound of

the dog barking earlier, the crash in the side yard. "Maybe the bricks have always been there. I just don't remember the window being open when I left. My dad must have opened it. Or he forgot his key and climbed in through the window." She drew in a breath and let it out. "Thanks for walking me home."

"Not so fast. Let's go inside and make sure everything is okay."

They walked around to the porch, where Lauren slipped her key into the lock and opened the door. The open window was in the adjacent dining room, and she walked over to close it. Nothing seemed out of the ordinary.

"Abby? Is that you?" Her father came out of his bedroom wearing his yellow rain slicker and boots. "It's time to go fishing. It's storming out, better get your gear on."

Lauren exchanged a quick look with Charlotte. "It's not raining, Dad."

"Who's your friend?" Ned asked, squinting at Charlotte. "Is she coming with us?"

"No, she's going home," Lauren said. "It's too late to go fishing."

"Okay, then. I better change." He ambled back toward his bedroom.

Charlotte looked at her sympathetically. "It must be difficult to have him call you Abby."

Lauren shrugged. "It doesn't shock me so much anymore. I think she's always on his mind. Since I've come back she's on my mind, too. We need closure. We need answers." She paused. "I was thinking about what Abby was involved with in the weeks before she died, and I remembered that she was always taking photos for the yearbook. She had to cover every event."

"What are you getting at?"

"Maybe there's some clue in those photos."

"Did you look in the yearbook?"

"I'm more interested in the pictures that weren't published. Do you think the school keeps them?"

"Mrs. Weinstein would know. She's been running the yearbook staff for the last twenty years, and she still works at the high school."

Lauren nodded. "Then I know what I'm doing tomorrow."

"If you go to the school around three, I'll be finishing up my biology presentation in Coach Sorensen's classroom."

"Really?" Lauren said. "Maybe I'll see you there."

Charlotte smiled, but there was a worried look in her eye. "Be careful, Lauren."

"Careful of what?"

"I don't know, but I don't have a good feeling about any of this. If Abby's killer is still in Angel's Bay, you could be putting yourself in danger."

"Or I could finally find out who he is, and make him pay."

FIFTEEN

Lauren felt sixteen again when she pulled open the high school's front door just before three o'clock on Tuesday afternoon. She avoided the office and headed down the familiar halls. Through the open doors she could hear the murmur of lecturing teachers and chattering students. Classes would be out in just a few minutes, and she could only imagine how eager the kids must be to finish school for the day. She'd certainly always looked forward to that last bell.

Her old locker was near the girls' bathroom on the first floor. As she passed by it, she smiled, thinking of freshman year when she'd wrestled with the lock, anxiety running through her veins. She'd battled shyness and insecurity for most of high school; she'd never had her sister's self-confidence. She'd started coming into her own at the end of junior year, which was also when she'd met Shane.

He'd been a year older, and while she'd heard

about him and seen him around for years, they'd never spoken until a month before he graduated. They'd met outside of a party. He'd been on his motorcycle. She'd been looking for excitement, and boy, had she found it, in one smoking-hot teenager with a bad attitude. Her mother had been horrified when she'd taken up with Shane. Her friends, who were mostly quiet, studious types, had been confused. But she'd been completely swept away, and her feet hadn't touched the ground until almost a year later, when everything fell apart.

She moved on down the hall, checking out the trophy case and the main bulletin board, which was now a flat-screen monitor with an electronically generated calendar. Climbing the stairs to the second floor, she paused when she saw Chief Silveira waiting outside Tim Sorensen's classroom. Her heart began to beat a little faster. What was he doing here?

Joe looked just as surprised to see her. "Ms. Jamison," he said quietly. "What brings you here?"

"I was going to ask you the same question." Over his shoulder, she could see into the classroom. Charlotte stood at the front, while Tim Sorensen sat at his desk. Now in his late thirties, he was actually more attractive than she'd remembered, with light brown hair and friendly brown eyes. He looked like an approachable guy, certainly not like a murderer.

"What's your interest in Mr. Sorensen?" the chief persisted.

She stepped back from the door. "Probably the

same as yours. Mr. Devlin shared his thoughts with me about a possible relationship between my sister and her volleyball coach."

"What do you think about that?"

"I can't imagine that Abby would have gotten romantically involved with her teacher." Lauren wished she could infuse more certainty into her voice, but with every passing day she was beginning to question how well she'd known her little sister.

"Then why are you here?" he asked.

"I thought I should at least talk to him, but I'm not exactly sure what to ask," she admitted.

"Why don't you let me take care of it?" Joe suggested.

She was relieved that the chief was following up on it, although the fact that he was here also gave more credence to Mark Devlin's suspicions. "Do you have any more information about him and my sister than Mr. Devlin's speculation?"

"No, I don't. But I'm following up with everyone who was known to be in Abby's life those last few weeks. Since Mr. Sorensen was her coach and her teacher, he's on the list."

"The team traveled to some away tournaments that year, and other parents always went along. It was never just the coach and the girls, but he was probably more involved with the girls than an ordinary teacher would have been. Not that I think that makes him guilty—I still don't believe my sister would have gotten involved with a married man when she was only fifteen." She paused. "Will you keep me up to date on your investigation? I'd rather you speak to me and not to my father. He drifts in and out of reality, and I'm still worried that any new information about Abby, especially any facts that damage her reputation, might really set him back."

"I understand."

"Thanks." She headed down the hallway to talk to Mrs. Weinstein, to see if she could get her hands on the yearbook photos.

Joe was glad to see Lauren Jamison leave. It was bad enough to have Mark Devlin shooting his mouth off all over town; he didn't need the victim's sister in the middle of things. If Abby's killer had gotten away with murder for thirteen years, anyone who got in the way of his freedom now might end up dead, too.

He checked his watch—two minutes until the bell rang. Charlotte was taking questions. She looked beautiful in her short floral skirt and light blue sweater, her blonde hair pulled back in a ponytail. Her easy smile made his gut clench. He'd bet that the teenage boys in the room were enjoying her as much as her presentation about sex. He liked the way she interacted with the kids. She wasn't only a good speaker, she was a great listener.

Charlotte had the whole package: beauty, brains, and warm-hearted charm. No wonder the new minister was all over her. Yet she seemed to be resisting rekindling her old high school flame, and Joe wondered why. Not that it was any of his business. He had his own relationship to deal with.

He'd thought having Rachel here would mean a lot more time together, but she was often with Mark, allegedly checking out filming locations, or looking into real estate opportunities. She had hung her license with one of the local realty firms, but so far she hadn't listed any properties or made any sales. When he'd asked about the potential for work, she'd given him an airy wave and said she was exploring her opportunities—whatever the hell that meant. He'd thought he'd known his wife inside and out, but every day she seemed to become more of a mystery.

The bell rang, interrupting his thoughts, and he stepped back as kids poured out of the room, eager to be done with school. He was about to step inside when Charlotte came through the door, her attention so focused on her cell phone that she stumbled right into him.

"Sorry," she said, her eyes widening with recognition. "Joe. I keep running into you. What are you doing here? This isn't your usual beat."

"I go where the action is."

She raised an eyebrow. "Did I miss some action?"

He grinned. "I need to speak to Mr. Sorensen."

"Really?" she asked, her head tilting thoughtfully. "Will you tell me why?"

"No. You were good in there."

A warm pink colored her cheeks. "You were listening?"

"Just the last part. You were straight with the kids. I'm sure they appreciated that."

"Their parents may not. I kept the information pretty basic, but I'm sure someone will have a problem with it. I'd love it if teenagers were educated by their parents, but most of them aren't, and I'd rather the kids be informed. As an ob/gyn, I see what happens when they're not."

"So do I," Joe said. "Not so much here as in L.A., though."

"Don't be so sure about that. This may be a smaller town, but teenage hormones run just as high."

"Good point. Do you know Mr. Sorensen well? Was he one of your teachers?"

She cast a quick look over her shoulder. Tim Sorensen was still in discussion with one of his students. "I had him for biology when I was a junior in high school. We've had a few conversations since I came back to town, and he's a very nice, intelligent man." She lowered her voice. "Are you here because you think he had something to do with Abby's death?"

"Do you think that?"

"I don't know. Lauren mentioned that that movie guy suggested that Tim and Abby had some sort of relationship. I guess it's not completely impossible. But would he have stuck around here all this time if he was guilty? Would anyone have stayed here after getting away with murder?"

He shrugged. "In a case this cold, no possibility can be ruled out."

She gave him a frown. "You're very cagey, you know that? You often answer a question with another question or with some placating generality."

"Sorry. It's part of the job."

"I could be helpful," Charlotte suggested, a gleam in her eyes. "I know a lot of people in this town. You should use me."

Her words painted a picture that had nothing to do with sharing information. He swallowed and cleared his throat. "I think Mr. Sorensen is finishing his conversation. I should step inside."

"Good luck. Lauren is one of my best friends, and I knew Abby, too. I really hope you can find out who killed her."

"I'm going to give it my best shot."

"I have a feeling you're extremely good at what you do. You've got that—" Distracted by the ring of her cell phone, she checked the text message. "I have to go. Baby coming earlier than expected."

"I've got that what?" he couldn't help asking.

She grinned. "Something. You've got that something."

Before he could ask for a further explanation, she was halfway down the hall. *Something, huh?* He couldn't stop the smile that curved his lips. Well, something wasn't nothing.

As the last student exited the classroom, Joe turned his mind back to the job at hand. If he couldn't stop Mark Devlin from making his movie, he could at least make sure he got the villain right. While he wasn't convinced Tim Sorensen was responsible, his gut told him the murder hadn't been random; it had been personal. Whoever killed Abby knew her—maybe better than anyone else.

"I'm trying to learn more about the last year of my sister's life," Lauren told Mrs. Weinstein, the art teacher who had managed the yearbook staff for the past twenty years. Celia Weinstein was short in stature but tall in forthrightness, and so far she hadn't responded well to Lauren's request. "You can understand that, can't you?" she persisted.

"I do understand, dear, but I can't just turn over hundreds of photos to you. They belong to the school. At the very least, I would have to get permission from the principal, and Mr. Donohue is out until Monday. There's a terrible flu going around. If you want to come back next week, perhaps I can give you a different answer."

"I'm not sure I'll be here next week." Lauren thought about her options. The photo archives were in the file cabinets in the adjoining office. She just needed to get Mrs. Weinstein to help her. "Do you remember Abby?" she asked.

"Of course I do. I never forget a student. She was a very friendly girl, a team player who worked well with others. It was very sad, what happened to her."

"The police think that Abby knew the person

who killed her. I'm trying to find out more about who she was spending time with in the last month before she died."

"I'm certain her friends could give you that information."

"They did, but there seem to be gaps. I think she had a crush on someone, and her yearbook job might have given her a good excuse to take lots of pictures of him."

Mrs. Weinstein shook her head. "The staff photographers had very strict instructions. They were to take pictures of everyone at every event, not just their friends. I used to go through the film to make sure that no one was spending all their time taking their best friend's photo." She paused. "I'm sorry that I can't help you, Lauren. If you want to come back next week and speak to the principal, you're welcome to do that. Or perhaps you and Mr. Devlin could join forces."

"What?" she asked in surprise.

"He was here yesterday asking to look through the photos. I gave him the same answer that I gave you. I'm sorry, but I must go now. I have a parent-teacher conference."

"Thanks for your time," Lauren said, as she left the room.

She had to find a way to get to the photos before Devlin did. She wanted to find Abby's killer, but she also wanted to protect her sister.

*   *   *

"What the hell is going on? First some movie producer and now you?" Tim Sorensen asked, anger brewing in his eyes.

Joe didn't like the fact that Devlin had gotten to Sorensen before him, but that was his own damn fault for not getting on top of this movie from the start. He'd figured Devlin would give up and go home after a few futile days, but the man was proving to be more of a bulldog than he'd expected.

"I told the police everything I knew about Abigail Jamison when I was questioned after the murder," Sorensen continued. "Abby was a gifted student, a talented athlete, and she fit in well with the group. She wasn't bullied, she wasn't one of the mean girls, and she seemed to have both male and female friends. That's all I know."

"Did she ever speak to you about any problems with her friends or family?"

"Not that I recall."

"I have a report that Abby and a friend of hers, Lisa Delaney, were spotted sitting in a car outside your house the Saturday night before Abby was killed. Do you know why the girls might have been there?"

"I have no idea. There were a couple of teenagers who lived on my street. Perhaps they were there to see them."

Joe was usually good at reading people, but Sorensen wasn't giving much away. He was irritated, but his anger wasn't necessarily indicative of guilt.

"Why don't we cut to the chase?" Tim suggested

tersely. "There was nothing inappropriate about my relationship with Abby or any of my other students, and I don't appreciate my name being brought into this case. Do you know what rumors like this can do to a male teacher's career? They don't even have to be true. I work hard at my job, and I have three kids to support. I don't want unfounded gossip killing my career."

"No one is accusing you of anything. I understand you took the volleyball team to some away tournaments, overnight trips with stays in motels."

"With parent chaperones. There were four girls to a room, and we had strict curfews. I've always been very careful never to place myself in a situation that could be misconstrued. Is that it?"

"For the moment. Thanks." Joe left the classroom. Either Tim Sorensen was a very good liar or he'd truly had nothing to do with Abby's death. Just because Abby and her friends were spying on their coach didn't mean that Tim was aware of it or had encouraged it. On the other hand, if he had been involved with Abby, he certainly wasn't going to volunteer that information.

One thing was certain: no one in town liked Mark Devlin. Maybe if he pissed off a few more people, he'd give up and go home.

Hours later, Lauren paced restlessly around the living room of her father's house. She'd had dinner with her dad before he'd gone off to see an old war movie playing at the dollar theater on Main Street. He wouldn't be back for a few hours, which gave her just enough time to put what was probably a really stupid plan into motion. She grabbed her coat and left the house before she could think twice.

Shane was on his boat when she arrived at the dock, breathless and determined.

He raised an eyebrow as she hopped onto the boat. "I thought it was a one-night stand, yet here you are again."

"This isn't a booty call. I need your help. Abby told me that there was someone she couldn't have. I'm certain she was writing about that person in her diary the morning of the day she died, because she was very secretive. I've searched the house looking for that journal, but I can't find it. I'm betting it went missing because it implicated the murderer."

"That's quite a leap," Shane said. "I thought her entire book bag was missing, with her wallet and cell phone."

"Which led the police to believe there was a robbery motive, although Abby didn't have anything of value in that bag. She couldn't have had more than twenty dollars in the wallet, and if someone wanted cash, why not just take the bills and leave the rest behind?"

"Where are you going with all this?"

"There has to be another way to find out who Abby liked. Her friends have never been able to come up with a name, but there has to be some evidence somewhere, and I think I know where."

"Okay, let's hear it."

"Abby was a photographer for the high school yearbook. In the few months before she died, she always had her camera with her. Everywhere she went, it went, which means she recorded a lot of her life."

"Or other people's lives. She wasn't taking pictures of herself."

"Sometimes she did. Sometimes she used to hand me the camera so I could snap a shot of her and her friends. If Abby liked someone, I think the answer is in those pictures." She drew in a breath, seeing the confusion in his eyes. "I was a teenage girl, Shane. I know what teenage girls do when they're in love. They write the boy's name over and over on binder paper and put their first and last names together, like they're married. They toilet-paper the guy's house, and take his picture, and put him in their diary. And they do everything they can to be close to that boy, like bumping into him accidentally on purpose. Abby had a camera and a reason to be at every event. If she liked someone, she would have taken his picture, and I'm betting she took it over and over again."

"Did you write my name over and over again?" he asked curiously.

"We're not talking about me."

"All right," Shane said, a small smile curving the corner of his mouth. "I can see you think you're on to something. So did you look in the yearbook?"

"Yes, but I don't know which of those photos Abby took, and they only publish ten percent of all the pictures taken. I went down to the high school today and spoke to Mrs. Weinstein, the yearbook teacher, who has all the pictures from the past twenty years in her back office. She said every staff photographer turned in an envelope with their printed photos once the yearbook went to press. How about that?"

"Impressive. Do you have the pictures?"

"No. She wouldn't give them to me—some privacy concern. She told me to come back next week to talk to the principal, but I have a better idea."

Shane immediate shook his head, a warning look in his eyes. "I don't want to hear it, Lauren."

"Yes you do, because it involves you."

"No way."

"Please, Shane." She put her hands on his shoulders, shamelessly pressing her breasts against his chest.

His hands remained firmly at his side. "I'm not that easy."

"Are you sure about that?" she asked as she slipped her hands under his T-shirt.

He cleared his throat. "What exactly do you want me to do?"

"Help me break into the high school tonight."

"Are you out of your mind? Why don't you just talk to the principal next week? He'll probably hand the envelope over to you."

Disappointed, she said, "Next week is too far away. I don't even know if I'll still be here, and he could say no."

"Then talk to the police. Get them to request the pictures."

"Jason Marlow works for the police department. I don't want him to have access to those pictures until I see them. The photos are just sitting in a file drawer, Shane. We're not stealing them, we're just taking a look." She stroked his back with her hands, her fingers kneading the tight muscles.

"That's quite a rationalization you've got going there."

"You didn't used to be a chicken."

"Trash talk? You're pulling out all the stops now. Do you really think calling me a coward will work?"

"The boy I used to know never met a rule he didn't want to break. And it's not like I'm asking you to do something you haven't done before—I know you're the one who put the goat in Principal Calvin's office."

"The girl I used to know was terrified to get into trouble. She never wanted to break the rules or even bend them."

"I'm not a girl anymore." She looked into his eyes. "I need to find out who killed Abby, and so do you. You could clear your name once and for all. You're going to help me in the end, so just say yes, and we can get on with it."

"I don't know. I'm kind of enjoying your persuasive tactics. If you drop your hands a little lower, I'll probably say yes to anything."

She stepped back, realizing by his grin that he'd been playing her, too. "You rat."

"I wanted to see how far you'd go to get what you want."

"I knew I wasn't going to have to go far," she told him. "You *are* that easy."

"Where you're concerned, that seems to be true. I'll get my jacket and a flashlight."

"Do you think we'll be able to get in?"

"I have no idea. I'm guessing the school has improved its security in the last decade, but you never know."

"We'll find a way," she said confidently. It felt good to be taking some action. Maybe she was wrong and the pictures wouldn't prove a damn thing, but at least she'd know for sure.

SIXTEEN

The high school sat on the edge of town, backed into a hillside and surrounded on three sides by tall, thick trees. Shane drove through the parking lot and down a narrow path that ran along the baseball field, stopping behind the shadow of the grandstand. If anyone came by, they wouldn't be able to see the motorcycle from the street.

Lauren slid off the bike and took off her helmet. There was a determined sparkle in her eyes tonight. She had changed, he realized. She wasn't nearly as shy and intimidated as she'd once been. She'd come into her own. They walked past the gym, the cafeteria, and through the quad where they used to eat lunch.

As he led her down a path behind the back of the school, she said, "This is spooky. Where are we going? The main building is over there."

"I'm hoping Ramon is still a creature of habit."

"The groundskeeper? Wasn't he like a hundred years old when we were in high school?"

"Probably close to that, but he's still alive. I've seen him and his grandson at the Crab Shack." He headed toward a small shed by the soccer field. There was a padlock on the door, and he handed the flashlight to Lauren while he twirled the lock. When it popped open, he felt a surge of relief. The shed was filled with gardening supplies and other maintenance items, and there was a battered old desk in one corner. Shane opened the bottom drawer on the left, dug through screwdrivers, wrenches, and pens to pull out a key ring with six keys attached. "Bingo."

"How did you know those were there?" Lauren asked in amazement.

"Ramon always kept an extra set in his desk."

"And the combination to the padlock?" she asked as they left the shed, and he stopped to refasten the lock.

"Ramon used his birthdate. A long time ago, we bonded over cigarettes and tequila. Let's just hope they still work." He headed back toward the main building and inserted a key into a side door. He tensed, hoping he hadn't set off an alarm, but all was quiet. He walked in and quietly shut the door behind Lauren, who wasn't looking nearly as cocky as she had when she'd first come up with the idea. "You all right?"

"What if we get caught?"

"It's a little late to be worrying about that."

She tucked her hair behind her ear, a nervous

habit from years ago. "True. Though if someone catches us, I'm sure they'll think this was your idea, not mine."

He liked her smile. "Good point. Where's the art room?"

"Second floor."

They made their way upstairs and down the dark hall to Mrs. Weinstein's classroom. Shane tried several keys in the door, finally finding one that unlocked it. There was a small office at the back stocked with six file cabinets. His heart sank. This could take a long time. He had no idea if anyone patrolled the school at night, or if a nightly cleaning crew would descend on the building.

"You look through the cabinets. I'll keep watch by the door." He set the flashlight on the desk, pointing the beam toward the file cabinets. "And hurry."

"I'll do my best," she promised, reaching for the top drawer.

He returned to the classroom and stood near the door. There was no way to lock it from the inside, so if anyone came by, they'd be able to get in. There was a small square window at the top of the door that he could look through, but the interior hallway was in deep shadow.

The classroom was more like a workroom, with round tables and chairs, easels along one side, artwork dotting the walls, mobiles hanging from the ceiling. He'd never taken art while in school. He had absolutely no talent for anything creative, not like

Lauren. He could still remember the cake she'd made for his nineteenth birthday. She'd somehow made it into a sailboat with her name on the side. She'd laughed and said if a boat could be called the *Gabriella*, why not the *Lauren*?

They'd made love that night at the beach. He'd wanted her with a hunger and a desperation he could still remember. Even then, he'd known that whatever they had was going to be short-lived. She'd known it, too. Lying in his arms afterward, she'd asked him why he had to leave. He'd told her because he had to. She'd hated that answer, but he couldn't give her a better one. When she'd started to ask him more questions, he'd cut her off with a kiss. He'd used his hands, his tongue, his whole body to make her forget about the future, to make himself forget that one day the night would only be a memory.

A memory he still couldn't forget.

He started as a whistle broke the quiet, along with the sound of footsteps and something rolling down the hallway. He dashed into the back room, turned off the flashlight, and pulled Lauren down under the desk. She started to ask him something, but he put his hand against her lips.

The whistling grew louder. A locker slammed. He heard muffled voices. A door opened and closed. It was probably a janitorial service. They had to get out before the cleaning crew got to this classroom.

"Hurry," he told Lauren. "I don't think we have a lot of time."

Her eyes were big and worried. "Should we just go? There are a lot of files."

He didn't want this trip to be for nothing. "Five more minutes," he said, pulling her out from under the desk. He turned the flashlight back on, and they each pulled open a drawer. He rifled through the folders as fast as he could, shutting one drawer, then moving on to the next. Lauren worked just as quickly.

Finally she pulled out a thick manila envelope. "Got it," she said with relief. "There are stacks of photos inside."

"We'll go through them somewhere else."

"If Mrs. Weinstein goes looking for it, she'll know I took it," Lauren said.

"Hopefully that won't happen before we get the information we need." Shane grabbed the envelope out of her hand and stuffed it inside his jacket. "In case we get stopped," he said at her inquiring look.

"In which case *I* should be holding them. This was my idea."

And there was no way he would ever let her take the heat for this. "Do you want to argue, or do you want to get out of here?" He moved quickly toward the door and opened it a few inches. Two doors down across the hall, the lights were on.

He stepped out, Lauren right on his heels. He relocked the door and they walked quickly toward the stairwell. They jogged down the stairs and opened the outside door as quietly as possible. Then they broke into a run, not stopping until they got back to the shed. He returned the keys to the desk and resecured the padlock.

"I can't believe we did that," Lauren said, her hand creeping into his as they moved away from the shed. "I think my heart is about to jump out of my chest."

He didn't reply. He wouldn't take a real breath until they were on his bike and heading back to the marina.

They were just crossing the road between the buildings and the baseball field when a car suddenly turned onto the property, the headlights catching them dead center.

"Shit!" Shane could see the strobe lights on the roof of the car.

"Oh, my God, it's the police," Lauren said, panic in her voice, her fingers squeezing the blood out of his hand.

"Stay calm, and try not to act guilty."

"We *are* guilty."

"They don't know that." The car stopped a few feet away from them, and as the officer stepped out, Shane realized it was Jason Marlow. This might just be his lucky day. Jason and Kara were good friends, and he doubted Jason would want to arrest Kara's big brother.

"Who's there?" Jason asked sharply. "Shane, is that you?"

"It's me, and Lauren Jamison," Shane said as Jason moved forward. "You remember Lauren, don't you, Jason?"

"Lauren?" Jason repeated, his gaze settling on her face.

"Jason?" Lauren echoed. "Jason Marlow?"

"Right," he said with a nod. "I heard you were back in town." He gave them a considering look. "What are you two doing out here?"

"Just taking a trip down memory lane," Shane said.

"It might be easier to see in the daylight," Jason said, a note of suspicion in his voice.

Shane couldn't blame him. Jason wasn't a stupid man, and they had no good reason to be on school property. He was still thinking of something to say when Lauren jumped in.

"I'm glad we ran into you, Jason," she said. "I recently learned that you were better friends with my sister, Abby, than I realized. I wanted to ask you some questions."

Jason straightened. "About what?"

"About your relationship with her. Lisa said that she and Abby hung out with you a few times, including two nights before Abby was killed. Lisa didn't mention it before because she didn't want to get in trouble for leaving her house. But I don't remember you coming forward and sharing that information."

Jason shrugged his shoulders. "Nothing to come forward about. I drove them around. We checked out a party and listened to music in my car. Then they went back to Lisa's house. That was it."

"Did you like Abby? Did she like you?"

"We were friends."

"Close friends?" Lauren persisted.

"Not particularly. I assume these questions are coming up because you've spoken to Mark Devlin about his movie. I wouldn't put much credence in what he says. He's making things up as he goes along." Jason paused. "What are you two really up to out here?"

"Like Shane said, I just wanted to drive around town, relive some old memories," Lauren replied.

"We used to make out behind the grandstand," Shane added.

"Don't tell him that," Lauren protested.

He was happy she was playing along. "And behind the gym, under the bleachers, by the tennis courts—"

"Enough! You're embarrassing me. We should go—my father is probably wondering where I am."

"Lauren, our department is working on your sister's case," Jason said. "If anything was missed, we're going to find it."

"I appreciate that. If there *is* anything that you knew about Abby that you didn't tell anyone, I hope you'll reconsider. She deserves justice. It's been a long time coming."

"I wish I could help," Jason replied. "But I'm sure you knew your sister better than anyone." He walked back to his patrol car and got behind the wheel.

"He's not leaving," Lauren muttered as they returned to the motorcycle. "He's watching us."

"And he'll see us go," Shane said as they strapped on their helmets, then sped down the road.

Jason's patrol car followed them back downtown and veered off as Shane pulled into the harbor parking lot. They walked quickly down the docks and onto his boat.

Shane followed Lauren down the stairs, turning on the interior cabin lights and shutting the door behind them.

Her cheeks were red, her hair mussed from the helmet and the wind, and there was a bright gleam in her eyes.

"Oh, my God," she said. "That was terrifying and strangely exhilarating."

Shane smiled. "Life in the fast lane, baby."

"I've never done anything like that before, not even when we were in high school. You got into trouble without me. You never took me along."

"I never wanted you to be in trouble."

"And you were going to take the blame for me tonight. That's why you put the envelope in your jacket."

"Nah. I just didn't want you to drop the damn pictures, after all the effort it took to get them."

She leaned into him, planting a hot kiss on his mouth. "Thank you for protecting me."

His mouth was still tingling when she pulled away.

"I can't believe Jason Marlow caught us," she said. "His name keeps popping up every time I turn around. You talked to him like you know him."

"I do know him. He's been friends with Kara and

Colin for years. Jason's been by her side a lot since Colin's injury, so I've run into him a few times. I've never had a deep conversation with him, but Kara likes him, and she's a good judge of character."

"Lisa implied that Jason had a thing for Kara."

"Maybe so, but she married his best friend. I'm glad he's the one who caught us. I figured his relationship with Kara would keep him from dragging us down to the police station for questioning."

"He was suspicious."

"But you cleverly threw him off by putting him on the defensive. I think he was as eager to get away from you as you were to get away from him."

"I wonder why, if he has nothing to hide," Lauren mused.

Shane unzipped his jacket and pulled out the envelope. "Hopefully we'll find out. Let's see how many times Jason popped up in front of Abby's camera." He dumped the pictures onto the middle of the bed. Some were rubber-banded together with sticky notes detailing the date and the event, others were loose, but there had to be at least a hundred.

Lauren sat on one side of the bed and stared at the photographs. "I'm almost afraid to look." She lifted her gaze to his. "I feel like I'm standing on the edge of a cliff. I can't back away, but I also can't jump. I'm afraid of what I'll find, yet I'm scared I won't find anything at all, and this will have been a big waste of time."

"Not knowing is harder than knowing—whatever the truth may be."

"I'm not sure that's true."

He wasn't sure, either. Some secrets were better left untouched. But he knew Lauren would drive herself crazy if she didn't finish what she'd started. "Let's find out." He settled on the bed across from her. "How do you want to attack this?"

"I guess we should start piles for people whose pictures repeat. We don't need any posed pictures of sports teams or clubs. Let's concentrate on the candids."

They worked quietly for about ten minutes. Shane knew a lot of the kids in the photographs, most of whom he hadn't seen in years. He was surprised by some of the couples featured in the pictures. He'd been so caught up in his own problems in high school, he'd tuned out the rest of the world. He'd had hook-ups, not relationships. And once he quit playing sports, he'd had little in common with his male friends. He'd spent most of his time on his bike or on his dad's boat, dreaming of sailing off into the horizon. He'd wanted to be anywhere but Angel's Bay—until he'd met Lauren. The year that Abby died he hadn't been in school; he'd been working for his father.

"All I've learned so far is that Pamela Baines was a big slut," Lauren announced. "Five pictures with her tongue in a different guy's mouth."

Shane cleared his throat. Lauren gave him a quick glance.

"No, you're not one of them." Her eyebrow arched. *"Were* you one of them?"

"I don't remember." He gazed back at the photo in his hand, a smile curving his lips. "Here's one of us at that car wash fundraiser. You look hot in your shorts, and you look like you want to eat me up."

She took the picture and blushed. "Oh, my God, I look like a lovesick puppy. How could you stand me?"

He laughed. "You were cute."

"I can't believe Abby took this picture! How embarrassing."

He grabbed the photo from her hand. "I can't believe I never figured out a way to get your T-shirt wet. What a waste of a car wash."

"Thank heavens that shot didn't make the yearbook. Anyone would think—"

"That you were in love with me?" he offered.

"Let's move on, shall we?"

When she looked back at the pictures on the bed, he slipped the car wash one onto the night table.

A moment later Lauren said, "There are quite a few shots of Jason, usually with Kara and Colin, but a few alone. Here's one with Lisa and Jason, and—" She stopped and pulled out another picture. "Jason and Abby." She held it out.

Jason had his arm around Abby and the two were smiling. The photo had been taken at some beach, a bonfire burning off to the side. "Jason said he knew Abby. This doesn't prove anything," Shane pointed out.

"What about the rest?" she asked, holding up the

pile. "I think Jason was her crush. Why else would she take so many pictures of him?"

Shane handed her the pictures he'd collected. "I wouldn't jump to any conclusions yet. Coach Sorensen was also a popular shot."

Lauren frowned. "Maybe she just wanted to make sure the volleyball team got enough coverage in the yearbook."

"They're not all at volleyball games. There are a couple of him in the stands at the basketball game, and at a pizza parlor with some other girls."

"Volleyball players," Lauren said. "It must have been a team party."

"Here are some from what appears to be a hotel room."

"One of the away tournaments. But these shots aren't of Abby and the coach. He's with other girls in every single picture. We don't know if she was taking shots of him or of her friends."

Lauren was definitely fighting the idea that Abby could have been involved with her coach, and Shane couldn't blame her. He didn't like that scenario much, either.

She sighed. "This was a dumb idea."

"We're not done yet. Don't give up."

"I've seen enough." She scooped up the photos and began shoving them back into the envelope. "I can't do this anymore. I can't keep imagining Abby and a married man—" She swore as the envelope ripped.

Shane put his hand over hers, stilling her frantic

action, and pulled the envelope out of her grip. He set it on the table, then hauled her into his arms. She resisted for only a fraction of a second and then gave in, resting her head on his chest, sliding her arms around his waist.

He held her trembling body against his. She was struggling to keep it all in. He wished he could do something to ease her turmoil, but there were no words that could take away her pain, so he just held on tight as she cried. Her small, muffled sobs tore him apart. When she'd first lost Abby he'd wanted to hold her, but she'd pushed him away. He'd give her what comfort he could now.

Finally she was spent, and he got up to get her some tissues. She blew her nose, then stretched out on her side, closing her eyes. "I'm so tired. I just have to close my eyes for a minute."

He pulled a blanket off the bottom of the bed and covered her with it. Then he stretched out beside her, putting his arm around her waist. Her hair tickled his nose, and as he inhaled the scent of her shampoo, he knew he was never going to forget her sweet smell, no matter where he went or what he did. She'd gotten under his skin, into his heart. They might not have forever, but for now, he'd hold on to her until he had to let go.

"Shane," she murmured.

He tightened his hold on her. "What?"

"I did love you back then."

"I know." He just wished she loved him now.

SEVENTEEN

Joe awoke to what he thought was the sound of sirens. He rubbed his eyes and glanced at the clock. One thirty-five, and it was quiet now. Had he been dreaming?

Then the phone rang. Adrenaline surged through his body and he grabbed the receiver. "Silveira."

Jason Marlow was on the other end, and Joe listened to his report with growing uneasiness. "Thanks. I'll be there as soon as I can." He hung up, his heart beating hard and fast. He stood up, grabbed his uniform out of the closet, and began to get dressed.

Rachel sat up, blinking the sleep out of her eyes. "Joe? What's going on? Is something wrong?"

"Yes."

"Do you have to go to the station?"

"Not the station, the hospital." He buttoned his shirt, stalling for a moment. He had to tell her, but he really didn't want to.

"What's happened?"

"Rachel, you need to get dressed and come with me." He reached for his jacket and put it on.

"Why? The only people I know in this town are you and . . ." Her voice trailed away.

He saw the sudden fear in her eyes and moved back to the bed. He sat on the edge of the mattress, taking her hands in his. "It's Mark."

She immediately shook her head in disbelief. "No."

"He was in an accident. He's being taken to the trauma center in Montgomery."

"That's not possible. I spoke to Mark an hour ago, right before we went to bed. He was fine. He was just going to have a drink at the bar. He was fine," she repeated, desperate to make it true.

"He was hit by a car, honey," Joe said gently.

"Oh, God." She put a hand to her mouth. "Is it bad?"

"It's very serious. Do you know where his family is? We need to contact them."

"They're all on the East Coast, in New York and Connecticut." Rachel climbed out of bed and began to throw on her clothes. "Mark will be all right," she said with determination. "He's young, strong, and healthy. He'll survive this."

Five minutes later they were on the road. The drive to the trauma center reminded Joe of the last time he'd made this trip in the middle of the night, when Colin had been shot. Then he'd had Kara in the passenger seat. Kara hadn't spoken a word the entire time, but he'd felt her panic as well as his own. He could feel Rachel's fear now.

He wanted to comfort her, but she seemed completely closed off. Her gaze was turned toward the window, her arms folded across her chest. He had no idea what she was thinking, which wasn't unusual since he didn't have any idea what she was thinking most days. They'd once shared every thought. Now they rarely shared dinner. But she was his wife and he was her husband, and that stood for something, didn't it?

He'd married with every intention of staying with her forever. He'd never taken his commitment lightly; he'd never been unfaithful. And he believed she'd been faithful to him, but there was no question that they'd drifted apart. Even though they'd both said they wanted to get the marriage back on track, neither of them seemed able to make that happen. Their sex life was more habit than passion. But maybe that was to be expected since they'd been together for years. Passion died down, didn't it?

Or was he just making excuses? That's all he seemed to do lately. He shook the thought out of his head and concentrated on the dark highway.

When they reached the hospital they were told Devlin was in surgery, so they went up to the third-floor waiting room. It was empty, the hospital eerily quiet.

Rachel sat down while Joe got Jason back on the phone. "We're at the hospital now," he said. "Can you give me more details on the accident?"

"Mr. Devlin left Murray's Bar at approximately one a.m. He was struck near the corner of Second Street. Roger Harlan saw a car speeding away but couldn't give any further details. He found Mr. Devlin in the street and called 911. The paramedics and I arrived about three minutes later," Jason reported.

"How's he doing?"

"He's in surgery. Was he conscious at the scene?"

"He mumbled a few words, but I couldn't make sense of them. I'm at the bar now, trying to find out if anyone had an altercation with him or if anyone left drunk. I'll check out the Blue Pelican and the Sunset Bar, as well."

"Keep me posted." Joe ended the call with a bad feeling in the pit of his stomach. Mark Devlin had been stirring up trouble in Angel's Bay for weeks. Maybe someone wanted to scare him off, or shut him up for good.

Rachel gave him an inquiring look. Her white skin was even paler under the harsh lights and her dark eyes were filled with concern.

"Hit-and-run," he said. "We don't know anything yet."

"Someone hit him and left?" she asked in surprise. "Do you think it was deliberate, Joe?"

"It's possible. He's been all over town questioning people about a murder."

"You have to find who did this to him."

"I will. Don't worry about it now."

"I can't stop worrying." She dropped her gaze to her clenched hands. "I feel so helpless. I just want to make it right. Mark is a good guy. I know you don't like him, but he's a great person." Her voice caught and she choked on a sob.

He sat next to her, putting his arm around her shoulders. "It's going to be okay, honey."

"You don't know that." She shrugged off his arm and stood up. "I need to use the restroom."

She didn't return for nearly fifteen minutes, and when she did, she sat in a chair across from him. There was barely three feet between them, but Joe felt like they were on opposite ends of the earth.

"Rachel," he began.

"Don't," she said quickly, her gaze meeting his. "I can't talk right now. You don't even like Mark."

"I don't dislike him. I certainly don't want him to be hurt."

"Fine, but I just want to concentrate on Mark making it through surgery." She leaned back in her chair and closed her eyes.

He watched her for more than an hour. He didn't know if she was asleep or praying, but she was definitely somewhere far away from him.

Finally a doctor came into the room dressed in surgical garb. Rachel jumped to her feet and Joe followed, hoping there would be good news.

The doctor was a man in his early thirties by the name of Ron Waxman. He was reluctant to give them any information since they weren't family, but Joe's badge persuaded him.

"Mr. Devlin has fractures in both legs," Dr. Waxman stated. "He also suffered a broken rib, a concussion, and some internal bleeding. We were able to stop the bleeding. His condition is serious but stable, and we believe his prognosis is good."

Rachel let out a breath. "Can I see him?"

"He'll be asleep for several hours. You might want to come back tomorrow."

"I'm not leaving," Rachel said immediately.

"I'll have the nurse get you when he's out of recovery," the doctor replied.

"Rachel, we should come back in the morning," Joe said when they were alone. "You're exhausted."

"I don't care. You can leave. I'll take a cab when I'm ready to go home."

"I'll stay with you."

"No, you have to work in a few hours, and I want you to find whoever did this to Mark. You should get some sleep."

He was reluctant to leave her alone; he needed to show her that he was there for her. "If you're staying, I'm staying."

She stared at him for a long moment. "Okay." She sat back down in her chair.

He took the seat next to her and put his arm around her shoulders once again. She resisted for a moment, then rested her head on his chest.

"I'm so scared," she said. "This is my fault. I got Mark involved in Angel's Bay. I encouraged him to spend time here because it was nice to have a friend nearby. Now he's hurt."

"It's not your fault, Rachel. And this may be just an accident."

"I don't think it was."

He didn't, either.

It was dawn when the nurse came to get them. Mark was awake but dazed when they entered his room. He had casts on both legs, a bandage around his head, and was hooked up to IVs and a heart monitor. His face was bruised, and he looked like hell.

Rachel put her hand on Mark's arm. "You're going to be all right. Just rest, and I'll be here when you wake up."

The look on Rachel's face made Joe's stomach turn over. She clearly had feelings for Mark. But how deep did those feelings go? Was it just the concern of friendship, or something more?

Rachel caught his stare, read his mind. "He's just a friend, Joe. A really good friend."

Was she lying to him? Or was she lying to herself?

"I'm going to work," he said abruptly. He needed to leave before he said something he couldn't take back.

Lauren slipped out of Shane's bed just as the dawn light streamed through the windows. Shane was still asleep, his thick hair mussed from the pillow, a shadow of beard on his jaw, and his beautiful lips slightly parted. Her heart ached with a yearning that only got worse the more time they spent together. The boy she'd hated was blurring with the boy she'd once loved and the man she was getting to know. What had once seemed so black and white was now a confusing gray.

Shane suddenly stretched and opened his eyes. She should have left when she had the chance.

"Sneaking out?" he asked her, his morning voice undeniably sexy.

"I was trying not to wake you up."

"What's your hurry? Are you sure you don't want to stay and have some . . . breakfast?"

Desire swept through her at his barely veiled invitation. By the look in his eyes, he wasn't talking about pancakes.

"I have to go." She didn't even bother to make up an excuse, because they both knew why she was leaving. "Don't ask me to stay." As she said the words, they echoed in her mind. But she wasn't the one who had said them before; he was. "That's what you told me the last time we were together. You said, 'Don't ask me to stay in Angel's Bay for you, Lauren, because I can't.'" She gave him a thoughtful look. "Why couldn't you stay for me? Or why couldn't you ask me to go with you? I might have said yes."

He sat up, his dark gaze on her. "I needed to leave town. I needed to breathe different air, to be around people who didn't know me, who didn't have any expectations."

"I wasn't expecting you to marry me. I was seventeen."

"It wasn't just your expectations. I had other issues."

"Other secrets," she said with a nod. "They're always between us—even now. How could I ever be with a man who won't let me all the way in, who can't trust me with his soul? I can't, Shane. I deserve more than that."

The color left his face, his jaw setting in that familiar forbidding line. She willed him to speak, but he remained silent.

There was nothing to do but leave.

Charlotte had seen Joe at the Water's Edge Fitness Center a few times, a perk of her early morning workout. She usually hit the streets for a jog, but the weather had turned and the cold fog had sent her indoors. She'd finished off an hour on the elliptical machine and was headed for a shower when she saw Joe working a punching bag.

He wore black shorts and a gray tank top with LAPD on the front. His arms were muscled and tan, his legs just as strong, and he wasn't carrying an extra ounce of weight. But he did appear to be carrying an unusual amount of pent-up energy; he was beating the crap out of the punching bag. She'd never seen him so physical before, and so very, very male.

Feeling hot from her workout and her thoughts, she grabbed a paper cup at the water cooler and filled it, then turned her back to drink it. She had no business ogling a married man, but she couldn't help wondering what had gotten him worked up. He was usually so calm and even tempered when she saw him, though that was usually when he was on the job. She'd always suspected he had a hot side.

While she sipped her water she took a look at the bulletin board, hoping for a distraction. Maybe she'd vary from her usual solitary exercise routine and take a kick-boxing class. Or maybe she could go a few rounds with Joe—boxing, of course! She bit back a smile at her thoughts and tossed her cup into the trash. As she turned around, she saw Joe heading toward her. He had a towel around his neck now and was wiping away the sweat from his forehead.

"Charlotte," he said, an odd note in his voice.

"Joe." She cleared her throat. "Did the punching bag survive? You were pounding the hell out of it."

"I had a rough night."

"Anything you can talk about?"

He hesitated. "I'm sure you'll hear the news as soon as you leave here. Mark Devlin was hit by a car last night. He's in the hospital in serious condition."

She was shocked. She hadn't spoken to anyone on her way to the gym, nor had she picked up the morning newspaper. "That's terrible."

"I doubt it was an accident. He's pissed a lot of people off."

"That's true, but it's difficult to believe someone would deliberately run him down."

"Maybe someone who didn't like his questions."

"Like the person who killed Abby. That would mean he's still here in town." A shiver ran down her spine. "Do you think you can find him?"

"I'm going to do my best."

"I'd love to help."

He gave her that slow smile that always made her heart beat a little faster. "You already have."

"How's that?"

"You're a good listener."

She studied his weary face and wondered if Mark Devlin's accident was all that was bothering him. "You must not have gotten much sleep last night."

"About an hour. And it's going to be a long day."

"Why don't you let me buy you a cup of coffee? They make a great vanilla latte at the snack bar."

"I don't go for whipped cream drinks."

"Not macho enough, huh?" she teased. "I think they have straight black coffee, too."

"Can I have a rain check? I need to get to work."

"Any time." She paused. "Your wife must be really upset about Mr. Devlin. They're good friends, aren't they?"

"She hasn't left his side," he said heavily.

And as he walked away, Charlotte had a feeling he'd just given her the real reason he hadn't slept all night.

Lauren slept for a few hours, showered and dressed, then headed down to Dina's Café to find her father and, she hoped, some lunch. She felt restless and unsettled, her mood amplified by the dark storm clouds blowing in from the ocean. The photographs she'd looked at hadn't provided the definitive evidence she'd been hoping for. She needed to go through the rest of them, but she'd left the envelope on Shane's boat. She'd go by later, maybe take her father as a buffer.

She picked up her pace, taking side streets to avoid the marina and to drop some bills off at the post office. At least she could keep her father's lights and electricity on while she figured out how to handle his living situation. As she turned down the next street, she came face-to-face with yet another of her past dreams.

Martha's Cakes and Cookies. The bakery was now just an empty storefront. Its name was still etched on the glass, but the counters were empty, the wallpaper peeling, and the floor was covered in dust. She'd worked at Martha's all through high school, helping sixty-five-year-old Martha and her daughter, Rosemary, make cakes and pastries. She'd told Martha that when she grew up, she was going to open her own bakery and they'd have cookie wars.

But Martha had died two years ago and Rosemary had moved, and no one had wanted to keep the bakery alive. It was a shame. It had a great location, not far from the marina. The local fishermen always picked up hot breads before their early morning trips. And the elementary school was only a few blocks in the other direction. Her mother had often taken her and Abby to Martha's after school for a treat.

As Lauren looked through the dirty windows, she imagined fresh paint on the walls, shiny counters, and sparkling glass shelves stocked with cookies, pastries, cakes, and pies. She could see small tables set up and a coffee bar in one corner. In nice weather there would be more tables outside, with bright red umbrellas over them.

She gave herself a mental kick at her wayward thoughts. She was *not* going to refurbish Martha's. Just because she could see the possibilities didn't mean she should do it. She had a job she liked in San Francisco, a job that she would need to get back to next week. She had her own bills to keep up with.

Dina's Café was just around the corner, and as she stepped inside she saw her father and his friends at their corner table by the window, where they could see all the comings and goings. The warm, inviting restaurant had both character and good food. The dining room was decorated with assorted knickknacks that Dina picked up whenever she went antiquing, and they were displayed on every available counter and wall space. There were a dozen or so tables, and a long counter with bar stools fronted the kitchen. Almost every seat was taken, and the smell of pancakes and bacon was in the air.

Her father waved her over with a cheerful smile. "Lauren. You remember Mort," he said as she joined them.

"Yes, hello."

"And this is Will Pachowsky and Don Lowenstein," he added. "Fishing buddies of mine."

"It's nice to meet you all," she said with a smile.

Her father grabbed a chair from a nearby table. "Have a seat. Don just made an incredible discovery," he added, excitement in his voice. "Show her, Don."

As Lauren sat down at the table, the white-haired man held up what appeared to be a gold coin. "I found a half dozen of them on the beach," he said. "They're from the *Gabriella*."

"Really?" Her heart leaped with anticipation. As a teenager she'd gone diving with her friends in search of missing treasure, and they'd routinely scoured the beaches and the rocks at low tide. They'd never found anything of interest, but they'd always had high hopes.

"Check out the date," her father told her.

Don handed her a coin. The numbers jumped out at her, 1849; the ship had gone down in 1850. Of course, many other Gold Rush ships had made their way down the coast, too.

"Can't you feel the pull of the past, Lauren?" her father asked. "When I held the coin in my hand, I felt like it was taking me back in time."

As the men began talking among themselves, the coin actually grew warm in her hand. As she stared down at it the symbols and words started to blur, and she felt shaky, almost off balance.

The boat pitched beneath her feet. It was all she could do to stay upright. Tommy was desperately trying to steer them through the storm, but the waves were too big, the ocean too angry. He looked over at her, and in his dark eyes she could see the world ending. Her big, strong man, the love of her life, was afraid—and he was never, ever scared.

"We'll be okay, Tommy. We'll make it," she said.

One of the other sailors grabbed the wheel as Tommy

came toward her. He pulled a velvet pouch out of his pocket and handed it to her. "You'll need this," he said.

"No." She knew what he was trying to do. "We're going to make it through this storm."

"We're filling the lifeboats now. You and Jeremy will be on the next one."

"Not without you."

"Leonora, I'm the captain. I go last."

Which meant he wouldn't go at all. They both knew the boat had taken on too many passengers.

"We have to stay together," she pleaded.

He closed her fingers around the sack of coins. "There's enough money for you to start over, to raise your son, to have a life."

"Not without you." She shook her head, tears sliding down her face. "We fought so hard to find each other again. I can't lose you now." She had left her life behind to run away with him, to be with her one true love. God couldn't be so cruel as to take him now, before they'd had a chance to really live, to really love.

"If I could stay with you, I would." His dark gaze bored into hers. "But you have a son, and he needs you to live. Go now, Leonora. Before it's too late."

She didn't have a choice. She was a mother first. "We'll find each other again," she promised. "Someday, we'll be together the way we were meant to be."

"Lauren? Lauren?"

She jolted, suddenly aware that her father and the other men were staring at her.

"Are you all right?" her father asked with concern.

She set the coin on the table with a shaky hand. What the hell had just happened? She'd felt as if she were Leonora. The coins—were they the same ones that had come with Leonora to the shore?

"You felt the draw, didn't you?" her father asked.

She'd felt something—something very strange.

"Who needs coffee?" Dina asked as she stopped by their table with a pot in hand. Dina's hair had grayed and she'd put on some weight over the years, but her generous smile was just the same. "Lauren, I didn't see you come in. My goodness, honey, you look white as a sheet. Are you feeling all right?"

"Coffee, please." Lauren's voice was hoarse, as if she'd been screaming into the wind like Leonora, begging her lover to come with her. After Dina filled her cup, she took a gulp to clear her head.

"Can I get you something to eat, hon?" Dina asked. "Cheeseburger and fries, maybe?"

"You read my mind."

"They were always your favorite."

"How could you possibly remember that?" Lauren asked in amazement.

"I remember all my customers. I'll tell Sam to put extra pickles on your burger."

"Sold," Lauren said.

Joe Silveira entered the café. He wore a suit and tie today, and there was grim determination on his face. She tensed, wondering if Jason had told him about catching her and Shane at the high school last night.

"Hello," he said as he stopped by their table. "Ms. Jamison, may I speak to you for a moment—outside?"

"Of course," she said, getting to her feet.

"Is something wrong, Chief?" her father asked. "Is this about that Devlin fellow?"

"Your daughter will fill you in." Joe waved her toward the door.

"What did my father mean?" Lauren asked as they stepped onto the sidewalk. "What's up with Mr. Devlin?"

"You didn't hear?"

"I just got to the café five minutes ago."

"Mr. Devlin was hit by a car last night. He's in the hospital in Montgomery. His condition is serious."

"My God!"

"I don't believe it was an accident," the chief continued, his gaze sober.

"You think someone tried to *kill* him?" she asked slowly.

"Or scare him off. Either way, he's going to be out of commission for a while."

"Why did you want to talk to me?" He didn't think she was responsible for the accident, did he?

"To tell you to be careful. Someone is getting nervous."

"Do you have any idea who that is?"

"I have a few thoughts." He paused. "By the way, where were you last night around one o'clock in the morning?"

"I was on Shane Murray's boat. We were together."

"Did you drive to the marina?"

"No, I walked."

"So your car was parked in front of your father's house all night?"

"It still is," she said.

He nodded. "I stopped by your house before I came here. If you see Mr. Murray, let him know I'd like to talk to him. I left him a message, but apparently he's out at sea."

"Shane doesn't even have a car."

"I'd still like to speak to him."

She watched him walk away. It was a good thing Jason Marlow had followed them from the high school to the marina; he could attest to their whereabouts. If Jason was on patrol all night, he was probably the officer who had responded to the scene of the accident. How ironic that a man who had every reason to be unhappy with Mark Devlin's movie was the one called to save his life.

She shivered as a gust of wind rocketed down the street. There was definitely a storm coming . . . or maybe it was already here.

EIGHTEEN

Colin's room felt cold, and Kara tucked the blanket around his body. She glanced toward the window, noting the spatter of raindrops across the window. She'd never liked storms. She preferred bright sunny days filled with promise. It was only a little after two o'clock in the afternoon, but it felt like ten o'clock at night. She turned on the bedside lamp, trying to warm up the room and erase the sense of foreboding that had been weighing her down the last few days.

The door opened and one of the nurses popped in. "Everything all right, Mrs. Lynch? Can I get you anything?"

"No, I'm fine. I'll probably spend the afternoon here." She'd brought along her needlework. She knew her mother's friends were making a quilt for the baby, but she'd wanted to make something special as well, something to be passed down from mother to daughter.

The nurse smiled and pulled the door shut. Kara

moved a chair closer to Colin's bed and sat down, feeling weary. She picked up Colin's left hand and played with the gold wedding band on his finger. The nurse had taken it off during his initial surgeries, but Kara had put it back on, wanting to keep that bond between them. It had gotten loose in the past few weeks. She was afraid if he got any thinner it would fall off, and she couldn't bear the thought of that. It would be another symbol that she was fighting a losing battle. But she *couldn't* give up.

She rubbed her abdomen; her muscles felt tight and crampy. A tiny foot kicked against her rib cage. "It's okay, baby. I know you're getting impatient, but we have to wait for your daddy."

Her body felt so warm compared to Colin's hand. She rubbed his fingers, trying to increase his circulation. He got physical therapy three times a week. Had anyone been in today? She got up to check with the nurse, and suddenly she felt a swoosh of fluid between her legs, followed by a sharp abdominal pain.

She gasped, realizing that her water had just broken.

"No," she said in shock, putting her hand to her abdomen. She sank back down on her chair, feeling panicked. She couldn't go into labor now; she wasn't ready. But the water on the floor told her it was too late.

Drawing in several deep breaths of air, she gathered her strength. Okay, if this was it—this was it. She scooted her chair up against the bed and grabbed Colin's hand again, squeezing his fingers tightly. "You have to wake up," she said forcefully. "It's time. I'm going into labor. Our baby is coming."

He didn't respond, not even the tiniest flicker of his eyelid. She stood and pressed his hand to her belly. If he felt the baby, somewhere in his mind he would know that he had to wake up. The childbirth instructor had told her that first labors could last hours, and she wasn't leaving until he opened his eyes. He'd be there to see their baby come into the world. She wasn't going to do it without him.

Shane brought his fishing charter back at four o'clock, the large waves having sent one burly ex-football player heaving over the side. It wasn't much of a storm yet, but too big for a pleasure trip. He was relieved, actually. His mind was on Lauren, and for the first time in a long time he'd been eager to get back on land.

He'd spent most of the day thinking about what she'd said to him, how she couldn't give her heart to a man who couldn't be completely honest with her. He didn't blame her. He'd wanted to tell her the truth for years, and maybe it was time to do just that.

The idea had been brewing in his mind for a while. Before he could talk to Lauren, though, he had to see Kara. She was the most vulnerable member of his family right now. He needed to feel her out, to see if she could handle what might follow.

He parked his motorcycle at the Bayview Care Center and entered the long-term-care facility. A couple of elderly people sat in wheelchairs in the lobby, one watching television, the other staring into space. While the room was decorated in warm, happy colors, there was no disguising the medicinal smells or the scent of sickness. How could Kara stand to come here every day?

The fact that Colin was even here was a crime. He was in the prime of his life. He had a wife and a baby on the way. He shouldn't be lying in a bed, with no purpose or joy to his existence.

After getting off the elevator, Shane walked down to the end of the quiet corridor. Colin's door was closed, so he gave a short knock, then pushed it open.

Kara sat next to the bed, her hand in Colin's. When she saw Shane, her eyes widened with fear. There was a fine sheen of perspiration on her forehead, and the hair that fell against her face was also damp. There was more than fear in her eyes; there was pain.

"He has to wake up, Shane," she said, desperation in her tone. "Dammit, Colin, wake up!" Her voice broke in defeat.

Whatever composure Kara had been hanging on to all these months had snapped. She was obviously on the edge of a breakdown; he needed to get her out of this room. "Why don't we get some coffee, take a break?"

She shook her head and bit down on her bottom lip, a moan escaping. Her pain wasn't just emotional, it was also physical.

"Kara, what's going on?" He rushed to her side.

She drew in quick, sharp breaths, her hand pressed against her abdomen, and he suddenly realized . . . "Oh, my God, you're in labor, aren't you?"

"I'm just having a few cramps. I'm fine."

He saw the lie in her eyes. "I need to take you to the hospital."

"I'm not leaving," she said with stubborn determination. "Colin will sense that the baby is coming, and he'll wake up. I *have* to stay here, Shane."

She was beyond reason. He had to get her to the hospital, but aside from physically throwing her over his shoulder, he wasn't sure how to do that. "I'll call the nurse, then."

She grabbed his arm. "Don't you dare! She'll get some orderlies to drag me out of here, and I'm not going. If you love me at all, you will not call the nurse."

He had to call *someone*. "What about Charlotte?"

"Not yet. I have lots of time, Shane. It's not that bad, really."

"Okay, but I am calling Lauren. You need a woman here with you." This was definitely not his area.

She gave a weary nod. "Fine, but don't tell her I'm in labor."

Shane punched in the number of Lauren's house. It was still burned into his brain from his high school years. She answered on the third ring. "Lauren, I need you."

He heard her quick intake of breath. Then she said, "Where are you?"

"Bayview Care Center, room twelve, second floor. I'm with Kara."

"What's happening?"

"Just come," he said, hanging up the phone. "She's on her way," he told Kara.

"You still love her, don't you?" Kara asked, her eyes searching his face.

"I don't know."

"Yes, you do, Shane. Why are you so afraid to admit it to yourself? Or better yet, tell her?"

"There are things between us. I haven't been honest with her, and she's moved on. She's planning to leave next week."

"So make her change her plans. Whatever it is you've been keeping from her, tell her. And don't wait too long. Life is short." She glanced over at Colin. "There are so many things I wish I'd said to him. You think you have time, but you never really know if you do." She bit down on her bottom lip again and closed her eyes.

Shane put his arm around her. "Just breathe. You can do it."

A moment later the pain seemed to ease, and she looked at him through teary eyes. "I'm glad you're here."

He was wishing he was anywhere else. But she was his little sister, and he couldn't let her do this alone. He just hoped that Lauren could talk her into getting help.

"What else is going on with you, Shane?" Kara asked. "There's something between you and our parents. I can feel the tension every time you're near each other, especially when Mom is in the room."

"You're imagining things." He couldn't get into this now; Kara had enough to worry about.

"I'm not," she said, shaking her head. "Dee, Michael, they've both noticed it, too. Even Dad, I think, although he's always kind of adorably clueless. Can't you tell me? Maybe I could help."

He shook his head. "That's a story for another day."

"*Will* you tell it another day? Or just stonewall me?"

"I don't want you or anyone else to get hurt."

"Like you've been hurt?" she asked, her gaze searching his face.

"Me? I'm fine," he replied, wishing she wasn't trying to distract herself with his problems.

Kara gave him a shaky smile. "You always say that, but it's not true."

"It's not true for you, either, Kara. You need medical attention. You can't just wish this labor away."

"Later," she promised. "Give Colin a chance. I know he's coming back to me."

Shane got to his feet as Lauren flew through the door. Her hair was damp from the rain, her blue eyes worried. He'd never been so happy to see her.

"What's wrong?" She looked from Kara to him.

"Kara is in labor, and she doesn't want to leave," he said shortly.

"Colin knows I'm here," Kara told Lauren. "When the contractions come, I put his hand on my belly so he can feel the baby. I read about a man who woke up when his wife went into labor. He knew he was needed, and that's going to happen to Colin. That's why I'm staying here."

He could see by Lauren's expression that she was just as flummoxed by Kara's declaration as he was.

"We should call Charlotte," Lauren said immediately.

Kara shook her head. "No way. She'll try to make me go to the hospital."

"We could just ask her how long she thinks you have before the baby comes," Lauren said. "I know you want Colin to wake up, Kara, but you have to think about your child, too. You don't want to do anything to jeopardize your baby's life."

"The baby is fine," Kara said firmly. "She's kicking. I can feel her. She wants to see her daddy. Oh, God, here comes another one." Kara grabbed Colin's hand and put it on her abdomen as she gritted her teeth against the pain.

Shane couldn't stand it a second more. He was not going to sit idly by while his sister made a huge mistake. He grabbed Kara's purse, pulled out her cell phone, and found Charlotte's numbers. Kara was too caught up in her contraction to stop him. He reached the receptionist in Charlotte's office and told her it was an emergency. A moment later, Charlotte's voice came over the line.

"It's Shane," he said. "Kara is in labor. She's in Colin's room, and she won't leave."

"When did it start and how often are the contractions?" Charlotte asked.

He looked to Kara. "How long have you been in pain?"

"I told you not to call her."

"Answer the question," he ordered.

"A little while. We have plenty of time for Colin to wake up. First babies take forever to be born."

He gave his sister a grim look. "She says not long, Charlotte, but I don't believe her."

"She can't have her baby at a long-term-care facility. They're not set up for that," Charlotte said.

"Well, unless you want me to throw her pregnant body over my shoulder, you're going to have to come here and tell her that."

"I'll be there in ten minutes. In the meantime, keep her calm, comfortable, and time her contractions."

Shane hung up the phone. "She's on her way."

Kara glared at him. "I hate you."

"I don't care. You need a doctor."

Kara stood up and leaned over the bed, cupping Colin's face. "It's time to wake up, honey. This is it—our big moment. Our little miracle is ready to be born." She pressed her mouth to his lips. "Come back to me," she whispered. "Come back to us."

Kara's pains began coming one on top of the other. Lauren held her hand and offered reassurances while

Shane paced around the room. She'd never seen him so rattled, but couldn't blame him. She was counting the seconds for Charlotte to arrive. The medical center was only a couple of miles away and Charlotte should have been here by now.

Shane sent her a pleading look, clearly wanting her to do something, but she didn't know how to answer him. When Kara wasn't gasping for breath, she was talking to Colin, telling him she needed him, that their baby needed her father. Every word made Lauren's heart break.

"Kara, let me take you to the hospital." Lauren tried again. "You don't want to have your baby here. Or I could get one of the nurses or doctors to give you something for the pain."

"I don't want drugs. I have to be alert for Colin. And if either of you leaves this room to get someone, I will never speak to you again." Kara's fierce gaze turned desperate as she looked at Colin. "Honey, please, I can't wait much longer." She gripped his fingers tightly. "I *need* you."

Lauren walked over to Shane. "She's so stubborn. I hope Charlotte can get through to her."

"So do I. This is killing me."

"It's killing her. She can't accept that Colin might miss this."

"He might miss everything," Shane said grimly.

"Don't say that, Shane," Kara ordered, her ears acute to any negative judgment regarding Colin's condition. "Either believe in Colin or get the hell out of here. And that goes for you, too, Lauren."

"We're not going anywhere," Lauren said. "We're here for you, Kara, and for Colin."

Charlotte finally came through the door wearing her doctor's coat and carrying a medical bag.

Kara sat down and put up a hand to ward her off. "I can't leave, Charlotte. Colin needs to be here for this. It will make him wake up." She gasped as another contraction hit, and doubled over.

Charlotte squatted in front of her. She glanced down at her watch, timing the contraction. "How often are they coming?"

"Every now and then," Kara said vaguely.

"One right after another," Shane interjected. "She's lying. She needs to go to the hospital."

"You can deliver the baby here. *Please,* Charlotte, this could be the moment that brings Colin back to life," Kara said. She had barely finished speaking when she let out a sharp scream and grabbed her abdomen.

"Shane, get the nurse and tell her I need a gurney in here," Charlotte ordered.

"I'm not going anywhere," Kara repeated as Shane left the room.

"You're going to lie down," Charlotte told her. "I'm going to check your cervix and see where you are. Then I'm going to make a decision."

A moment later Shane returned with a nurse, an orderly, and a gurney. Charlotte explained what was going on to the nurse while Lauren helped Kara onto the gurney.

The nurse wanted to call an ambulance, but

Charlotte asked her to wait until she examined Kara.

"We don't have time to move her," Charlotte said a moment later. "You're already dilated ten centimeters, Kara. Your daughter is on her way." She turned to Shane. "Why don't you stand by Kara's head and be her coach?"

Shane swallowed hard, then did as Charlotte requested.

Now that Charlotte had taken charge, Lauren felt confident that everything would be all right.

Kara held out her hand to Shane. "I need you to be strong for me. I can't concentrate on Colin and the baby at the same time."

"Just concentrate on getting this baby out," Shane said, taking his sister's hand.

She gave him a pained smile. "Push me as close to Colin as you can. I want to hold his hand, too."

Shane moved the gurney next to the bed while Charlotte laid a sheet over Kara's lower half and checked her cervix. When another contraction hit, Kara hung on to Shane and Colin, gasping through the pain. Lauren hovered nearby, not knowing what to do except pray. Kara was fighting for her family, for her love, for her future, and Lauren had never admired anyone more.

Time passed in a blur of chaos. A doctor from the facility stopped in to offer help. Then it was time for Kara to push. Shane moved behind his sister, holding her shoulders as she sat up and leaned against his chest. His strong, calm voice seemed to keep her panic down. She clung to her brother, to her husband, to her belief that everything would be all right.

Charlotte coached Kara through the contractions with a calmness that impressed Lauren, and she watched in amazement as a tiny head finally appeared, followed by shoulders and a body, squirming arms and legs. Then she heard the baby's first cry.

Kara collapsed on the gurney, breathing hard, as Charlotte told her she had a perfect baby girl, with ten fingers and ten toes. The nurse wrapped the baby in a blanket, and Charlotte placed the child on Kara's chest. "Here's your daughter," she said with a smile.

Kara's mouth trembled. "I can't believe it. She's really here."

Shane moved next to Lauren, his hand slipping into hers as they stared at the baby. She had red hair and her brown eyes were filled with wonder, as if she couldn't believe what had happened.

Kara turned to look at her husband. "Colin, we have a daughter. Our baby is here. She wants to see you. She wants you to hold her, to talk to her, to be her father." She waited, long seconds ticking by, the silence in the room growing louder.

Lauren squeezed Shane's hand, her heart about to break. Kara's face began to crumple, then she broke. "God dammit, Colin, wake up! Wake up. Wake up," she cried.

Charlotte took the baby out of Kara's flailing

arms and Shane rushed to his sister's side, trying to take her hand, but she jerked away, her attention only on Colin.

"I can't bear this anymore. I can't do it," Kara said, choking on her sobs. "I need you, Colin. I *need* you. You have to come back to me." She started to shake, the agony of her loss ripping through her. Shane put his arms around her, and she finally collapsed against him, the grief pouring out of her.

Tears slid down Lauren's cheeks. Why couldn't Colin come back? They were good people. They loved each other. And they had a child who needed two parents. Sometimes life was unbearably cruel.

Charlotte moved next to her, the baby in her arms. "Can you hold her for a minute? I want to get Kara ready to go to the hospital."

Lauren took the baby and gazed down at the tiny, angelic face. She could see Kara's features in the shape of her daughter's nose, the curve of her lips, the downy red hair on her head. The baby's mouth turned down and she began to whimper and squirm, obviously not happy about the situation. She wanted her mother, but Kara was lost in her own pain right now.

"It's okay, sweetie," Lauren whispered, trying to comfort the child in her arms. "Your mommy will be back. She just needs a little time. But you are going to be loved like no other child, because your mother has more heart than anyone I know. Your daddy, too." Lauren blinked back the tears. "He loved your mommy from the first second he saw her, and he's going to love you when he wakes up." Kara couldn't fight for Colin anymore, but Lauren could—and that's what Kara would want her to do.

Fifteen minutes later, Colin's room had been cleaned up and an ambulance had taken Kara and her baby to the hospital, with Charlotte following close behind. Lauren had stayed with Shane to gather up Kara's things. Now that everyone was gone, the room seemed unbearably quiet.

Shane's hair stood on end, and there were beads of sweat on his forehead. There was also frustration and disappointment in his eyes. "This should have been the happiest day of Kara's life," he said.

"I know. But she did it the way she wanted— with Colin by her side."

Shane glanced over at the man who slept on. "Kara has loved him since she was a kid. I don't think there was ever anyone else. She had such hope that the baby would wake him up. If this didn't do it, I don't know what will."

"I don't, either. I kept praying he'd open his eyes."

Shane pulled her into his arms, then rested his chin on the top of her head. "I've never believed in miracles, but for a while there I thought Kara might get one. She had such faith."

"Maybe she still will," Lauren said, unwilling to give up completely.

"Right now she's so devastated she couldn't even look at her baby. I don't know how she's going to be a mother all by herself."

"She'll figure it out. She's a tough, stubborn Murray. We certainly saw that today." She gazed up at him. "You were great, Shane. She couldn't have done it without you."

"Or without you. Thanks for coming when I called."

"Thanks for asking me. I think it was the first time you ever have," she said, realizing how much it meant to have Shane need her for anything. How pathetic was that? She stepped out of his arms. "You should get to the hospital."

"In a minute." He gave her a long, thoughtful look. "It might have been the first time I said it, Lauren, but not the first time I felt it."

She didn't know how to respond to that. The more they were together, the more confused she became. Shane was the king of cryptic comments that were close to being what she wanted to hear, but not exactly. He was like a dancer on hot coals. He could never put his foot all the way down, never commit fully to the heat. But maybe that was good—because, in all honesty, she no longer knew what she wanted him to commit to.

"You should call your parents and siblings," she said, changing the subject. "The Murray clan will want to meet their newest member. I wonder if the ladies at the quilt shop have Kara's baby quilt ready yet."

He didn't reply, his gaze on her unnerving.

"I should go home, check on my dad."

"You're not coming with me to the hospital?"

"No. I need to spend some time with my dad." She walked over to the bed, pressed her fingers to her lips, and then to Colin's forehead. "We're still counting on you to come back," she said, then headed toward the door.

As they walked out of the facility, Lauren said, "In all the excitement, I forgot to ask if you heard about Mark Devlin's accident."

"Yes," Shane replied. "The marina was buzzing about it. I also had a message from Chief Silveira to give him a call. I must be on his list of suspects."

"I already spoke to him. I told him you don't have a car."

"That probably won't matter. I could have borrowed one."

"Well, if you are under suspicion, I am, too, because Jason Marlow saw us together last night. Anyway, the chief said he's worried that Abby's killer might be getting nervous—which means he believes that her killer is still here in town."

"It certainly looks that way."

A chill ran down Lauren's spine. "I wonder what Mark Devlin knows that we don't."

"Let's hope he gets a chance to tell someone, before something else happens."

NINETEEN

Joe spent the better part of the afternoon rereading the notes Devlin had compiled on Abby's case. He also sent officers door to door in the vicinity of the accident to locate possible witnesses. Every body shop and mechanic within a hundred miles had been alerted to be on the lookout for any cars brought in with front bumper damage.

He checked in with Tim Sorensen, Lisa Delaney, Kendra Holt, Lauren Jamison, and a number of others who were featured in Mark Devlin's notes. He left another message for Shane Murray and had a long conversation with Jason Marlow about his relationship with Abby and Lisa while in high school. He very much wanted to believe that Jason wasn't involved in the case, but for now he asked Jason to step aside from the hit-and-run investigation. He couldn't afford a potential conflict of interest.

As Joe pulled into the hospital parking lot, he automatically scanned for anything out of the ordinary. He'd asked hospital security to place a guard outside of Devlin's room—not just for Devlin's sake, but for Rachel's as well. She hadn't left Mark's side, and he didn't want her in the line of fire.

He sighed, remembering the way Rachel had looked at Mark when she'd first seen him after surgery. He wanted to believe that his marriage would survive this bumpy patch, but how long could he tell himself they were just having growing pains?

He didn't believe in quitting just because things were tough. He could fight for Rachel's love. But he didn't know how to fight this deep friendship she had with another man. Was he being ridiculous not to want his wife to be so emotionally connected to Devlin? Or was he a blind fool not to see what was happening right in front of his face?

He shook his head as he got out of his squad car. First things first—he needed to get Rachel to come home with him.

When he got to the room, Rachel was sitting next to Mark's bed, watching television with the sound turned down low. Mark was dozing. She clicked off the TV and met Joe at the door, putting a finger to her lips as he started to speak. She walked into the hall with him and down the corridor, out of earshot of the security guard.

"Have you found out who did this?" she asked.

He saw the dark shadows under her eyes. She was exhausted, but also angry. She wanted someone to pay for hurting Mark. She expected him to deliver that person to her, and he really wanted to.

"Not yet." He felt like he was letting her down again.

"Someone must have seen something."

"Everyone in the department is working on the case. In the meantime, I've asked the hospital to make sure Mark has twenty-four-hour security."

"You think someone would still try to hurt him?"

"I just want to be careful. How is Mark doing? Has he said anything to you? Did he see the car that hit him?"

"The last thing he remembers is walking out of the bar. He talked to some people there, but no one he hadn't spoken to before. He's going to have a long recovery. He needs to go back to Los Angeles and recuperate there."

"That sounds wise," he said, trying to keep a neutral tone.

"Don't even try to pretend you're not happy," Rachel said crossly. "You've been wanting Mark to leave since the minute he got here."

"Not like this. Let me take you home, Rachel. You've been here for hours. We can pick up some dinner, some wine, and relax. You can come back first thing in the morning."

She stared at him like he'd just suggested they fly to the moon. "I'm going to stay until Mark goes to sleep."

"He's asleep now."

"I mean later tonight. He's my friend, Joe. He doesn't have anyone else. I don't want him to be here alone."

He hesitated, about to take a step he probably shouldn't take, but he was damn tired of hearing about her *friend*. "Mark is more than a friend, Rachel, isn't he? The way you look at him—it's the way you used to look at me."

She swallowed hard. "Don't be ridiculous. Nothing has ever happened between Mark and me."

"Nothing yet. I want you to come home with me now."

A few seconds ticked by. "I can't."

He let out the breath he'd been holding. He didn't know if she was talking about now or ever, and he couldn't bring himself to ask.

Shane was on his way to Kara's hospital room when he saw his mother standing outside the nursery window. She'd gotten to the hospital in record time. Her gaze was focused on the first bassinet, and she appeared mesmerized by her granddaughter. He couldn't blame her. The baby was beautiful, an angel face with gorgeous red hair, just like Kara.

When Moira turned to him, she had tears in her eyes. "I heard that you helped deliver this little beauty."

"Kara did all the work."

"I can't believe she had the baby at Colin's bedside. Or maybe I can. She's stubbornly refusing to move on without him. I told her that she should come home with me when she's released, but she threw me out of her room."

Shane would have liked to see that. If any one of his siblings was a match for his mother, it was Kara.

"I don't know where she gets her faith," Moira added, her expression bewildered and sad. "It's not like I don't want Colin to wake up. But I'm a realist, and Kara needs to be, too. She has a baby now. Eventually she'll have to return to work. Your father and I will help, of course, but she has a long road ahead of her, and it won't be easy if she doesn't face facts. Talk to her, Shane. She listens to you."

"She's never going to quit on Colin while he's still breathing. She loves him. And she wants to have her family together." As he gazed through the window at his niece, he realized that while he'd always thought love was a pretty illusion and mostly for suckers, this little girl embodied the love of her parents. "Did Kara give her a name yet?"

"Not yet—another thing she wants to wait on until Colin wakes up."

"Well, there's no hurry. She can take her time."

"I'm surprised she didn't want the baby with her. She said she just wanted to be alone."

"Kara is exhausted," he said, knowing that it was more than that. He'd seen Kara turn away from her child when she realized Colin was still comatose. But she'd come around; Kara was innately nurturing. She just needed to catch her breath.

"I think it's more than that. Kara seemed very upset, very unlike herself. I do want the best for her, for all of them. Colin is like a son to me. I adore him."

"Just give Kara a little space. She has to figure out how to deal with reality in her own way."

"I suppose she does." His mother tilted her head as she turned her gaze back to the nursery. "You had such dark hair when you were born. You came out wide awake, alert, and curious, ready to take on the world. I knew you would challenge me every step of the way, and you did." She drew in a deep breath and slowly let it out, then turned toward him. "I want to set you free. I should have never made my burden yours to carry. I was wrong, and I've regretted it for a long time. I never thought it would change your life the way it has. Whatever you need to do to be happy, you should do."

Shane couldn't believe what he was hearing. He'd waited years for her to say those words. Why had she said them now? Was she really setting him free, or trying to make him carry a bigger part of the burden?

When he remained silent, she said, "I thought you'd be happier."

"I don't trust you."

She sucked in a painful breath. "I guess I deserve that. But I'm being sincere, Shane. You paid a big price for my past. It was easy for me to pretend you were having a wonderful time, traveling the world, living out your dreams, but I was just trying to make myself feel better. You're my son—I love you. I know it doesn't mean anything to you to hear that, but it's the truth. This little baby reminded me that you were once that innocent, too. I'm sorry, Shane." She put a hand on his shoulder. "I hope someday you'll forgive me."

He didn't know if he ever could.

Kara stared at the ceiling of her hospital room. It was nine o'clock at night and she was exhausted, but she couldn't sleep. She was a mother now. She had a child. And she was alone.

Well, not completely alone. She could hear her family chattering outside. They'd already been in to visit, offering a never-ending stream of well-intentioned smiles. No one mentioned Colin. They just went on and on about the baby.

She wanted them to go home. She didn't want to talk anymore, or cry or think. She just wanted to sleep. But when she closed her eyes, all she could see was Colin's still body. She'd been so sure he would wake up when the baby came. Now her hope was gone.

It was over. Colin was lost to her.

The nurse came into the room with a warm smile. "Your daughter is awake. Shall I bring her to you? Would you like to give breast-feeding a try?"

"I'm too tired," Kara said listlessly. "I can't do it right now."

The nurse looked a little surprised. And why not—didn't all new mothers want to see their babies? Kara felt horribly guilty and even more depressed, but she just couldn't give any more of herself right now.

"All right," the nurse said. "We can give her

a bottle in the nursery. Is there anything else you need? Are you having any pain?"

Did the pain in her heart count? "I'm fine. Could you tell my family that I'm going to sleep and they can go home?"

"Of course." The nurse left, hitting the light switch and shutting the door behind her.

A stream of moonlight peeked through the part in the curtains. The storm had passed, but not for her. Her bottom lip trembled and she wanted to cry again, but there weren't any tears left. She and Colin were separated by only a few miles, but the distance between them had never been so great. This was not the way it was supposed to be.

The door opened again and she stiffened, ready to order whoever it was out of the room, but Charlotte's determined expression gave her pause. She swallowed a knot of emotion as she saw the baby in Charlotte's arms—her baby. No one else had dared to bring her daughter to her. They'd all tiptoed around her feelings, too afraid of how she'd react.

Charlotte turned on the bedside lamp and sat down next to Kara. Kara knew that look of steel in her eyes; she wasn't going away without a fight.

"I was sleeping," she said.

"No, you weren't. You were lying here thinking about how screwed up your life is. And it is, but you have a beautiful child. She needs you, Kara. And you need her."

Kara didn't know why it was so difficult to look at her child. She'd wanted this baby more than anything in the world. They'd struggled for years to get pregnant. She had danced with joy when she found out they were expecting, but now . . .

"Look," Charlotte ordered. "She has your beautiful red hair and your pretty eyes and your big mouth—she's been wailing up a storm in the nursery. But I think she might have Colin's nose. Hopefully she'll grow into it."

"She does not have his nose," Kara protested, her gaze drawn to her baby. But she was wrong; that narrow nose was all Colin. Her breath stalled in her chest. Reality hit her in the face.

Her baby was real. She was *here*. She lived and breathed. And Kara knew why it was so hard to see her: because as happy as she was to finally meet her baby, her daughter's birth meant the death of her other dream—of Colin waking up in time to see his child come into the world. And if he hadn't woken up now, maybe he never would.

But that wasn't her daughter's fault.

And now that she was looking, Kara couldn't tear her gaze away. Her heart filled with love. She held out her arms, and Charlotte placed the baby within her embrace.

The hole in her heart didn't feel quite so big anymore.

"Hello, baby," she whispered. Her daughter squirmed a little, her mouth bunching up as if she were about to cry. "It's okay. Mommy's here." She looked at Charlotte. "Thank you."

Charlotte smiled back at her. "You're very welcome. I'll be back in a little while. If you get tired just buzz the nurse, and she'll take the baby back to the nursery."

As Charlotte left the room, Kara settled back against the pillows. It felt so strange to have her baby in her arms instead of inside of her. She played with her child's tiny fingers, amazed that she and Colin could have created this little person.

A few minutes later she felt an odd warmth in the air, as if someone had just turned the heater up. A small breeze blew against her face. She looked toward the door, wondering if it was open, but it was still closed. The room was dim, lit only by the table lamp by her bed, and in the shadows she saw a ghostly shape take form.

It was Colin. Her heart stopped. His green eyes were open, looking right at her. He was smiling. He was happy. He was upright and talking . . .

"Our daughter looks just like you," he said. *"She's beautiful, Kara, and so are you. My girls."*

"She has your nose," Kara said. "And her toes curl in just like yours. We made a beautiful little girl."

"Yes, we did."

"We need you, Colin."

"I'll always be with you—in your heart."

"I want *more* than memories. I want to hear your big, booming laugh and listen to your tall tales, and feel your touch on my skin and your kiss on my lips. I want my husband back. It's so lonely without you."

"I miss you, too."

"How can I go on without you? Every time she smiles or cries, I'm going to be looking for you. When she crawls and takes her first step, I'll want her to be able to run to you. I'll want you to be able to catch her when she falls. But most of all, I want to share her life with you. We're partners."

"I want all that, too. But whatever happens, you'll be all right. You'll tell her about me." He smiled at her. *"You may not have me, but you have my heart, always. Be happy. I couldn't bear it if you weren't. Don't wait around for me; go on with your life. Raise our little girl. I love you, Kara."*

"Don't go," she cried, but he was already fading. "We love you, too."

Her words hung in the air and the room had gone from warm to cool. She was overwhelmed by fear. Had Colin found a way to say good-bye?

She reached for the phone by her bed and punched in the number she knew so well, then asked the nurse to check on Colin, to make sure he was all right. She held her breath until the nurse came back on the phone and told her Colin was just the same, no change.

Hanging up the phone, Kara cradled her daughter tighter in her arms. "It's going to be all right," she told her. "I didn't want to do this alone, but I'm not really alone, am I? I have you." She drew in a breath as a tear slid down her cheek. "And your daddy wants us to be happy. So we're going to have to try—for him. For better or worse, we're in this together. You and me, kid. You and me."

TWENTY

The sun always comes up. Colin used to say that whenever she was depressed or worried. And as the nurse entered her room after breakfast and handed her daughter to her, Kara realized it was true. Not only was it a new day, but she was blessed. Her child was healthy. That's what mattered most. She tried not to think about the long future ahead as a single mother; there was too much darkness in that thought to be beaten down by a few rays of sunlight.

A knock came at her door, and Jason stepped into the room. She smiled, happy to see him out of uniform. He'd been working double shifts so he wouldn't think about Colin, and it had been taking a toll on him. But today he looked relaxed in his jeans and sweater, younger and more carefree. In the future, she couldn't let him continue to be a stand-in for Colin. He needed to have his own life, and she needed to make sure he had it.

"I see you decided to have this kid without me,"

Jason said as he approached. "And after you made me watch that disgusting movie, too. You owe me big time."

"She was determined to come out. Believe me, I tried to stop her. And you should thank me for not calling you—the real thing was a lot worse than that movie."

"I would have come if you'd called."

"I was well taken care of. I had Shane, Lauren, and eventually Charlotte. I didn't want to leave Colin's side; I was convinced that my labor would make him wake up. I pretty much drove everyone nuts."

"There's a big surprise," he said with a grin.

"I know I can be stubborn. And I'm not giving up on Colin, but there's no time table anymore."

Jason tilted his head thoughtfully. "Something's changed. You sound more . . . accepting."

"I'm a mother now. I have to put her first, before myself and before Colin. He'd want it that way."

"He would," Jason agreed. "And he'd be very proud of you. I know I am."

"I'm kind of proud of me, too," she said with a sheepish smile. "I managed to breast-feed her last night, and I've even changed a diaper. I think I might be good at this."

He grinned. "Just don't get too confident. I hear babies undergo a personality change when they leave the hospital. They don't actually sleep all the time."

"Really? Because this has been pretty easy so far."

Gazing down at the child in her arms, he teased,

"It's hard to believe any baby this pretty has Colin as a father."

It was the kind of thing Jason would have said if Colin were here, and for a moment it made her feel like he was. "Do you want to hold her?"

"Oh, I don't think so."

"You won't break her, Jason." She put the baby in his reluctant arms and he held her awkwardly, but with all the care in the world.

"You're a lucky girl," he said, gazing down at the baby. "You have two great parents, the best in the world." Then he looked at Kara. "I can't believe she's so small."

"She didn't feel small coming out of me."

"You can skip the details." The baby scrunched up her face. "Uh-oh, she's not happy. She wants you." He quickly handed her back to Kara.

"And here I thought you had a way with the ladies," she said, rocking her daughter back to sleep.

"I like them a little older," he said with a familiar twinkle in his eyes.

She was glad to see his lighter side returning. "So tell me what's going on outside this room. I feel like I've been in isolation the last couple of days. I heard about Mark Devlin's accident. Any leads?"

"As a matter of fact, yes," Jason said. "The chief is interviewing her right now."

"Her?" Kara asked in surprise. "Who on earth are you talking about?"

"Erica Sorensen."

"The coach's wife? *She* ran down Mr. Devlin? Oh, my God!"

"She must have thought that Devlin had something on her husband," Jason said.

"Which would mean . . . that Coach Sorensen was somehow involved in Abby's death?"

"It's possible."

Kara couldn't believe it. "He was old and married!"

"He was only in his mid-twenties when Abby was in high school, and all the girls thought he was good-looking."

Kara shook her head. "Are you sure Erica didn't run Mr. Devlin down by accident?"

"We'll find out. I must admit, I'm a little relieved to have Tim Sorensen as a suspect in Abby's death," Jason continued. "I didn't like the scenario featuring me as the killer."

"That was a ridiculous theory—although you haven't been very open with me. I get the feeling you knew Abby better than you've said."

He dug his hands into the pockets of his jeans and sighed. "I hooked up with her one night after a party. I didn't think it was a big deal, but maybe she did. I don't know. I hooked up with a lot of girls. I was a teenage boy."

"So you were with Abby and Lisa a couple of nights before she died?"

"Yes, but that was a couple of months after Abby and I hooked up. I thought we were cool. And it was the three of us; Lisa was there, too. We just drove around. If we were spying on the coach's house, I didn't know about it."

"I believe you. And with Erica's arrest, maybe the police can finally solve Abby's murder."

"That's the hope. Unfortunately, even if we can tie the hit-and-run to Erica, we're a long way from arresting anyone for Abby's death."

"I did it to protect my husband," Erica Sorensen told Joe. "Mark Devlin was making up lies, tarnishing Tim's reputation. We have three children, and we can't afford to lose Tim's salary. I wanted to scare Mr. Devlin off, that's all. I didn't mean to really hurt him."

Joe stared at the woman sitting in the chair across from him in the interrogation room. Erica looked like she was on something. Her eyes were dilated, and there was a nervous edge to her movements. She kept crossing and uncrossing her legs, twisting her fingers together, biting down on her bottom lip. She was terrified, and she had good reason to be. She hadn't done a very good job covering up her crime. The left front bumper on her car was damaged with what appeared to be traces of clothing and blood evidence that he believed would link her car to Mark Devlin. Erica had taken her vehicle to a mechanic fifty miles away, but it hadn't been far enough. The mechanic had alerted them immediately.

Once he'd told Erica they had evidence that tied

her car to the hit-and-run, she'd caved, admitting that she'd run down Devlin in a moment of panic.

"I didn't mean to hurt him. I just wanted him to go away," Erica reiterated, her words slurring a little. "I saw him, and something in me snapped. I hit the gas, and I don't remember anything else."

Joe looked up as Rick Harrigan opened the door. Rick was one of several defense attorneys in town, and Joe had anticipated his arrival.

"My client is done talking," Rick told him.

"My husband is a good man," Erica declared. "He didn't have anything to do with that girl's death, and that man was telling everyone that he did. Do you know how vulnerable a male high school teacher is to accusations of misconduct?"

"Mrs. Sorensen, don't say anything more," Rick said firmly.

She sank back in her chair as Rick took the seat next to her.

Joe left the room and found Tim Sorensen pacing in the hallway. The man looked far less sure of himself than he had when they'd spoken earlier in the week.

"This is a mistake," Tim said. "Erica wouldn't hurt anyone."

"She said she did it for you," Joe told him, gauging his reaction. Sorensen looked upset, but he didn't seem that surprised. "To protect your reputation," Joe added. "You told me you didn't know Abby Jamison outside of school, so why would your wife be worried about whatever Mark Devlin came up with?"

"I want to speak to Erica."

"I'll bet," Joe muttered.

"You're not going to hold her, are you?"

"Your wife is in serious trouble."

"This is a big misunderstanding. Erica is suffering from postpartum depression. She's not herself. She imagines things that aren't true. She's been paranoid for months, thinking that I'm falling out of love with her because she weighs more than she used to. She's not herself. Whatever she did, she didn't do in her right mind. I need to see my wife." Sorensen moved past him and entered the interrogation room.

Tim's assessment of his wife's mental condition jibed with Joe's, but her mental state at the time of her crime was something for the court to debate. And confession aside, Joe had a gut feeling they'd have enough forensic evidence to tie Erica Sorensen to the hit-and-run. Now he just had to figure out how to tie Tim Sorensen to the murder of Abigail Jamison. Obviously his wife had had suspicions. Tim had an alibi for that night, but Joe intended to check it out more thoroughly.

Unless . . .

Was he on the wrong track?

Erica was her husband's protector. She didn't want his reputation tainted, his job put in jeopardy. Was it possible that she had committed murder to protect her husband thirteen years ago?

*   *   *

The moon was high when Lauren moved through the side yard next to the Murray house. Shane had called her a half hour earlier and asked her to meet him in the old treehouse. He'd told her that he wanted to tell her *everything*. She wasn't sure what *everything* meant, but she definitely wanted to find out. She also wanted to talk to him about what was going on in town. He'd been out on his boat all day, and she had no idea if he knew Erica Sorensen had been arrested for the hit-and-run.

There was nothing at the moment that tied Erica to Abby's murder, but certainly there was an assumption of some connection.

She tripped over a tree root and stumbled, knocking into a trash can. Great. She'd have Shane's parents out here any second. She waited a moment, but no one came out. Maybe Shane's parents were at the hospital with Kara.

As she made her way through the backyard, she was reminded of the last time she'd been in the treehouse. She'd gone looking for Shane because he'd gotten in a fight that day, and she'd wanted to find out if he was all right. He hadn't been happy to see her at first, but one thing had led to another, and they'd ended up making love.

It was like taming an angry beast with long, deep kisses; she'd felt the tension go out of him with each touch. She'd reveled in the thought that she could ease his pain in a way that no one could. And Shane had made her feel beautiful and wanted, treating her with a tenderness that had surprised her. She could still remember him putting his hand under her head to cushion it from the wood floor as he moved inside of her.

The old memory blended with the more recent ones, and the potential to make new ones. She was playing with fire coming to see Shane, but she couldn't seem to stop herself. Well, it would all be over soon. But while next week was coming closer, reality was getting farther away. She barely remembered her life in San Francisco, her friends, the men she'd been dating. It was all Angel's Bay, Shane, her father, Charlotte, and Kara. She'd even gone by Martha's Bakery again, wondering what the rent might be on that space, as if she was going to do anything about it.

She wasn't ready to make that commitment. She wasn't ready to give up a life that was safe and controlled for one filled with the potential for more pain and disaster. But she had to admit that she was weakening.

"Lauren? Is that you down there?" Shane called.

She cleared her throat, realizing how long she'd been stalling. "I think this is a bad idea, Shane."

"You said you wanted me to tell you everything."

"Does it have to be here?"

"It's where it all started."

She had no idea what that meant, but she'd come this far. She had to juggle the plastic container in her hands while she made the climb, but eventually crawled into the treehouse with a breathless smile. "Okay, that was easier when I was seventeen."

Shane gave her a slow, lazy smile that sent the usual thrill down her spine and told her she was in big trouble. Unfortunately, she had a feeling it was the kind of trouble she'd enjoy—a lot. He slid a familiar envelope across the floor to her. "I brought you the photos in case you still want to look through them. What did you bring?" he asked, eyeing the container in her hand.

"Cookies. But you don't get these until you tell me why I'm here. You were awfully mysterious on the phone." She picked up the envelope and stashed it in her purse, then scooted against the opposite wall of the treehouse, stretching out her legs as a barrier between them.

The moonlight provided just enough light to see his face, and while he was smiling, she sensed a tension in his body.

"Do you remember the night we made love here?" Shane asked. "I was in a bad mood, angry with the world. I didn't want you here but you pushed your way in, and you wouldn't leave."

"I had to push, or you would have kept me out."

"I thought you were shy and really sweet when we first met, but you had a stubborn side. You kept coming back even when I told you to go away."

"Because you didn't really want me to go away. You wanted me, even though you didn't want to. I could see the battle in your eyes, and I was determined to win, to make you see that I was perfect for you."

"But I wasn't perfect for *you*. I had a lot of—

issues. I shouldn't have gotten involved with you, but you drove the demons away with your beautiful blue eyes, your honest smile, your generous spirit. You let me take way too much from you, Lauren."

"Now you make me sound like a doormat. I took from you, too—your strength and your confidence. You made me try things I'd never tried before. You made me feel brave and special. At home, I was second best to Abby. At school, I wasn't particularly smart or athletic or gorgeous. But when you picked me over all the other girls, I felt a lot better than average."

"You were never average," he said with a frown. "You didn't believe in yourself, that's all. You let other people's opinions mean too much. You tried to make everyone else happy before yourself."

"You knew me pretty well." She paused, giving him a long look. "But I didn't really know you, did I? Isn't that why you asked me to come here tonight?"

He nodded. "I'm still working up to it."

"I figured. Did you hear about Tim Sorensen's wife being arrested for the hit-and-run?"

"Yeah, the chief filled me in this morning when I returned his call. He said there's no evidentiary link that ties Tim Sorensen to Abby's murder, but I'm guessing there will be."

"I still can't believe Abby was having an affair with her teacher. I'd need solid proof to accept that. And I can't imagine how my father will react when he hears that. She's become a saint in his mind."

"She was fifteen. We all made mistakes back then," Shane reminded her.

"Are you going to tell me about your mistakes now?" she prodded. "The secret you're keeping for someone else?"

"Yes." He drew in a deep breath. "It's why I went to the law offices the night Abby died."

"Okay. But if you tell me something that changes the investigation regarding Abby, I can't promise I won't let the police know."

"It's not about Abby, but you can decide what you want to do with the information after you hear it." He crossed his arms in front of his chest. "So here goes. My mother had an affair almost thirty-two years ago—and I was the result."

Surprise rocketed through her. Shane's parents had always been so tight. The whole Murray family had seemed close to perfect. "When did you find out?"

"Sophomore year. I came home early one day, and I overheard my mother talking on the phone to my biological father. Our family was going through tough financial times, and she wanted his help. She thought he owed her that."

"What did you do?"

"I confronted her. She begged me not to tell my dad. He didn't know that she'd cheated on him, that I wasn't his son. She said it had been a moment of temporary insanity and one that she regretted ever since."

"But she didn't regret you," Lauren said quickly.

She could tell by the hard gleam in his eyes that he didn't believe her. "Shane, she *didn't* regret you."

"By the time I found out, the affair had been over for years," he continued. "My parents had gotten back on track, and they had had three kids after me. When I learned the truth, Patrick was away at college, Kara was a freshman in high school, and Dee and Michael were just little kids. My mother felt sure my father would divorce her if he knew about the affair, and I couldn't break up the family. So I said I'd keep her secret."

"But it made you crazy—reckless and angry," she murmured, his past making so much more sense now. "I never understood where the pain in your eyes came from. People told me how you'd changed, how you used to be friendlier, not such a loner."

"I was furious, and I didn't know how to handle it. I couldn't tell anyone. So I'd just ride my motorcycle and count the days until I could leave home. I felt like an impostor every time my father called me *son,* and when he talked about leaving the business to me someday.

"I couldn't stand to be around him," he added. "I couldn't stand to see him with my mother. I hated her, because she was the one who made me lie. She was the one who betrayed the man she supposedly loved. So how could I ever believe her when she said she loved me? It made me sick to my stomach."

Now Lauren understood where Shane's inability to declare his love for her came from—his unwillingness to commit to anything long-term, his restless feet, and dark moods. How could his mother have asked him to keep such a secret?

She'd always liked Moira Murray; she never would have suspected that she'd cheated on her husband, or lived a lie for thirty years and asked her son to go along with it.

"Oh, Shane." She moved across the clubhouse and put her hand on his arm. She could feel the tension in his muscles. "I'm so sorry. Your mother should never have asked that of you. It was wrong."

"It was for the greater good, and she was right. My siblings got to grow up with two parents living together in the same house, and what they didn't know didn't hurt them. If I'd told the truth, my father might have moved out. I couldn't take the chance that that would happen."

She couldn't believe how much Shane had taken onto himself. "God, I'm so angry with your mother! Do you know who your biological father is?"

"No. That's why I broke into the law offices that night. I was sure that one of those men, Rick Harrigan or Jeff Miller, was my real father. The office phone number was listed on our telephone bill. I just didn't know which man my mother had spoken to, and she refused to tell me. She was afraid that I'd confront him. They were both married men with kids. Everywhere I looked, I could see that I was going to hurt someone, but I couldn't get it out of my head. I just wanted to know who my real father was."

"I can understand that." She wanted Shane to look at her, but he was avoiding her gaze, and in the shadows she couldn't get a clear read on his emotions, which was why he'd probably wanted to have the conversation here. He wasn't a man who was comfortable with showing what he was feeling. He'd closed himself off a long time ago, and those walls were now almost impenetrable. But there were tiny cracks, and she was determined to get through. "Tell me the rest."

"There's not much more. I had the crazy idea that I might be able to find evidence in their offices—a note from my mother, an old check written out to her, something. There had been some contact over the years, some exchange of money, and I figured any proof would be at the office, not at home. I even thought I'd swipe a used glass or a comb and see if I could get a DNA test done on it. I had a lot of ideas."

"What did you find?"

"Nothing. That's the worst thing of all. I went through the entire office, and I came out empty-handed. I was so pissed. Abby said I looked like I wanted to kill somebody. I told her that's exactly how I felt, but I didn't know who to kill."

"And you didn't tell her the rest?"

"No. If I was going to tell someone, I would have told you." He put his hand over hers and gazed into her eyes. "When I dropped Abby off at the high school parking lot, she gave me a hug and said I should go and find you, that you'd make me feel better."

His words hurt. She could see Abby in her head, hear her voice, and knew that might have been the last good moment her sister had had.

"It doesn't sound like Abby knew she was heading into danger."

"She was a little on edge, but nothing out of the ordinary. At least I didn't think so. Later I wondered if there was something I'd missed, something that I should have seen. I felt horrible for leaving her alone in that parking lot, and not telling you what had happened compounded my guilt. I wasn't just carrying my mother's lie around anymore; I was also carrying my own. I wanted to be there for you, Lauren. But you were so angry with me, and then all the speculation arose about Abby and me. I didn't know what to do. I tried to say as little as possible, but that only made things worse. And then you left."

She let out a long breath, realizing she'd been holding it for some time. "I never imagined that your lie had such deep roots. I needed to blame someone for the horror that had become my life, and you were handy. When you wouldn't talk to me, it drove me crazy. That last day, I almost took a swing at you."

"It probably would have made us both feel better."

"I hated you all the way up the coast. I tried to hang on to that feeling for a long time, because while I hated you, I also missed you like crazy. I'd tell myself that I was a fool, that you had hit on my sister, that you were a liar and a cheat—but then a part of me wouldn't believe it, and I'd make up excuses. I went around and around in circles."

"I'm surprised you gave me that much thought. I figured out of sight, out of mind."

"Well, you figured wrong. Our relationship wasn't that trivial. Maybe it was for you—"

"It wasn't," he said, cutting her off. "I couldn't forget you, Lauren. I'd keep myself busy during the days, but at night I'd think about you, and wish things could have been different."

She wanted to believe he'd been equally as devastated by their breakup, but it was difficult. She'd worn her heart on her sleeve, while Shane had kept his in hiding. But they'd been teenagers caught up in the throes of first love. Their breakup had come during a time of tragedy. Every emotion she'd had was heightened by Abby's death: the love, the hate, the guilt ... It had eaten her up for weeks. But eventually she'd gone on, and so had Shane.

"Did you ever find out who your father is?" she asked.

He shook his head. "No. After Abby's murder, I was on the hot seat. I couldn't breathe without someone writing it down. I was followed all over town. It was ironic that at one point I thought I might have to get a lawyer, maybe Harrigan or Miller, but my dad talked to someone else for me. Once I could leave town, I left. I didn't think I'd ever come back."

"I didn't think I would, either," she said. "But here we are."

"Here we are."

As they stared at each other, the air seemed to crackle between them. Lauren could feel the pull and tried to resist, but it was impossible.

She reached out and cupped his face with her hands. Shane had truly been the black sheep, the one who didn't belong, the outcast—no wonder he'd started to act that way. She kissed him on the mouth, lingering there for a long moment, wanting to show him what she couldn't put into words.

When she lifted her head, she said, "Thanks for telling me." He'd finally given her what she'd always wanted from him—trust. "Aren't you afraid that I'll say something and destroy your family?"

He gave her a small smile. "No, because I know you. Your heart is big and generous and kind."

Her eyes blurred with emotion. "Why did you tell me now? As you said, your mother's affair and your trip to the law offices had nothing to do with Abby's death. I didn't need to know."

"I didn't want there to be any more secrets between us."

"Really?" Her pulse quickened with anticipation and fear. Things were happening too fast, and she could see where this was headed. She could hear the words she'd wanted him to say hovering on his lips . . . but she couldn't let him speak; not now. She wasn't ready.

She scrambled to her feet, and was halfway down the tree before he called after her.

"Lauren, wait."

She ignored his command, jogging out to the sidewalk. He caught up to her at the end of the driveway. "I'll give you a ride home."

"I can walk—it's only a few blocks."

"I'm not letting you walk home alone—not after what happened to Mark Devlin last night."

"I'll be fine," she said, but he stayed right on her heels. "Erica Sorensen is in custody."

"Her husband isn't. Dammit, Lauren. Why are you running away from me?"

"I'm not running away, I'm just going home."

He grabbed her arm and forcibly stopped her. "That's crap and you know it. Talk to me. Tell me what you're thinking."

His demand was mind-boggling and oh, so ironic. "Do you know how many times I asked you to tell me what you were thinking, to say three simple words, 'I love you,' but you never did? I'd declare myself, and you'd smile or kiss me or change the subject. You always wanted to keep your options open."

"I was eighteen."

"You're not a teenager anymore, but what's really changed? You live on a boat. You don't have any roots. You can leave at a moment's notice, and you probably will."

"Or I can stay forever," Shane said.

"Really? You, the ultimate wanderer? I don't think so."

"Why don't we stop talking about me and focus on you? What do *you* want, Lauren? Do you even know?" he challenged.

"No—I don't," she answered. "I'm tempted to stay here. My dad needs me, and I love being with Charlotte and Kara again, and it feels more like home than I thought it would."

"And me?" he asked. "Where do I fit in?"

She sucked in a quick breath and let it out. "I look at you, and I think maybe I could have everything I ever wanted. But then I remind myself that it's you, and you hurt me, and that getting over you was the hardest thing I ever had to do. I can't do it again."

"Who says you would have to?"

"Are you saying I wouldn't? Are you really ready to put it all on the line, Shane?" His hesitation was all she needed to hear. "I didn't think so."

"You're the one who's running away now. Do *you* want to put it all on the line?"

"No, I don't. I can't, and we shouldn't have this conversation until we know how we want to finish it."

She yanked her arm away and walked home, his long shadow following close behind. He didn't speak; neither did she. She told herself that's the way she wanted it.

But she was a liar. She wanted so much more.

TWENTY-ONE

Later that night Lauren sat cross-legged on Abby's bed, the yearbook photos spread out across the comforter. She was tired, but she wouldn't be able to sleep with so much on her mind. She still felt rattled by Shane's confession, and that he'd finally put his trust in her. He hadn't just put himself on the line, but also his family: she could destroy the Murrays with just a few words. He'd taken a big risk . . .

So why was she so scared to take one?

Because a part of her felt that she was so close to the biggest dream she'd ever had for herself, and another part of her said she was a fool to think that divulging his secret meant Shane loved her.

The real question was, did she love him?

She'd gotten to know him as the man he was now, and he'd gotten to know her. They had their own life experiences, and while they'd moved on in many ways, they'd never really moved past each other.

Maybe they never would. Maybe like Leonora and Tommy, they were destined for each other.

Leonora and Tommy hadn't gotten their happy ending, but they hadn't been afraid to go for it. Why was she such a coward?

With a sigh, she made herself concentrate on the photos. The last stack had been taken at awards night. Most of the shots were of people she didn't recognize. The last few had been shot outside the school, with lots of kids milling around a dessert table.

Her breath caught as she pulled a torn photo out of the stack. It had been ripped in two, a third of it missing. In the portion remaining was Tim Sorensen. He was standing on the outskirts of the crowd, and he had his arm around someone. She could see a pink sweater, a feminine shoulder, but that was it. Tim was looking down at whoever he was holding, and his gaze was extremely serious.

Lauren's heart skipped a beat. Was he looking down at Abby? Had someone else taken the photo with Abby's camera? Had Abby seen the picture and ripped it in two, so that no one would know about her relationship?

That pink sweater looked familiar . . . like one she'd taken out of the closet the other night and put in the trash bag for charity. Lauren rushed over to the bags and opened one after another, going through each one until she found the sweater. She held up the sleeve, comparing it to the photo.

Her heart sank. It was a match.

She tossed the sweater back on top of the bag and sat on the bed. Her mind was racing, but really, what did she have? A lot of girls could have had a similar sweater. And she didn't *know* that it was Abby in the shot, though it certainly seemed likely.

She rolled her neck back and forth, feeling the crack of her tight muscles. It was late. She needed to sleep. She gathered up the rest of the photos and put them in the envelope, then she glanced over at her side of the room. The sheets and blankets that she'd tossed there a few days earlier reminded her that she really needed to get over the last hurdle and make up her bed.

She shivered at the thought, or maybe it was the cold. She could hear the wind howling and the scrape of the tree branches hitting the window.

Abby had hated those branches. In the moonlight, she'd thought the tree outside their room looked like a monster with a hundred arms.

But it was just a tree, Lauren reminded herself. And it wasn't an imaginary monster that had hurt Abby; it was a human, and probably someone she'd trusted.

Feeling more chilled, she went to the old wall heater, turned the knob, and waited to see if it would come on. It had always been erratic, and most nights she and Abby would give up and just grab another blanket.

Squatting down, she put her hand in front of the

slats to see if any warm air was coming through the vent.

She couldn't feel anything—but she could see something red between the slats. Her gaze narrowed; her pulse sped up. She pulled on the front panel of the heater, but it resisted. She tugged harder, and it finally came off. Tossing it aside, she stared in amazement at the red cover of Abby's journal.

Adrenaline roared through her veins. She'd found it! Abby must have stashed it there before she left that night.

Lauren was terrified to open it. Would she finally learn the truth?

With a shaky hand, she pulled the journal out and sat on the floor at the foot of her bed. Her hand trembled as she opened to the first page. Abby had never wanted her to read her private thoughts. Was it wrong to read them now?

But if she didn't read it, how could she help Abby? She couldn't turn the book over to the cops without knowing what was in it. She had to protect her sister.

This journal began seven months before Abby was killed. Lauren drew in a hard breath. Thankfully, the early entries weren't scary; they were just rambling thoughts about whatever was going through Abby's head. She talked about wanting to become a marine biologist, fishing trips with Dad, a zit on her forehead.

Lauren began to relax. She could see Abby now, hear her voice through the words on the page. She'd begun to think Abby's life was a dark, shadowy place of horror, but she could see now that wasn't the case. It was ordinary. It was a little boring, and sometimes it was really, really sweet. Lauren teared up when Abby talked about her, about hoping Shane was treating her right. She'd never known her younger sister had ever worried about her. She'd been so determined to forget the pain that she'd forgotten everything else, and now it was coming back.

As she neared the entries from the days preceding Abby's death, the tone of the journal changed. Abby's thoughts were restless, yearning. She talked about a boy she simply called J. Though a lot of the people in the journal were only referred to by their initials, it quickly became clear that J was Jason Marlow.

Abby wrote about how much she liked him, but he only had eyes for Kara. She mentioned a dance where she and Lisa had found him drinking with some other kids, deep in the trees outside the high school. He'd given her a beer, and she'd taken it because she wanted to fit in.

Abby wrote how happy she was when Jason put his arm around her. When he kissed her, her heart was beating so fast she thought she might have a heart attack. They'd gotten into his car and he'd put his hands on her breasts, and she thought it was wrong, but she didn't care, because she really, really liked him. But the next day he didn't even talk to her, and Abby wondered if he even remembered being with her. As the weeks passed, she realized that it hadn't meant anything to him, but she still liked him. Maybe one day he'd ask her out again.

Lauren felt a wave of anger toward Jason. He shouldn't have taken advantage of her sister like that, and obviously they'd been more than just friends as he'd claimed.

Lauren skimmed the next couple of pages as Abby veered into discussions of marine life. Then her focus turned to Lisa.

"I'm worried about L," she wrote. *"She's drinking too much and making out with everyone. I know she has this big, crazy need to be loved. She doesn't think her parents love her, especially her dad, who ran out on her. But I'm afraid for her. She's doing stupid, dangerous things. I keep telling her to stop. This isn't her, but she's not listening to me. She's listening to other people, people who don't love her like I do."*

Lauren frowned as she turned to the next page.

"I feel like I'm not being a good friend. I have to find a way to make L stop, before she gets in trouble. She thinks she's in love with Coach, but he's not in love with her. And he's married. He's not going to leave his wife for a fifteen-year-old girl. She's going to hate me, but I have to stop her. I have to stop him. This isn't right. He's using her; he's going to hurt her, I know it."

Lauren sucked in a sharp breath. *Oh, God!* It was Lisa, not Abby, who had a crush on Tim Sorensen. She felt sick to her stomach. Abby must have threatened to reveal their relationship, so Tim Sorensen had killed her.

Why hadn't Lisa come forward? Why hadn't she told the police?

Had the coach threatened Lisa, too? Was she afraid to turn him in, terrified she'd be next?

But if that were true, why would Lisa have stayed in town all these years? Why wouldn't she have left, put some space between herself and Abby's murderer?

Lauren remembered the shock on Lisa's face when she'd walked into this room a few days earlier, seeing it look exactly like it had thirteen years ago. She'd asked about the journal, probably knowing that Abby had written about her. Was she still afraid her affair would come out?

Lauren's eyes began to water, and she drew in a breath that turned into a cough. The door to the bedroom was closed, but the air had become smoky. She glanced toward the heater, wondering if it had sparked, but there was no heat coming from it. Had her father gotten up and started cooking again?

She jumped to her feet and ran to the door. It was warm but not sizzling hot, so she opened it— and gasped. Heavy smoke was billowing down the hall and flames were coming out of the kitchen, licking their way up the wallpaper in the hallway.

Why the hell hadn't any smoke alarms gone off? She ran down the hall, pulling her sweater over her mouth and nose to protect her from the smoke. Her father's door was closed; she pushed it open and found him asleep. When she shook him, he didn't wake up. Had he passed out from the smoke? He seemed to be breathing. She ran to the window and tried to open it, but it wouldn't budge.

She had to get him out. She had to call 911. Which to do first?

Across the hall flames came out of David's old bedroom, and there was plenty of fuel in there, with all the paper and old magazines. She grabbed her father's hands and tried to get him into a sitting position. He began to stir.

"Dad, wake up!" she yelled, but as she did so, she took in a blast of smoke and began to cough.

He looked at her blearily. "Lauren?"

"We have to get out of here. The house is on fire!" She put his arm around her shoulder and helped him up, but he started coughing and couldn't catch his breath. He sank to the floor, taking her down with him.

"Go," he said. "Save yourself, Lauren. Go."

"I'm not leaving without you, Dad. Come on." She struggled to get him back up to his feet, but he'd fallen unconscious. She grabbed his hands and pulled him toward the door. Half the hallway was on fire, and the curtains in the living room were going up now. The kitchen was consumed with flames. How had the fire spread so *fast*? There was no way to get to the back door, and in another minute they might not be able to make it to the front, either.

She dragged her father down the hall, coughing from the smoke, trying not to breathe too deeply. If she passed out, neither of them would ever wake up.

*   *   *

Shane rode his motorcycle back into town, feeling just as restless as when he'd left. He knew what he had to do. He had to put it all on the line. Lauren was running scared, and he couldn't let her go without trying to convince her to give their relationship a chance. Though it was late now, maybe she'd still be up.

He turned down her street and saw the smoke, then the flames.

Lauren's house was on fire!

Where the hell was everyone? No neighbors were out on the street, no alarms going off, no sirens in the distance. He stopped his bike, pulled out his phone, and dialed 911. He gave Lauren's address, then ran up the steps. The front door was locked. He hit it with his shoulder, once, twice, finally breaking through.

The house was filled with smoke and fire, the heat intense. He stumbled through the living room. Lauren was in the hall trying to drag her father out, but his weight was slowing her down.

She cried out with relief when she saw him.

"Get out of the house! I'll take your dad."

But she waited while he grappled with her father's dead weight, finally getting the man over his shoulder. "Go!" he told Lauren, urging her ahead of him.

But she didn't listen, running back down the hall.

Shit! He rushed through the front door and laid her father on the grass, then went right back inside. He was not going to leave Lauren in a burning house.

What the hell had she gone back for?

Abby's diary had been missing for too long to be lost now. Her father would be all right. Shane would get him to safety. The smoke was thicker when she re-entered her bedroom and it took a moment to find the diary. She stuffed it in her purse, with the envelope of photos, and headed back into the hall, but the fire was roaring now, the flames barring her escape, the heat unbearable. She saw Shane enter the other end of the hall, but they were separated by a wall of fire.

"Go back!" she shouted, then ran into her bedroom and tried to open the window. *Dammit*, it was painted shut! Her throat burned from the smoke and flames were licking at the doorway now, just inches away from the plastic bags filled with Abby's clothes. In minutes the room would be an inferno. She dropped her purse, grabbed the desk chair, and hurled it at the window, shattering the glass.

As she gulped in fresh air, Shane appeared at the window and laid his jacket over the shards of broken glass. Lauren quickly grabbed her purse and climbed out, falling into Shane's embrace.

His arms enfolded her, his face buried in her hair for one glorious moment, then he pulled her away from the house.

"What the hell were you thinking?" he yelled as they ran across the lawn, past the firefighters who'd arrived on the scene.

"I found Abby's diary. I couldn't let it go up in smoke."

"You could have been *killed.*"

"I'm okay," she said, her throat still raw. She paused on the sidewalk, suddenly aware of the fire trucks and the neighbors coming out of their houses. "Where's my dad? Is he all right?"

"He's over there. He's okay."

Her father was sitting on the curb across the street. He had on an oxygen mask, and a paramedic was attending to him.

Lauren ran over, relieved to see his eyes open, and sat down next to him.

Her father reached for her with a shaky hand. "I was so afraid," he murmured, his gaze on her face. "I didn't know where you were, Lauren. I was terrified that you might not make it out. I couldn't bear to lose you."

She swallowed hard at the love in his eyes, love she hadn't really seen since she was a little girl. She squeezed his fingers reassuringly. "I had to get something of Abby's out of the house. I found her diary earlier tonight."

"Her book?" he asked in amazement. "It was there, all these years?"

"Yes, tucked in the heating vent. Abby had found the perfect hiding place."

He let out a sigh, his gaze turning toward their

house. Fire was shooting out of the windows and roof. It was hard to believe that the house that had been in their family for so many generations was going up in smoke. She couldn't imagine the pain her father was suffering; this was his life—the life he'd been so desperate to hang on to.

"Everything will be gone soon," he said heavily, echoing her thoughts. "Not just my memories now, but the house, and all that's familiar to me."

A tear slid down his face. Lauren put her arm around his shoulders, feeling the frailness of his body. She wished she could tell him it would be all right, but nothing would be the same for him again after this night. Maybe they could rebuild, but that would take time, and who knew how much time her father had left?

"We'd like to take your father to the hospital to check him out," the paramedic told her.

She nodded. "Dad, you need to go with them."

He shook his head. "I have to stay here. This is my home and Abby's, too." His voice cracked. "Her room will be destroyed, all of her things. I can't stand it. I'm losing her again."

His eyes were filled with so much grief, she could hardly look at him, but she couldn't turn away. He needed her. "They were just things, Dad. Abby was more than what was in her room. She was a vibrant, beautiful girl, and her spirit is everywhere. It's in all of us."

"I won't be able to remember her without the re-minders. I need to see her things."

"No, you don't. She's in your heart, not just in your head. I know, because she's in mine, too."

Her dad sighed and gave her a sad smile. Then he leaned over and kissed her cheek. "You'll remember her when I can't, Lauren. Promise me that."

"I'll never forget her. I couldn't. Now, you should go to the hospital." She helped him to his feet.

He paused, his hand on her shoulder. "You're in my heart, too, Lauren. Don't ever doubt that."

She bit down on her bottom lip as the paramedic helped him into the ambulance. She didn't like how weak he sounded, how resigned, almost as if he were giving up. She didn't want to lose him yet; they were just getting to know each other again.

"Are you all right?" Shane asked.

She shook her head and turned into his arms, burying her face against his solid chest. He held her for long minutes, and amid the chaos of the fire and the trucks and the milling neighbors, she felt safe and protected.

She didn't want to let him go. She didn't ever want to let him go.

Lifting her head, she gazed into his eyes. "How did you know to come to the house?"

"I was lucky—and almost too late," he said, anger in his eyes. "I never should have left you alone tonight. After what happened to Mark Devlin, I should have stayed by your side."

His words struck her hard. She hadn't had time to think about how the fire had started. She'd assumed it had been an accident, that her father had left something on the stove. But the flames had been everywhere. "Do you think this was deliberate?"

"It's a possibility we can't ignore. You did find Abby's diary there," he pointed out. "Do you know who killed her now?"

"I'm guessing Tim Sorensen," Lauren replied. "But it wasn't Abby who had the affair with him, it was Lisa."

"Are you serious?" he asked in surprise.

"Yes, it's all in her journal. Abby wanted to stop it. I think she went to the high school that night to confront Mr. Sorensen, to tell him that she was going to turn him in, and he killed her."

"Tim Sorensen didn't kill your sister," Chief Silveira interrupted.

She turned her head, shocked to find him so close. She hadn't seen him arrive. "How do you know that?"

"Because I've spent most of the day checking out his alibi. It's airtight. He was out of town at a symposium that night. There were plenty of witnesses to verify his whereabouts."

"Then why would his wife run Mark Devlin down?"

"She said she didn't like Mr. Devlin's insinuations."

"You don't hit someone with your car unless you're afraid of something serious," she said.

But maybe Erica wasn't afraid that Devlin would implicate her husband—maybe she was afraid he would implicate *her*, Lauren mused.

If Abby had gone to Tim's house, she could have

told his wife about the affair. Maybe that's how she'd tried to stop it.

"What about Erica? Did she have an alibi?" she asked.

"Mrs. Sorensen was allegedly at home with a small baby. We'll continue to investigate," Joe said. "Not only the accident, but also your sister's murder, and now this fire. I'll let you know what we come up with. In the meantime, do you have friends you can stay with?"

"She's staying with me," Shane said, tightening his arm around her.

"Good. Keep her safe."

As the chief got into his car and drove away, Lauren realized she'd been so caught up in her dizzying thoughts that she hadn't told him about Abby's diary. It was just as well. She wanted to read through it one more time before she gave it up to the police.

"If Tim Sorensen didn't kill Abby, then maybe his wife did," she said to Shane. "She might have thought Devlin was getting too close to her. It's hard to believe, though. Why would she kill Abby for telling her that her husband was having an affair with another student? Why wouldn't she have gone after Lisa?"

"Maybe she snapped," Shane suggested. "Maybe she saw Abby as the biggest threat, because she wanted to expose the affair."

"But Lisa was the one having the affair," she reiterated, her mind stuck on the things that weren't adding up. "Lisa came by here the other day. She almost fell over when she realized that Abby's room was exactly the same; she'd thought that my parents cleaned it out years ago. She asked me if I'd found the diary, so she knew it was still missing. She was worried that it would come to light."

With each word that Lauren spoke, a certainty began to grow in her head. "Where's your motorcycle?"

"Right over there," Shane said. "Lauren, we should go to the police."

"No, this is personal. Lisa grew up in my house. She was practically Abby's sister. I want to see her face. I want to look into her eyes. I want her to tell me the truth. If you won't take me, I'll drive myself."

"I'll take you," Shane said. "I have a few questions for Lisa, too."

TWENTY-TWO

It was only a five-minute ride to Lisa's house, and as they drove down the familiar streets Lauren remembered all the times Abby had walked or ridden her bike to see Lisa. They'd had so much fun together during childhood. Their friendship had been deep and loving.

Shane parked in front of Lisa's house. There was a light on upstairs and Lisa's car was in the driveway. Lauren ran up to the door, impatient to get the answers she'd wanted for so long. She rang the bell and pounded on the door, shouting Lisa's name. She heard Shane calling the police from his cell phone. She didn't care if they came, but she was going to talk to Lisa first.

"I smell gasoline," she said, wrinkling her nose. She lowered her face. The door handle reeked of gas. "We have to get in there."

"If she set fire to your house, we should wait for the cops."

"If she didn't set the fire, then maybe whoever did is after her, too. Tim Sorensen is still roaming free."

Shane drew in a breath. "Good point. Give me some room." He moved back a few steps, then tackled the door like the linebacker he'd once been. It groaned on the first hit, then snapped open on the second. They stumbled inside.

Lisa came flying out of the kitchen, her dark red hair tangled, her eyes wild, her face white, and her hands covered in dripping wet towels. She saw Lauren and froze in her tracks.

"What happened to your hands?" Lauren asked, but she already knew the truth. She'd been trying to convince herself that the only thing Lisa had done wrong was sleep with her volleyball coach, but that wasn't the case. "You burned them, didn't you?" she said. "You burned them when you set fire to my house."

She moved toward Lisa, who immediately began backing away, but there was nowhere for her to run.

"My God!" Lauren cried. "You could have *killed* me. You could have killed my father! How could you do this to us? We were your family. Abby was like your sister."

"Abby turned on me," Lisa said bitterly. "She betrayed me. She was going to ruin everything."

"You mean she was going to tell everyone that you were having sex with Coach Sorensen."

"He loved me. He loved me like no one else loved me!" Lisa cried. "You didn't know what it was like to grow up in this house. You didn't have to watch my mother bring men in and out. You didn't have to lock your bedroom door in case one of those men decided to take a side trip in the middle of the night. You and Abby had the perfect family."

"Abby *loved* you," Lauren said, still in shock, even though the truth was right in front of her. "She loved you, Lisa."

Lisa shook her head. "You're wrong. She hated me when she found out what I was doing. And you know why? Because Abby wanted him for herself. She didn't like the attention he gave me. She was used to being the star."

"That's not true," Lauren said. "You're not going to turn this on Abby."

"You don't know what's true."

"I know she didn't have sex with the coach."

"No, because he was in love with *me*. Tim was the man Abby couldn't have. He's the one she wrote about in her diary." Lisa stopped abruptly, her gaze narrowing. "You found it, didn't you? That's why you're here. I knew it was in the house. I tried to look after she died, but you wouldn't let me in. You and your parents, who supposedly cared about me, had no use for me after Abby died. I wasn't part of the family anymore." She spat out the last part of her sentence.

"So you decided to burn my house down, just in case the diary was there?"

"I figured everyone would think your father had done it."

"But you didn't count on burning your hands." Lauren saw Lisa's gaze slide toward the bedroom. Through the open door, she could see the suitcase on the bed. "You were going to run."

"Who says I still won't?" Lisa challenged.

"I do," Shane said, stepping in front of her.

"Always the big hero," Lisa said sarcastically. "Why would you help her? She didn't stand up for you when they accused you of murdering Abby."

"As I recall, you were more than happy to tell the police that I'd been hitting on Abby, even though it wasn't true," Shane said. "You wanted me to go to jail for her murder."

"Better you than—" Lisa cut herself off.

The truth suddenly hit Lauren between the eyes. Tim Sorensen had an alibi. Erica Sorensen was supposedly home with her baby. But Lisa . . .

"You? You did it? You killed Abby?" She flew across the room and grabbed Lisa by the shoulders, ignoring her scream of pain as Lisa's burned hands were pinned between them. "Say it! Admit it, damn you!" Furious tears blurred her vision. "How could you kill your best friend?"

"I had to—she was going to ruin everything! I tried to talk to her. I begged her to just leave it alone. We weren't hurting anyone, it wasn't her business. And Tim—he would have lost everything. He was so scared."

"He knew that you did it?"

"He told me to find a way to stop her. He knew she'd caught us because of that damn camera she always had in her hand. She loved sneaking up on people and taking their picture. That's how she found out about us." She drew in a ragged breath. "Don't you get it, Lauren? I loved him, and he loved me, and he was the only one who did," she sobbed.

Filled with a violent rage, Lauren wanted to put her hands around Lisa's throat and strangle her like Lisa had done to Abby. How terrified and angry her little sister must have been when Lisa had gone after her. How betrayed she must have felt.

She grabbed Lisa's throat, saw her eyes widen in shock. "How does it feel?" she asked, squeezing her fingers around her neck. Lisa tried to struggle, but her hands were too burned to fight.

"Stop her," Lisa begged Shane.

Shane moved toward her. "Lauren, let go," he said firmly.

"Why do you care what happens to her? She wanted you to go to prison," Lauren said.

"I don't care about her—I care about you. The police are coming. They'll arrest her. "

Lauren didn't *want* to let go. She wanted Lisa to suffer the way Abby had.

"Lauren, your dad needs you. He can't lose another daughter," Shane told her.

His words finally got through to her. She let go and Lisa slumped to the ground, crying hysterically that it wasn't her fault.

Then Joe Silveira and two uniformed cops came in.

"Lisa killed Abby," Lauren told him. "She did it

to save herself and her lover, Tim Sorensen. Abby was going to reveal their affair."

She looked back at Lisa, who was being hauled to her feet by one of the officers. "Do you know what Abby wrote in her diary, Lisa? She said she was worried about you—that she loved you, and that she didn't want you to ruin your life. She didn't want to hurt you; she wanted to save you. And you killed her."

"I'm sorry," Lisa whimpered. "I'm sorry." The officers led her away.

"You found her diary?" Joe asked, a somber expression in his eyes.

"Tonight. I forgot to tell you earlier. Lisa guessed it was in the house; that's why she set the fire. She was going to leave but she hurt herself, and that delayed her escape." She looked around. "Where's my purse?"

"It's here," Shane said, retrieving it from the floor where she'd dropped it.

She pulled out the diary and handed it to Joe. "I'd like to get it back when you're done with it. It's the only thing of Abby's that I have left."

"No problem. Are you all right?"

She let out a sigh. "No, but I will be. I just want to make sure that Lisa pays for what she did."

"She will," Joe promised.

"Let's go, Lauren," Shane said gently. "You've done all you can do. The rest is up to the police."

*   *   *

Before going to the boat, Lauren went to the medical center to check on her father. He'd been admitted for observation and was dozing in his room. Oxygen tubes ran into his nose, but he seemed to be breathing normally. The nurse had told her that barring any unforeseen developments, he'd be released in the morning.

Lauren studied him quietly for several minutes and was about to leave when he opened his eyes. He blinked a few times, then his gaze settled on her face.

"Lauren," he said, relief in his eyes. "I couldn't remember what happened to you. I was afraid. No one knew where you were."

"I'm here." She smiled at him. "Are you doing okay?"

"I was dreaming about the old days in the house, when we were all together—you, me, your mother, David, and Abby. We had some good times."

"We did," she agreed, battling a surging wave of emotion. She didn't know how much more she could take tonight.

"Your mother loved that house. I remember when we first moved in, we painted all the rooms together. She'd get more paint on her face and clothes than on the walls, but she didn't care. She was so happy then."

"Dad, let's not do this now."

"I want to tell you everything," her father said.

His words echoed Shane's from earlier that night. "We can do that later. You need to sleep."

"I don't know how much time I have left."

"Don't talk like that. You have more good days than bad."

"That could change at any moment. I know you don't want to talk about the past—"

"Yes, I do," she said. "I want to hear all of your memories. I want to write them down and pass them on to my kids and David's kids." She saw happy tears gather in his eyes, and it was all she could do to hang on. "I know it's important to you, and it's important to me. Even if you forget us, we're not going to forget you." She leaned down and kissed him on the cheek. "Get some rest, Dad. We'll talk in the morning."

Shane was waiting for her in the hallway. When they walked down the quiet corridor and out of the hospital, she stopped in the front courtyard and drew in a deep breath of fresh air. A million stars surrounded a brilliantly full moon that was dipping toward the horizon. Dawn was approaching.

"Let me take you to my boat or wherever you want to go," Shane said.

"I just want to sit for a minute," she said, walking over to a nearby bench.

Shane took off his jacket and put it around her shoulders.

"Now you'll be cold," she said with a smile.

"I'm a man. I can take it."

"You never told me why you came back to my house tonight," she reminded him.

"Haven't you had enough talk for tonight? You must be a little overwhelmed right now."

"That's an understatement. But I don't think I could sleep even if I tried."

"Did you tell your father about Lisa?"

She shook her head. "Not yet. I still can't believe she's the one who killed Abby. I never in a million years would have thought it was her."

"She was a mixed-up girl, desperate for love," Shane said. "The most ironic thing of all is that the man who's responsible for all of this is going to lose the least."

She frowned. "What do you mean?"

"Tim Sorensen had sex with a fifteen-year-old student. But it was Lisa who killed Abby, because she wanted to protect him and their relationship. And it was his wife who ran down Mark Devlin, because she also wanted to protect him. Erica knew her husband was having an affair; she was just mistaken in thinking it was Abby and not Lisa."

"So Lisa gets tried for murder and Erica for attempted murder—and what happens to Tim?"

"I'm sure he'll lose his job."

Lauren shook her head in disgust. "That doesn't seem right. He should go to jail, too. He had sex with an underage minor."

"Thirteen years ago. I wonder what the time limit is for statutory rape."

"Lisa would probably say it was consensual just to save him. I can't believe that Abby felt sorry for her. I wanted to kill her. I've never felt such rage before. Were you worried you were going to witness a murder?"

"Not in the least," he said with a small smile. "I know you, Lauren."

"You keep saying that."

"Maybe you should start believing it."

For a moment there was nothing but easy quiet between them. Lauren couldn't remember when she'd felt so at peace, with so many questions finally answered—except one. She turned to him, drawing his gaze to hers. "Shane, you still haven't told me why you came to my house tonight."

"I wanted to tell you that I love you," he said simply.

Her heart skipped a beat. "I think I must be high from smoke inhalation. Could you repeat that?"

His smile broadened. "I love you, Lauren. I'll say it as many times as you want. And I'll say it for the rest of our lives, if you'll let me." His gaze turned serious. "I knew you were the one for me the first time you got on my bike and slid your arms around my waist. You hung on like you weren't going to let go, and it was the first time I'd ever *wanted* someone to hang on. It scared the hell out of me. The only person I ever wanted to commit to was you, and I couldn't have you. After I left I tried to forget you, but it didn't work. No one else ever came close." He let out a deep breath.

She could see the worry in his eyes that his declaration wouldn't be enough, that it was too late. Silly man. "I love you, too, Shane. I always have."

"Thank God!"

His heartfelt relief made her smile. "So what are we going to do about this?"

"Whatever you want, Lauren. I can move to San Francisco if you want. I can move anywhere, as long as you're with me."

"That's one good thing about loving a man with a boat," she said lightly. "But I think I want to stay here for a while. I want to get to know my dad again, while he's still well enough to know me. Except we don't have anywhere to live now."

"So we'll buy a place."

She raised an eyebrow. "You mean a house on dry land?"

"I can live on dry land."

"Without the waves rocking you to sleep?"

"I guess you'll have to rock me to sleep," he teased. "I do love you, Lauren. God, it feels good to say that out loud. I don't know why it sounded so scary in my head."

"Because you've been hurt by love—but that's going to change," she promised. "We have our second chance, just like Leonora and Tommy." She gave him a tender kiss. "Let's go home."

"To *our* home," he said.

She smiled. "I like the sound of that."

EPILOGUE

Two days later, Lauren entered the Bayview Care Center with Shane, Kara, and her baby, now named Faith.

Kara paused in the hall outside Colin's room. "The days I spent in the hospital are the longest Colin and I have ever been apart. I know I need to do this, but I'm a little scared. Her eyes filled with tears. I have to tell Colin that while I love him, I have to put our daughter first. I have to say good-bye."

Lauren blinked back her own tears. The love between Kara and Colin was so powerful, so deep, and she couldn't imagine having to go through what Kara had been through.

Before Kara could open Colin's door, Charlotte, Joe, and Jason stepped off the elevator and came toward them.

"We thought you might want a little more support," Charlotte told Kara. "If it's too much, we'll wait outside."

Kara smiled. "Thanks, but you can come in. You're all Colin's friends. You're all my friends." She pushed open the door and walked over to the bed.

The group gathered behind her. Colin looked exactly as he had the last time Lauren had seen him. She glanced over at Shane, whose expression was grim. He'd been against this visit. He'd wanted to take Kara straight home from the hospital, but she'd insisted on making the stop.

"Colin," Kara said. "I brought your daughter to see you. Her name is Faith, because you always had faith that she'd be born perfect, and she was. We have our little girl. And I'm going to make sure that she knows everything about you." Kara drew in a deep breath. "But I won't be able to come here every day. I'll need to stay with her. I know you'll understand." She paused, and then laid the baby down on Colin's chest. She lifted Colin's hand and placed it on the baby's back.

Long seconds ticked by.

Lauren could hardly breathe. The scene was so poignant, so sad. Shane slipped his hand into hers, holding on tight. She knew he wanted to make things right for Kara, but there wasn't a damn thing he could do.

"So I came to say good-bye," Kara continued. "I thought it would be hard, but it's even worse," she said, her voice breaking.

Shane started forward, but Lauren held him back. She knew Kara needed to finish this.

Kara drew in another deep breath of courage. "I

felt your spirit in my room the other night, Colin. You came to me when I was scared. You said our little girl is beautiful. I know you can see us from wherever you are. And we'll always be with you."

As Kara bent over to lift the baby back into her arms, Colin's eyelids began to flicker. At first Lauren thought she was imagining things, but then she heard Kara gasp.

They all surged forward as Colin opened his eyes—his bright green eyes.

For a long moment, the air sizzled with electricity, expectation, hope.

Colin looked at his chest, and he reflexively held his tiny daughter close. "Is this our baby?"

Kara let out a cry of joy and disbelief. "Colin, you're awake!"

He stared at her in bemusement. "Was I asleep?"

Kara started to laugh and cry together.

Colin glanced around the room. "What's happened?" he asked in confusion.

"A miracle," Shane said, as he looked at Lauren. "Kara finally got one."

"We all did." Lauren smiled. "We *all* did."

Turn the page

for a sneak peek at

IN SHELTER COVE

the next heart-tugging Angel's Bay romance

from bestselling author

Barbara Freethy

Coming soon from Pocket Books

It was almost midnight when Brianna settled into bed. As she stared at the ceiling, watching the shadows dance in the moonlight, she tried to relax but still felt tense, jumpy. She wasn't used to the way the house breathed yet. And it was too quiet in Angel's Bay.

She was accustomed to falling asleep to the sounds of cars streaming down the highway next to her former apartment, the shriek of sirens from the nearby fire department, the loud thumps of her upstairs neighbors. While often annoying, those noises had comforted her, made her feel less alone.

As if sensing her need for noise, the puppy began to bark and whine, long, pitiful high-pitched cries. Despite her son Lucas's plea to let the dog sleep with him, she'd insisted on putting the puppy in its crate in the kitchen. She didn't want to set a precedent that she wouldn't be able to change. Unfortunately, the dog was testing her willpower.

Pulling the pillow over her head, she told herself that Lucas had learned to sleep through the night on his own and so would the as-yet-to-be-named dog. Lucas was debating among Oscar, Snickers, and Digger. After the damage the puppy had already done to the backyard in the short amount of time he'd been in it, Digger might be the best choice.

Ten more minutes of pathetic puppy cries finally drove her out of bed. She pulled a sweatshirt over her camisole and cotton pajama bottoms and walked into the hall. She stopped at Lucas's bedroom to pull the door shut, then went to the kitchen. The puppy bounded to his feet when he saw her, barking and yelping even louder. She closed the door to the kitchen, hoping the noise wouldn't wake Lucas.

Kneeling next to the crate, she gave the dog a firm look. "It's bedtime. You're supposed to go to sleep."

He barked in delight as if she'd just told him it was time for a walk. She stuck her fingers through the mesh, and he licked them with enthusiasm, bringing a reluctant smile to her lips.

"Okay, I get it. You don't want to sleep. But you can't keep barking." Maybe if she let him out, he'd run around and get tired. She took him out of his crate, and he squirmed in her arms, licking her face and hands and anything he could get his tongue on.

Then he ran around the kitchen, sliding into the table legs and the walls. They were going to need a little more room.

She opened the back door and watched in amazement as he flew around the dark, fenced-in yard, exploring the shadows under the bushes and trees. There was a lot of overgrown foliage; she'd need to do some gardening. It was nice to have such a big backyard. Lucas would have room to run and play and would enjoy it as much as the dog did.

Glancing next door, she saw lights on at the back of the house. Someone was up late. The Realtor had told her that an elderly woman owned that house. On the other side was a couple with three older children; she hoped she'd find a babysitter among them.

She wasn't all that eager to meet her neighbors, though. There would surely be questions about Derek that she didn't want to answer. But she wouldn't be surprised if everyone knew who she was before she knew who *they* were. News traveled fast in Angel's Bay, and the widow of the town's least favorite son would be gossip-worthy.

She returned to the kitchen and put on some hot water for tea. Maybe it would relax her enough to sleep. Like the puppy, she was finding it difficult to settle down in her new surroundings. While she waited for the water to boil, she unpacked one of the half-dozen boxes on the kitchen floor, one less task to do tomorrow. When the water was hot, she poured her tea into a mug and stepped out onto the deck.

The puppy was nowhere to be seen. He had to be under a bush or in a dark corner, she thought, as her uneasiness grew. She heard barking, an unfamiliar yap, and then a crash followed by male swearing—all coming from next door. When she walked into the yard, she saw the hole that the puppy had dug underneath—just big enough for a small dog to get through.

"Damn," she muttered, as the barks and swearing next door grew louder.

She ran down the side of her house and found a gate that led into the neighbor's property. As she slipped inside, a tiny white puff of fur ran around her, chased by her puppy and a very pissed-off man who was also wrestling with an irate, spitting cat.

"Digger! Puppy!" she yelled, though the dog had no idea what his name was and was too busy chasing another dog to pay any attention to her. She *thought* he was chasing a dog; the small furball had squeezed under the deck in a space so small that her puppy could only bark furiously at his escaped prey.

The man let out another curse as the cat sprang from his arms. He put a hand to his face, and as he stepped into the light, she saw a long red scratch down a face that was very familiar.

Her heart jumped into her throat. "No way!"

Jason looked as shocked as she felt.

"You can't possibly live here," she said. "I was told this house belongs to an elderly lady."

"It does—Shirley Pease. She had a stroke a few months ago and went to a care facility. Her daughter is living here now."

"You don't look like her daughter." Her gaze slid down his body. His jeans were slung low on his hips, and his button-down shirt was open, revealing a tantalizingly broad, muscular chest. His bare feet and tousled hair made him look as if he'd just rolled out of bed. She swallowed hard at the thought. She'd forgotten how sexy he was. Forgotten how his gaze had always made a tingle run down her spine. But Jason was the cop who'd ruined her husband's life, and she couldn't forget that.

"I'm housesitting for my father's girlfriend," Jason said. "And you need to get your damn dog under control. He's digging a hole under the deck," Jason pointed out.

He was right. Another minute, and her puppy would be under the deck with his dog. She ran over and grabbed Digger.

Jason got down on his knees and peered under the deck. "Come on, Princess," he called. "It's safe to come out now."

"Princess?" she echoed.

Jason scowled at her. "She's not my dog. I didn't name her."

"She seems to like you," Brianna said as the tiny fluffball threw herself into Jason's waiting arms, whimpering with relief.

"At least she likes you better than the cat. That's a nasty scratch it gave you."

"Shit! Where did the cat go?" Jason got to his feet and scanned the yard, but there was no sign of the calico.

"It's probably hiding," Brianna suggested.

"Yeah, until you and that little monster leave. He needs to learn some manners."

"He's a puppy. He's—exuberant."

"Is that what you call it? How long have you had him?"

"About eight hours. He was a present to Lucas from his grandparents." The puppy barked and began to lick her face again. "He's very friendly."

"I can see that. He looks like Buster, Derek's old dog."

"Apparently that was the intention." The mention of Jason's past friendship with Derek reminded her just who this man was to her. "I'd better get back."

"Hang on." He opened the door to the house and thrust Princess inside, then returned to the deck. "I need to find the cat."

She headed toward her yard, keeping an eye out for the cat, until a large shadow by the front windows of her house startled her. She stopped so abruptly Jason bumped into her.

"What's wrong?" he asked.

She wasn't sure. She took another step forward, knocking into the trash can. The shadow moved through the trees. "Someone is in my yard," she said in shock.

"Stay here." Jason moved past her quietly, quickly.

She obeyed for a moment, but the idea of Lucas being alone in the house propelled her forward.

Jason met her on the lawn. "I don't see anyone. It was probably just the wind moving the trees."

Maybe he was right. There were tall trees on both sides of the property, and it was pretty dark, the nearest streetlight three houses away. "I need to check on Lucas."

"Did you come out the back door?"

"Yes."

"I'll walk around with you."

Her back door was open the way she'd left it, her cup of tea sitting on the deck. She picked up the mug, then hurried inside to check on Lucas. He was still asleep. As she came out of the room, she saw Jason checking her bedroom.

"What are you doing?"

"Just looking around. Everything seems to be fine."

She walked into the kitchen and put the puppy in his crate, much to his dismay. He immediately started barking. "He really doesn't like this thing."

"I can't say that I blame him." Jason leaned against the door frame and crossed his arms in front of his chest, making himself a little too comfortable for her taste. Then again, it was nice not to be alone in the house.

She didn't know why she was so jumpy. She'd lived alone with Lucas for the past five years, aside from the weekends when Derek's parents, Rick and Nancy, would come to visit.

She refilled the tea kettle and turned on the stove. "Tell me again who lives next door?"

"Shirley Pease, Angel's Bay's head librarian, lived there for twenty years until she had a stroke a few months ago. Her daughter Patty is moving in. If she doesn't rope my father into marriage before that," he grumbled.

She gave him a curious look. "You don't sound as if you care much for Patty."

"She's an ex-stripper, which doesn't bother my father at all. She has certain large attributes, if you know what I mean."

"And she's going to be your stepmother?"

"I hope not. With my father, who knows? He's a romantic, up until the time he ends up in divorce court."

Brianna raised an eyebrow. "Has he been there more than once?"

"Three times."

"What number was your mother?"

A dark shadow passed through his eyes. "She wasn't a divorce. She died when I was seven."

"I'm sorry."

He shrugged. "It was a long time ago. My dad

took it hard. He couldn't get out of bed for months, and his business failed. We were running out of money, and then my uncle came one day, packed us up, and drove us here to Angel's Bay. I think he saved my dad's life—probably mine, too."

She didn't want to get to know Jason. She didn't want to see any other side to him than the one he'd shown the day he testified against Derek. Then he'd been a cold, ruthless, ambitious cop who was destroying Derek's life and hers, too. He'd been the villain in Derek's version of the story, but he didn't look so much like a bad guy now, with his tousled hair and bare feet. He looked like the guy she'd first met in the bar five years ago, the one who'd shamelessly flirted with her until he'd realized she was taken.

She turned away and rinsed out her cup, busying herself with getting another tea bag. She wanted Jason to go, yet she couldn't quite ask him to leave. He sat down on a stool by the counter. "When my father started to recover, he discovered there were loads of women eager to make him feel less lonely. They were also eager to marry him. Patty is just the latest in a string of women my father thinks might be the real thing." He shook his head. "He had the real thing. She died."

"Did you want him to stay single forever?" Brianna couldn't help asking.

"No. I want him to be happy. I want him to find love, but he looks in all the wrong places."

"Maybe they're just not the places you would look."

"Well, I wouldn't look to a stripper for love," he admitted. "Other things, maybe."

She had a feeling that Jason had no trouble getting women. The pot on the stove began to whistle, and she quickly turned down the flame. "Do you want some tea?"

"Not really a tea guy."

"That's all I have. I haven't gone to the store yet." She poured herself a cup, surprised when her hand shook. All the stress, she thought. It had been a bad couple of weeks.

"You're spooked, aren't you?" His sharp gaze didn't miss a thing.

"It's just the new house, new neighborhood. I'll feel better once I get unpacked and organized."

"Looks like that might take some time." His gaze drifted along the stack of boxes against the wall.

"Probably. I have more boxes coming on Friday from Derek's place." She stopped abruptly, realizing she'd just brought up the subject she'd been trying to avoid.

"Today must have been rough on you."

"There have been a lot of rough days in the past five years."

"I imagine so."

"You *can't* imagine," she told him flatly. "You really can't."

His gaze grew wary as the tension between them returned. "Okay." He took a breath. "Maybe you should have stayed with the Kanes tonight."

"I'm used to being alone and taking care of myself. We might have buried Derek today, but he's been gone a long time. And that's because of you," she finished, feeling a desperate need to remind both of them of that fact.

"Is it really that simple?" Jason challenged, his eyes darkening. "To blame me for everything that happened to Derek?"

His words hung in the air for a long moment. Logically she knew Jason hadn't done it alone, but he was the face of her pain—at least, he had been.

"It was simpler when you weren't standing in front of me," she admitted.

He drew in a sharp breath at her words. "I guess that's a start."

She immediately shook her head. "It's not a start. I'm willing to concede that you were part of a larger investigation, but you led the charge, and you took the stand and testified against Derek. You were the last one to speak before the verdict came in. Even though you were his friend. That should have mattered."

"If I could have taken myself off the case, I would have, but this is a small town with a small police department. I saw Jason on the museum grounds and talked to him just minutes after the guard was assaulted. I was subpoenaed to testify. I had no choice. I had to tell the truth."

"You *shaped* the truth to fit the case—but I'm not going to argue with you. What was just a job to you was the end of my dreams. Derek and I had so many plans, and now none of them will come true. Lucas is going to grow up without a father." A wave of anger ripped through her. "You ruined everything."

"Derek ruined everything," Jason said harshly. "Why don't you blame *him*?"

"Because he's dead."

Her words brought a stark silence to the room.

She felt hot, dizzy. It was too much. All the emotions of the past years, months, days assaulted her at once. She started to sway, her knees beginning to buckle.

Jason had her in his arms before she even realized he'd moved. His chest was solid, his body warm, his embrace secure. She wanted to sink into him, to lean on his strength and let him hold her up, because she'd been holding herself up for so long. But she couldn't. This was so—so absolutely wrong.

She pushed him away and staggered to the kitchen table, sitting on a chair before she fell down. Drawing in several deep breaths, she forced herself not to look at Jason, acutely aware that his gaze was fixed on her.

"Please go," she said, staring down at the table top.

"Are you all right?"

She had no idea how to answer that question. Finally, she lifted her gaze to his. "I will be."

He moved toward her, his eyes concerned. "I'm

sorry, Brianna. I never intended to have this conversation with you tonight."

"I was hoping we wouldn't have it at all. You have your opinion; I have mine. We're never going to agree."

"I wish you could see that I'm not your enemy."

"I wish you could see that it doesn't matter to me *what* you are."

He gave a tight nod. "Got it." Then he left, shutting the back door quietly behind him.

Experience the **excitement** of bestselling romances from Pocket Books!

Eileen Carr
HOLD BACK THE DARK
When a clinical psychologist and a detective investigate an unspeakable crime, they learn that every passion has its dark side.....

Laura Griffin
WHISPER OF WARNING
Blamed for a murder she witnessed, Courtney chooses to trust the sexy detective pursuing her. Will he help prove her innocence...or lead a killer to her door?

Susan Mallery
Sunset Bay
What if you got another chance at the life that got away? Amid the turmoil of broken dreams lies the promise of a future Megan never expected....